Take a Journey into the Mystic.

"Then, when you say she's a witch, then, you're... well... you don't mean it literally?" His demeanor changes into an intense study of my person.

"Of course I mean it literally. The blood of eight centuries of the MacIntyre and Montaigne lines flow in her veins. Her mother is an Adept. All of Morgan's extensive line of aunts all possess the insight... including the sisters in Scotland, Seamus' sisters, Vivien and Vanetta MacIntyre."

"What do you mean by... *insight*?"

"The ability to see beyond this base mortal plane into that which is consciousness." I sit dumbfounded, my world suddenly becoming much larger. "And to compound it... Morgan is what is referred to as *a Power Child*."

"A what?"

"Every line possesses them, every family, every species within the animal and plant kingdoms alike," he states matter-of-factly. "Just as energy ebbs and flows, sound and light vibrate within certain frequencies, water peaks and troughs... familial and genetic lines peak and ebb. Most members possess stasis. However, every few cycles and certainly within generations *a Power Child* is born... the peak of the frequency. Morgan is such a person." I stare at him in utter amazement. "Surely by now you understand that all of life, all of manifest reality, is frequency and vibration?" he asks and stares into the center of my being.

From *The Man Who Would Be Coyote*

Other books by M E Nyberg

The Profound Art of Omens

The Man Who Would Be Coyote

(The Memoirs of Morgan MacIntyre)

(Book 2 of The Shade Series)

~

Book design by Don Mangione

Cover Painting by M. E. Nyberg

ISBN (book) 13: 978-0-9970986-0-0

ISBN (ebook) 13: 978-0-9970986-1-7

Library of Congress registration #TXu 1-968-896

May 18, 2015

The Man Who Would Be Coyote

(The Memoirs of Morgan MacIntyre)

By M. E. Nyberg

To Yumiko, Sophia and Julien

Table of Contents

Prologue

This is the Shade
That which your father made
Of which you enquire
Its mystery desire

Each look, each feature
Shadow or eyther
Low or above
The crow or the dove

That which you see
Rather obliquely
Windward or lee
Yet, always me

The Man Who Would Be Coyote

I had no premonition of what I was about to get myself into. Like a fly on the windscreen just before a storm hits, I was sitting in the reading nook of Emerald Montaigne's Victorian on Sutter Street in San Francisco pouring over a volume on traditional Italian villas, when I hear the bell. Opening the door I'm surprised to find Lucien standing on the stoop.

"Willem m'boy, how are you?" After a brief pause he asks: "May I come in?"

"Yes, of course." I swing wide the door and he steps in, surveying the room. He sets his hat upon the end table and removes his tweed dispensing it upon the rack near the door. Taking the chair adjacent mine he uses the opportunity to eye what I'm reading.

"What are you studying? Italian villas. Interesting, for what purpose may I ask?"

"No particular reason. I found it on Emerald's shelf."

"Fascinating." His dark eyes glimmer. I wonder silently why it strikes him so. "How have you been keeping?" he inquires, withdrawing his meerschaum from a waistcoat pocket and checking the time-of-day with a gold timepiece on a chain. He extracts a pinch of shag from his tobacco pouch and tamps the bowl while I ramble on about the past few weeks. I feel the pangs of guilt, having been somewhat removed from company business since our return from Prague and the horrid business of *the Burning Man.*

"How about yourself?" I ask during a protracted silence.

"I've been well," he replies, lighting his pipe with a cedar match, filling the room in a gray haze. He studies me intently for a minute then asks: "Are you fit to travel?"

"Where?"

"The southwest… Arizona."

"Arizona? Why?" He takes the pipe from his teeth and exhales.

"The medicine man is refusing to fly." He is speaking about Grey, the Apache medicine man who had been flown from Arizona to deal with the odious situation at the Clay Street apartment. "Apparently the flight in was not to his liking. He's refusing the return flight. I've agreed to take him back personally."

"I see. When do you intend to leave?"

"Immediately."

"Immediately?"

"Indeed. He's preparing to hitchhike back to the reservation as we speak." I can scarcely believe it.

"Lucien… surely he can wait a day or so?"

"Of course I've asked this question of him, however he seems bent upon an immediate departure."

"But why?"

"He was less clear on that point," he says. "I would certainly refrain from bothering you over it, had I the proper credentials to manage a motor vehicle," he states flatly. "You can most certainly decline, I've no right to put you under any unnecessary duress."

"Of course. I'll prepare to leave at once."

"No." We both turn. She has quietly descended the stairs, the brow knitted beneath the folds of her dark hair. "I don't want him to go." I look into her lovely, but troubled, eyes.

"What is it Morgan?" Lucien asks.

"I don't know... but I don't think he should go." We both stare at her. "I feel something... something odd. Don't you sense it? An omen of some kind," she whispers.

"An omen? What sort of omen?"

"I'm not sure... but I don't think you should go. Have the police take Grey back... it was their business to begin with. It's the least they can do to repay all your sacrifices." There is a long silent exchange between them.

"Morgan, how long have you been away from home?"

"This is my home..." she responds absently.

"But I thought you live in New York," Lucien says and Morgan falls silent. "How long have you been away?" She suddenly grows impatient.

"A little over a month," she says crossing her arms as if feeling a sudden chill. "Uncle, are you implying I'm remiss in my professional career?" Lucien seems shocked.

"Morgan... you know I'm the last person on this earth who would criticize you professionally." She touches the side of her temple with just the fingertips.

"I'm sorry. It's just... first mother leaves abruptly, and now you both. Something's not right. Are you telling me you don't sense something?"

"Perhaps it's time to check on matters back in the metropolis my dear, reconnect with the center of your life," he says with care. Her eyes dilate, growing dark and begin to quell with moisture.

"I can't believe it Uncle Lucien, of all people." I watch as tears build in her dulcet green eyes. "Are you actually dismissing my concerns? If it were anyone else in the family you would consider what I'm saying, but because it's me..." We look at each other, her eyes glistening. I'm somehow unable to speak. She turns and ascends the stair. Lucien strokes the beard on his chin, a concerned expression etched upon his face.

"Hmm…" he mulls deep in thought.

"I'll talk to her," I say.

I tap on the door and let myself in. She sits on the edge of the bed gazing through the window at the wooden siding of the neighboring house. The bed is covered with photo prints, her cameras, a Macintosh laptop and a large three ring binder with headshots of beautiful models. Resumes and production reports are strewn about. I make some room and join her.

"What are you looking at?"

"Nothing," she says stoically engaged with the empty frame of the window. I reach down and take her hand. I roll the amethyst ring on her finger between my thumb and index.

"Morgan, don't be upset, we'll be back in a day or two." She looks into my eyes.

"I'm not upset Willem, I'm concerned. Do you understand the difference?" I ponder this a moment.

"What are you concerned about?" She closes her eyes –as if pained- and resumes her vigil out the window.

"I told you. You choose not to listen to me… so it doesn't matter." She gently pulls her hand from mine, placing it across her cheek between us. Her sudden aloofness stabs at me.

"What is it you feel?" I ask but she's fixated out the window. I stroke her shoulders and they suddenly seem so thin and fragile. I repeat my question. She rolls her head as if caught between two thoughts.

"Nothing… like what I'm feeling about mother." I see the tears forming in her eyes and I feel lost. "Uncle Lucien says my concerns about her are nothing… so… they're nothing," she says turning toward me and it takes everything I have to hold her wounded gaze. She lays her head into my shoulder and strokes the back of my neck with her fingertips. After a few minutes of silence she whispers in words barely audible: "You better go."

"Okay, I will," I say with aplomb. "It should only take a day to drive down, then a quick flight back," I say and cup her cheek in the palm of my hand and kiss her crimson lips that taste like the smell of wild orchids.

When I rejoin Lucien, he's sitting on the stoop, the smoke from his pipe wafting upwards, spiraling into strange shapes mixing with the gentle breeze. I look up into the immensity of *the big blue*. It's a stunningly clear morning. We begin to stroll down Sutter in the direction of Union Street where it will be easier to hail a cab.

"Are you alright?" he inquires.

"In what way?" I ask, a tinge of regret in my voice.

"You've bonded with Morgan, it's quite profound."

"She's a very... remarkable woman." Lucien eyes me intently.

"Undoubtedly... quite remarkable." He continues to study me closely as we walk.

"What is it?" I ask, for he seems unwilling to break off his scrutiny.

"How much did she tell you about herself, her family, during your time together?" he asks in a rather mysterious way. I muse over this for several moments.

"Not much I suppose. We talked a lot about art and literature... photography of course, and cinema... we've a lot in common."

"Unquestionably." We turn the corner onto Union Street. "Did she tell you, perchance... about her lineage?"

"What do you mean?" He stops and takes a seat at one of the bus stops.

"Well, did she mention she comes from a long line of authentic witches?" I'm astounded. I can scarce believe I have heard him correctly.

"I beg your pardon?" He pounds his pipe on the leg of the bench discarding the spent ash and gestures for me to sit down.

"The French line that was expelled from Acadia three centuries ago." I stand there in a state of confusion. "Do sit down old boy," he mutters, "let's discuss this rationally." I take a seat next to him.

"Are you actually trying to tell me… that sophisticated, contemporary woman… *is a witch*?" I ask with undoubtedly more than a hint of sarcasm in my voice. He doesn't answer immediately but studies me closely several moments while he refills his pipe. His eyes are keen and he seems to be looking not at me directly but more at some aspect of my person. He continues to elude my question as he lights the bowl with a cedar match shaking it out and discarding it into the gutter puffing on his pipe for several moments.

"Seamus MacIntyre was perhaps my greatest friend. I've not a *blood brother* per se but if I did, he would very much be this person," he says. "We shared much of our youth together in Scotland and England. He was instrumental in my development as *a human being*." He looks at me in a most intense manner. "Do you comprehend what I'm saying?" I nod but in truth am not entirely certain what he means by use of the phrase *human being* or his strange emphasis on the words. He nods and relinquishes his stare, diverting his attention across the street. "He was schooled as an anthropologist but his passion, his desired learning, was in mysticism, in particular witchcraft and sorcery. This is not unique within his family, this branch of the MacIntyre tree."

He re-lights his bowl and puffs several times causing the person next to him to relocate. "He was a storyteller and wrote extensively." I stare across the street at what I think he's studying but nothing more than shoppers and passersby scurry about upon the concrete walk. "Seamus fell in love with a young woman during his numerous trips to Louisiana, while conducting an extensive study of one of the French lines of witches and married her when she came of age." He looks at me squarely and I sense his meaning implicitly.

"Emerald?" I ask, less a question than a statement.

"Indeed. Morgan is their daughter and was prepared as a young girl for this line of study." I return my attention across the street and consider this. "Many people think the Creole culture endemic to the Americas but this is hardly complete. The culture is a mix of native societies and the French and European migrations, in particular the French. Deep within those amalgams exist the old lines of mystics and healers that left the old country to escape the religious persecution going on at that time in history." He pauses and studies me a moment. "You may be quite aware that many, many people including an inordinate amount of women were... *lost*, during that loathsome time under the proclamation of being witches."

"Yes, I'm somewhat aware of it."

"They followed the Huguenots and other persecuted sects to America, many the deep South, in particular the French enclave at New Orleans where they found fertile ground for the synthesis of their... for lack of a better phrase, *religious* pursuits. The French mysticism synthesized with the native nature cults and the result was a pure earth religion. I'm not talking about black sorcery here, nor the Obeah and voodoo cults that imbibe in the manipulation of the human emotional sphere. I'm referring to those adherents that interfaced with the energies of *Nature herself* and the boundless potentials of *the Source itself*, all for the benefit of the society as a whole; *a more confluent connection with Universal thought*." He pauses to look at me and I'm sure my detached expression conveyed my confusion. "I've a question for you. Did Morgan tell you how she became involved in the art of photography?" I return his gaze. His eyes are bright and lucid.

"She told me she started at a very young age." This makes him smile.

"Nothing more?" I admit this is all the detail she had divulged. He puffs on his pipe silently, deep in thought.

"Why?" I suddenly ask, keenly interested in knowing. He muses a moment in thought.

"I doubt she would object to my telling you. She probably wanted to, but not knowing you as I do, may have felt your reaction possibly an adverse one." I'm intrigued and press the point. "When she was a mere lass, she could see the spirit of a young girl and her cat meander about the old mansion in New Orleans. She had even given the girl, and the cat, names. One afternoon when she was perhaps seven or eight years, she requested the use of Seamus' Leica. It was her intention to photograph the girl spirit." He smiles, momentarily lost in memories of the time. When he looks back at me it's as if I can actually see Morgan as a young precocious girl, I even sense the grand old estate and its gardens. "Anyway, she was never quite able to get the picture of the *phantom child* she desired, however, a love for photography emerged. Now, as you know, she's a very successful photographer in New York City." He grows quiet again, seemingly lost in thoughts about his niece.

"Does she… does she still…" I stammer and Lucien interjects.

"See ghosts?" he asks finishing my question. "I'm afraid not my boy… living with all the constraints upon *her attention* that her profession interposes has deadened her keener senses I fear," he says wistfully. "Perhaps it's for the best, who can really say."

"Then, when you say she's a witch, then, you're… well… you don't mean it literally?" His demeanor changes into an intense study of my person.

"Of course I mean it literally. The blood of eight centuries of the MacIntyre and Montaigne lines flow in her veins. Her mother is an Adept. All of Morgan's extensive line of aunts all possess *the insight*… including the sisters in Scotland, Seamus' sisters, Vivien and Vanetta MacIntyre."

"What do you mean by… *insight?*"

"The ability to see beyond this base mortal plane into that which is consciousness." I sit dumbfounded, my world becoming much larger. "And to compound it, Morgan is what is referred to within known circles as *a Power Child.*"

"A what?"

"Every line possesses them, every family, every species within the animal and plant kingdoms alike," he states matter-of-factly. "Just as energy ebbs and flows, sound and light vibrate within certain frequencies, water peaks and troughs… familial and genetic lines peak and ebb. Most members possess stasis, however, every few cycles and certainly within generations *a Power Child* is born, the peak of the frequency. Morgan is such a person." I stare at him in utter amazement. "Surely by now you understand that all of life, all of manifest reality, is frequency and vibration?" he asks and stares into the center of my being.

"She's never mentioned any of this at all," I say for lack of anything more substantial. Lucien merely shrugs, puffing on his pipe.

"It's immaterial, they exist none the less. Some are of equal or greater ability than Emerald... primarily Monique Montaigne." He grows silent, suddenly deep in thought.

"Why haven't I met them?" I ask and the look from Lucien nearly makes my skin crawl.

"My dear lad, these persons are ill-disposed to journey out into the chaos and insanity of this world in which we reside. Emerald is very much the exception and this is due entirely to the influence of Seamus MacIntyre."

"How so?" I ask and he looks at me with an incredulous expression upon his face.

"I've already told you. The two met, were attracted to each other body and soul as two magnets interlock and she journeyed forth with him into the world. Followed him to Europe. Schooled at the great institutions on that continent and was able to channel her natural abilities within that course of study, and very much for the benefit of humankind I should add." He states this all so matter-of-factly that I find myself dumb and mute. "Hello..." he says pointing his stick. "The tram arrives."

The Muni bus screeches to a halt and hisses as it lowers itself to the curb. Lucien clamors aboard while I pay the driver our fares. He takes one of the single seats up front in the handicapped section, which is uncharacteristic for him and I sense the conversation about Morgan and her family is closed.

I gaze out the window as the bus climbs about the San Franciscan landscape. I think about Morgan, the last several days of our time together, the joy and mystery about her. Inside my heart I know what Lucien is telling me is very much in truth. Deep inside the pit of my stomach I feel a great longing for her, to get off at the next stop and retrace my steps back to her embrace.

As fancy gives way to a clearer sense of reality, I begin to recall moments when I found her staring off into space as if peering into another world, the pupils dilated fully. I would casually entreat her about her thoughts, but always the same response, a sort of shrug and resumption of the work upon the table or laptop, conversation instantly resuming regarding her photography or perhaps a restaurant or movie she was contemplating.

There was one exception. I had come down the staircase to find her staring fixedly out the large bay windows over-looking Sutter Street. This was shortly after our return from Prague. I questioned what she was engaged with. There was no response. I repeated the question to witness the same stoic disconnect. When I placed my hand upon her shoulder, she abruptly turned and her countenance shocked me.

"I need to call my mother," she announced and immediately took up her mobile phone in a very agitated state. Whatever the conversation that ensued I was not privy. She removed herself from the confines of the house into the back garden, pacing back and forth amongst the ferns in something of an animated state. I watched time to time from the window and felt a deep concern. After a period she rejoined me inside in a less than pleasant mood. I enquired about Emerald. She informed me that she was unable to speak with her.

"Is she alright?" I asked pensively.

"Yes... she's alright," she answered somberly.

"Then, why weren't you allowed to talk with her?" I asked and as if igniting a fuse she exploded.

"Those damn witches!" she railed slamming the cell phone down upon the teakwood table, shattering the screen. I stared at her in awe and she seemed to recoil from her anger. "I need to talk to Uncle Lucien," and immediately set about to leave. I suggested I would accompany her but she declined, asking I remain and *mind the house.* It was less a request than a dictate. I watched as she took her coat from the rack and was gone out the front door. Her sister Audrey came down the stairs asking about the commotion. I told her about the unsuccessful phone call to New Orleans.

"Oh, don't worry about it," she said. "Morgan's not always clear in her thinking about them."

"What do you mean?" I asked.

"Well, ever since her breakdown, she's been at odds with the family in New Orleans about her life," she said off-handedly.

"Breakdown?" I asked and Audrey seemed to freeze upon the stairs.

"Never mind. Everything's cool. Don't worry about it," she said heading back up the stairs.

"Audrey wait." She stopped and stared down at me. "Can you mind the house? I'd like to visit Lucien."

"Don't do it!" she interjected with intent.

"What?"

"Leave it alone. If you interfere you'll regret it," she said in a most disturbing manner. She didn't wait around for my reaction but headed up the stairs saying over her shoulder, "Besides, I'm getting ready for Europe."

I think over this reverie as the bus lurches uphill, the pink and beige stucco homes all at a distinct incline. I had thought at the time, Morgan's use of the word *witches* as nothing more than a derogatory term. Now I wasn't so certain. When she returned several hours later it was as if nothing had happened. She immediately engaged me in conversation and had brought cake from a French patisserie on Bush Street. I inquired if she had seen Lucien and she confirmed this, forwarding his regards. I said I felt I had been remiss in my exchange with him. She waved away my concerns saying he was very busy *with the old men*. When I asked her to elucidate, she looked at me squarely saying:

"You'd rather talk about a bunch of old men?" I took her face in my hands and we kissed.

I feel a sudden jab in my side and turn abruptly, Lucien poking me in the ribs with his cane.

"We get off here," he says looking at me oddly and disembarks. I gather my bag and exit into the throng on Union Square.

The square is alive with people. Women in fine dress and expensive jewelry entering and exiting Tiffany's while the homeless outside the doors pan for dimes with paper cups. Musicians are playing beneath the palms hovering over the square. Suddenly Lucien stops and gestures.

"Do you see this? Do you feel a vibrancy?" he asks. I gaze at the people about the square, rich and poor alike, some in business attire mingling with artists and transients. "*This is the Power Child*," he says, "*the ability to coalesce extremes*." He looks at me intently. I study the environ trying to realize his meaning. "The rich to poor, here and valid... this is the nature of the Power Child," he says. "Cities, nations in fact, take on attributes similar those of the individual personality, it's well documented. Some cities and nations are *old souls* some young, occasionally *the power child* emerges within the *family of states*, San Francisco is such a place."

"What do you mean by that?" I ask. He gestures about us.

"The answer lies before you… do you not see it?"

"I don't mean San Francisco Lucien, I mean… people," I say and he studies me intently.

"The ability to live multiple lives, multiple perspectives if you will, within the parameters of the one life, to see, or more appropriately *to feel* the experience of life through the eyes of another," he says. I wish we have more time to discuss it, however, Lucien turns and resumes his slow meandering path through the park toward the Saint Francis Hotel.

As we cross Powell Street, taking care to dodge the cable car that climbs its way toward the crest of the hill, I spy Grey, the odd old medicine man standing off to one side of the entrance to the hotel. He wears a white flannel shirt, faded blue jeans, dusty black cowboy boots and a new white broad-brimmed Stetson. He also wears his patented reflective aviator sunglasses. I realize the times we have met previously, he's never been without these glasses firmly in place.

He's amiable, immediately engaging Lucien in a spirited conversation. I'm amazed he is fully packed and ready to go. Lucien informs Grey we will need about an hour to be fully prepared for the journey and suggests he relax in the restaurant or one of the numerous coffee houses. Grey declines in lieu of the benches in the Square.

I follow Lucien into the St. Francis. He departs upstairs in the lift while I work with the concierge securing a rental vehicle for the forthcoming trip. When we are ready, I find Grey sitting stoically on one of the stone benches in the Square staring into the crowd.

"Sorry we were long in getting ready." He looks at me, his eyes hidden behind the dark lenses.

"This is a good place," he says. "Pretty good place." I glance about and nod.

"Yes, I like it too."

It's put to vote, Highway 1, 101 or Interstate 5? I ardently press for 5 due its expedient nature –I want to get this trip over with and return to San Francisco as soon as possible. I'm out voted in favor of Highway 1 –the slowest route- Grey wanting to see the Pacific Ocean and Lucien's desire to visit Big Sur and a particular acquaintance of his residing there. Thus we begin the slow arduous drive down Highway 1, tossing and turning about the undulating California coastline with its myriad of bays and inlets.

We stop in the seaside city of Monterey and indulge in an excellent brunch. We then take an hour's respite in Carmel for coffee with an acquaintance of Lucien's who proceeds to take us to his estate not far from the famous Pebble Beach. He graciously offers us use of the house for the night including an invitation to explore this quintessentially delightful area but Grey dissuades us. I feel an intense disappointment leaving the occasion behind.

We head south on the winding two-lane that skirts the stunning Pacific, colored an almost magical cerulean blue. The road meanders through the redwoods, dipping to sea-level at times then climbing to several hundred feet, the coastline dropping off in sheer cliffs toward the pounding surf below; the marvelous ocean incessantly tossing herself against the rock creating a most intense blue and white patterning.

By the afternoon we make Big Sur and its wild golden barranca. Grey and I have an extended dinner at a local distillery while we wait for Lucien –after being picked up by a most exotic blonde woman in an old beaten Jeep. Grey proves to be a man of few words and as he wears mirrored sunglasses obscuring his eyes, it seems an eternity before Lucien rejoins us and we are off in the direction of San Luis Obispo. At Santa Barbara we divert onto Highway 101 and the LA mainstream. By the time we're on Highway 10 toward Phoenix it's well onto twilight. We head east into the heart of the immense Mojave.

Highway 10 proves to be a long lonely road and our intrepid trio is not resplendent with conversation. Somewhere near midnight –quite unexpectedly- a large coyote darts across the road directly before the car causing me to break severely, just missing the animal. This awakens the two old travelers with a start, both inquiring as to what I'm doing.

"A coyote ran across the road in the headlights," I report.

"Which direction?" Grey inquires mysteriously.

"Beg your pardon?"

"Which direction was he headed?" he echoes resolutely.

"Uh… it happened fast…" I think out loud, wondering what possible reason for such a question unless to make idle conversation. "This direction," I say pointing north.

"Hmm," he mutters low and grows quiet. For some reason this piques Lucien's curiosity.

"What is it?" he asks Grey.

"Bad omen," the old Indian murmurs and both grow amazingly quiet.

Eventually, out of boredom, I reach down and turn on the car's radio. I twist the knob through the spectrum but only some lonely desert station comes in –oddly enough- playing Rap music. I can see Grey from the edge of my vision studying me when abruptly he reaches down and turns it off.

"You listen to music that would degrade your mother, your sisters and your very own daughters?" He stares at me implacably. I'm not quite sure what to say so I say the truth.

"It's probably the only radio station between here and Needles." He just stares at me in the darkness of the cab. "It's just to help keep me awake," I say and he reaches into his shirt pocket and withdraws a small beaded pouch and extracts a piece of what looks like ash wood and hands it to me. "Oh, no thanks, I'll be alright," I say but he's insistent.

"Just pinch it between your cheek and gum, you'll stay awake," he says. I take it, it's hard like wood and smells awful but I stick it in my mouth anyway and bite into it; the flavor is remarkably good, a mix between pine and ginger.

"It's good. What is it?"

"Root," is all he says and leans back in his seat pulling his hat down over his eyes. Soon I'm wide-awake, the root's flavor and zeal infusing a comfortable alertness that is very pleasing.

I push the car on into the night, the desert glowing for miles with a pallid iridescence under the moonlight. The rest of the journey is conducted in abject silence. Having never driven it, I have no idea of the vastness of the great American desert. The emptiness absorbs us. It takes all my energy to finally get us into Blythe and secure rooms for the remainder of the night.

The following morning starts agonizingly early, Lucien ringing my room at seven o'clock.

"Grey wants to get going, he's already been up over an hour." I want to point out that he had slept most of the trip from Los Angeles but instead ask for enough time to shower and meet up with them just before eight o'clock in the lobby of the tired old highway motel.

Grey seems pensive, less relaxed than the drive along the Pacific coast. Lucien actually questions him about his mood. He says he is anxious to get back home and check on things. I push the car eastward toward Phoenix and listen to Lucien and Grey converse on a number of topics including some unnerving details of the *cleansing of the Clay Street apartment* –which quite frankly made the hair at the base of my skull tingle- and the quiet coolness I have been harboring toward the old man begins to dissipate. Almost as if reading my thoughts Grey says:

"We travel over oceans, over mountains, across the deserts to do battle with evil creatures out of love for humanity. We call upon the Great Spirit for guidance and protection in these pursuits. This is the new battlefield of our age. In our hearts we are loving and forgiving, men and women of peace, but we're unafraid to go into battle with the formless world, the world of devils and apparitions that this world, this plane in which we live be made safe for the Great Mother. She who nurtures us gives us life." I look at him and he's looking directly at me, his eyes invisible behind the mirrored sunglasses reflecting the golden rays of the new sun.

We stop briefly in Phoenix for lunch and soon we are again pushing on eastward into the heart of *the Superstition Mountains*. Grey tells us there is good reason this range is named so, apparently replete with stories of mystical events and history.

"This was the last stronghold of the great Apache Nation, the last free American tribe." He looks at me. "We call ourselves Americans. We are the true original American people, the Indian people, the native American," he says with conviction. "These men fought for their freedom and way of life against the soldiers who came here, right up to the turn of the twentieth century. Our nation is a nation of warriors. Though we no longer carry the war baton we fight against oppression and ignorance. It's always been this way, since the beginning, the war against mankind's two greatest enemies, *Ignorance and Stupidity*."

He continues to tell us about the great Apache leaders, Cochise, Victorio and Geronimo, their ability to elude the army's plans.

"They could change shape... into animals or birds. They could sing to the mountain and the mountain would swallow them."

"They were skilled in the art of camouflage?" I question him and he studies me.

"Three thousand soldiers chased Geronimo and his band of two hundred men and women for over three years. They say the men *could disappear from the face of the earth or change into an animal, to fight again*."

The afternoon had become scorching hot. By the time we make the boundary of the reservation, it's well over one hundred degrees Fahrenheit. We turn off the Interstate and proceed down the dusty two-lane blacktop deep into the reservation. I notice –feel actually- a change, a sense of timeless emptiness. We pass enormous tracts of barren desert smattered with a few old derelict homes, gutted trailers void of life; relics from a by-gone era before the casinos came to the reservation. Tired broken fences made of old rough-hewn pine logs, miles from any discernible dwelling, baking in the sun, add an odd element to the surreal landscape; burnt rock and dust everywhere.

When we make the village it seems little more than a post office, a grocery store and a few ramshackle buildings flanked by a few old single story homes.

We turn off the main street onto a hot black-tar road passing the carcass of a dead steer beside a dried out saguaro and proceed east. Eventually we turn onto a gravel road that cuts a swath into the sagebrush. This chip-rock road dumps us onto a sandy two track that takes us to Grey's *ranch*.

I get out of the car, stretch and breathe in the dry air. Not a speck of moisture. There's an old single story cement-block house and a corral made of lashed up red pine poles with two impressive horses –one, a spirited black stallion and the other a gray speckled mare, an Appaloosa.

Completely out of place to the northwest *sits a new modern home*. It is into this house Grey requests I wait while Lucien follows him into the old weathered and well-lived cement-block house. As I make my way across the gravel and scrub he called *the yard* I spy several young Apache children playing under the shade of a stand of large cottonwood trees. Two mongrels –both very thin with ribs showing- are with them, one watching me closely, the other scratching itself and staring off down the ravine. At the door of the home I knock but there is no answer. It is only after my second attempt, slightly louder, that I hear a strange thin raspy voice clearly say, *'Come in.'*

Upon entering I'm astounded to find *absolutely no one within the house*. I search the entirety of the home yet not a soul is present to account for the odd invitation. Incredibly, the house is void of what one would consider the accoutrements of any normal home. There's all the necessary furniture sitting in place but nothing more. I call out several times, no answer. When I set my bag upon the living room table, I'm shocked when a caged mockingbird of black and white plumage, that I had failed to notice earlier, repeats the welcome. I stare at the bird and the bird stares back, its black eyes study my every move. I say *hello* and the bird says *hello* in return. A trained miner bird! I repeat my salutation and the fowl does the same.

I sit down on the brand new sofa. It is one of those L-shaped affairs and spotless. Adorning it are a set of end tables and a coffee table also new and polished. I begin to note that the entire home is immaculate and an odd thought hits me that it looks very much like a film set just prior to shooting, just before the set dresser and props persons ply their art to give *the set* a lived-in look. This home is literally showcase perfect in every detail. I study the strange environ and it seems odd, very out of place compared to its immediate neighbor, and the harsh exterior, outside.

The bird swinging in its cage twitters. I puzzle over the odd situation when the bird suddenly speaks again.

"Hello," it mimes flitting from one stanchion to another. I look at the bird staring at me intently. "Hello" it chirps again and more out of boredom I say *hello* back at which point the amazing fowl says distinctly: "Who are you?" *clearly couching the words as a question.* I'm amazed at how well the bird is trained when it repeats itself again and the words, the question, *creates a very odd feeling.*

I decide to retrieve my notebook and receipts and begin tallying the expenditures of the trip when suddenly the fowl says:

"*Let me out.*" This is quite remarkable. How ingenious I think, to teach a bird to say something of this nature. After an interval of perhaps four to five minutes the bird says again clearly: "*Hey you, let me out.*"

I'm awestruck for the animal says this in no uncertain language. I study the bird and his coal black eyes look into mine without blinking. Suddenly this amazing creature says in the clearest and plainest wording:

"Let me out, *please.*" This is too much. I rise and walk over to the cage and study it closely. I'm certain that someone has hidden a microphone as a joke but nothing in or around the cage indicates a pun is in progress, no wires nor electronics of any sort are evident anywhere near the bird and its cage. I tap on the bars several times. The bird flits about watching me keenly but remains steadfastly silent. I bait it with questions, '*Want a cracker?*' –and the rest. It isn't until I return to the sofa that the crazy thing says, *Let me out*, again clearly and in the plainest English. This is beginning to border on the bizarre. I study the beast and find myself intrigued.

"What did you say?" I ask and wait for an answer but the bird simply flits about its cage eyeing me in a most curious manner. I return to my notes and after several minutes the bird says:

"Hey…" I turn and look at it staring when it says clearly once again: "Let me out." This is beyond weird. I walk to the cage scrutinizing the animal closely.

"Do you want out?" I ask and the damn thing replies:

"Yes."

It's the oddest thing, knowing rationally that the creature is mimicking an already rehearsed set of words, yet experiencing first-hand a member of the animal kingdom responding to my own utterances in an extremely uncanny manner. I actually find myself playing with the door's mechanism as if to goad the thing on further.

"You want out?" I ask, loosening the latch, when in a sudden furious frenzy the crazy thing flies at the door snapping it open from my hand and escapes into the room, perching upon the rail of the curtain rod suspended above the large glass windows over-looking the desert to the southeast. I immediately go for the thing's legs and it flies across the room, bounces off one of the smaller windows before returning to its perch on the curtain rod. *Damn!* I say to myself. *How did I allow myself to let loose Grey's family bird?* I attempt its retrieval but every opportunity to gather the blasted thing fails. I begin to worry it might break its neck on one of the windowpanes, all –oddly- secured tight despite the desert sun that shines through them making the entire house uncomfortably hot. Eventually I conclude the best course of action is to get Grey. Perhaps they have already been through this little farce and possess the proper technique to capture the errant fowl.

As I proceed to carefully open the front door, I'm inexplicably confronted by the two curs that earlier had seemed so docile. They both come bounding over baring fangs and yelping at the top of their lungs. I'm forced inside the screen door for fear of being bitten. Then –just as shocking- when I crack open the door to shout at the dogs and bring them to their senses, the wily mocking-jay flies through the gap of the door and is gone.

I make quite a fuss about the escape and the dogs instantly cower off. Is it my voice suddenly full of irritation that makes them cower so? It strikes me as very odd behavior.

Dogs aside, there is nothing to be done about the situation but to report the loss of the pet to Grey. The dogs, weirdly, are now nowhere to be seen as I chance the journey across the yard and knock upon the door of the old house. A tall thin Indian girl with long ebony hair tied in a pink ribbon answers. I ask if Lucien and Grey are available and she leaves me standing outside while she goes to retrieve them. I look about at the controlled chaos of the yard. Saws, pine poles and chipped wood lay about. On the large rough-hewn picnic table, an assortment of horse tack and rope –lassos- sit beside a large bucket of what looks like lard and another filled with barley or oats. Laying about helter-skelter is a plethora of old discarded rusty cans and bottles.

Grey emerges from the dark interior of the house still wearing his reflective sunglasses. I marvel silently to myself that he apparently wears them inside his own home. He asks how I'm doing and I tell him about the bird. His look is one of distinct shock for he stares at me in length through the dark glass without saying a word until:

"Did he get out of the house?" which I readily confirm. I follow him across the yard to the house and watch as he inspects the cage and scans the interior of the home as if the bird might possibly still be there. I then follow him back to the old house and watch as he retreats inside without inviting me to enter.

Ten minutes later, Lucien emerges and squints in the bright desert sun and entreats me to sit with him at the wooden table fashioned out of knotty pine. He stretches out his right leg, wincing. I inquire how he feels and he says that the extensive car ride has tightened his leg. He fills his pipe and begins to smoke before turning his attention to me.

"So, what's all this about the bird?" I tell him what has happened and he grows surprisingly pensive, stroking his beard deep in thought. I inform Lucien that I will pay to replace the pet. "If it were only so easy," he says strangely. I assure him probably a car ride –lengthy as it is- into Phoenix will assuredly resolve the issue at which point he looks at me in the most intense manner, his dark eyes like coals of fire and says, "It's much worse than that," and begins to convey to me that the bird I have inadvertently released into the world is not a bird at all *but an incarcerated black shaman who has the proclivity of turning himself into a coyote and terrorizing the homes and ranches in the area!* This individual is so dubious, so caustic and evil of nature that he stalks persons walking at night and pursues them with such wild abandon as to create the deepest kind of fear and dread within the immediate and extended communities. He also has the penchant of unlatching corrals and coops and chasing, and oft times killing, the livestock. Several gruesome mutilations had been reported throughout the boundaries of the various tribal lands and a bounty had been placed upon the species although it had been known within the circle that much of the devastation was due this vitriolic character *and his insatiable appetite for fear and blood.*

Lucien finishes telling his tale, puffing on his pipe and stares at me without the least bit of humor in his approach. I chuckle outwardly wondering when *the pun* might wane but there is no reprieve in his severe countenance or in his steadfast gaze.

"You are joking of course?"

a

"Joking?" he echoes.

"Of course. You don't think for one moment that this story Grey has fabricated has any basis in reality... do you?" He looks at me in utter disbelief.

"Quite the contrary," he says matter-of-factly. "It is of the most serious nature." Eventually –with a certain air of incredulity- I inquire what is to be done about the situation. "I'm not sure," he says peering into the distant desert landscape. "They're discussing the matter now."

"They?" I inquire and he looks at me deadpan.

"The tribal elders," he says and returns his gaze toward the distant mountains.

No more than thirty minutes later a large white pickup truck roars up and parks. Four men, all in cowboy boots and hats, step out, gaze at Lucien and I a moment and then enter the old house. Soon the men re-emerge, followed by Grey, and slowly amble up beside where we sit. No one looks at me but all four are introduced and shake hands with Lucien. Grey and the men all speak together in the Apache tongue and in English when addressing Lucien. After about five minutes or so of this idle chatter they all suddenly turn about and face me, not menacingly, but neither light-hearted. Grey introduces me to the largest fellow, a man named Grant, who shakes my hand. He says a few words in Apache to Grey who shrugs and kicks at the burnt rock beneath his boot.

"The bird you let loose was a medicine man that went bad, couple years back," Grant says. "Pretty bad medicine, so we were keeping him here under lock, Grey was... so, now he's back out again." There's a long pause, several nods from the others. "So, we asked Grey to go back out and bring him in, but his eldest son is no longer here... so, he don't want to do it." The group looks at Grey who studies the ground and kicks at the pebbles beneath his boot.

"No," he says softly shaking his head. They all return their attention to me.

"So... someone's got to go out and bring him in," Grant says and the men all nod and voice their conviction. A short lean man in a long sleeved pink shirt and black hat steps up.

"We were hoping since you let him out, you'd go out and bring him back," and everybody is in distinct agreement about this idea. I look at Lucien who only sits and smokes, not saying a word. I look at all the men who stand resolutely before me waiting on my response.

"How do I find the bird out there?" I ask pointing at the wide and desolate wilderness and this makes the men chuckle softly.

"He won't be a bird no more," Grant says. "That was Grey's doing," and the other men all look at Grey with a distinct admiration upon their brown faces. They speak a few words together in Apache and laugh.

"Then, how do I find it?" I ask and a sort of hush falls over the group. They seem to be looking to Grey for some sort of answer to my question. He speaks with them quietly in Apache, all the while kicking at the gravel beneath his boot. All the men nod and answer in unison and Grant says:

"Grey's going to teach you. He'll sweat with you and ask for help."

"Help? From whom?" I ask and the question seems to confuse them. Grey says something in Apache, which makes them all laugh. This effectively ends the meeting, the two silent men immediately leaving together for the truck while Grant and the thin man remain for a moment longer speaking with Grey in their native tongue. As the thin man passes me he holds out his hand and we shake. His hand is hard, like dried leather, and his shake firm. Grant places his large hand on my shoulder.

"Don't worry Cochise, Grey is the best medicine man," he says and he and the thin man leave together saying something in Apache over his shoulder to Grey who responds in kind. We watch the truck roar off in a cloud of white dust. Grey continues to stare long after they are gone as if in deep thought. He sits down next to Lucien and they talk together so softly I can hear little of their conversation. Then he rises and says to me:

"We'll sweat tomorrow," nodding from behind his dark glasses before heading toward the house taking a moment to shout to the children who come running over to him and they all disappear into the house.

Lucien and I get into the rental car and head back into town, about a forty-minute drive through the empty desert scrub. Once we're clear of the reservation I ask:

"What's going on?"

"They're counting on you to undo your error," he says somewhat sharply.

"What, letting a bird go?" I ask incredulously and he grows silent a moment before saying flatly:

"The men are all in agreement that the bird you released, for whatever reason, is in reality a *black sorcerer*, an extremely dubious fellow who has damaged their flocks, herds and crops and has caused terror in their communities. A few months ago, Grey, with the assistance of his son, caught the rascal in his favorite guise, that of a coyote, and put him in captivity. When the rogue turned himself into a bird to fly, they had a net ready, and once in the cage he could no longer return to his true form as a man nor his preferred form as a coyote." I look at my mentor with bitter disbelief.

"Do you honestly believe in all this nonsense? That a man can change into an animal?" His look is stoic and hard.

"Why, yes in fact... absolutely."

"Seriously?" I ask astonished.

"You do not?" I think a moment then reply that I do not and he grows silent for several moments then says, "Every society, all cultures, hold to the myth, from the Scottish highlands to the darkest reaches of the African Congo, from the furthest reaches of the Saharan desert to the extreme wastes of the Eskimo lands."

"What myth?"

"That the human being is endowed with the ability to transform himself into animals or reptiles."

"What do you mean?"

"Exactly what I just said. The myth or story of Man turning himself into beast is replete throughout all cultures and societies save none. There is no living –or dead- society that doesn't embrace the concept in its pantheon or texts." I think about this for several minutes. I surmise that he is correct in his assertion.

"Still," I say eventually, "surely you admit this whole thing is completely far-fetched."

"How?"

"Come on Lucien... really? A bird, a sorcerer?"

"Are you actually trying to deny the gravity of the situation?" I don't know how to answer this question as I pull onto the main street of the tired desert town with its endless rows of dried out buildings and broken vehicles. "Let me ask you a question," he suddenly says. "Why did you let the bird out of its cage in the first place?" I admit to myself the question is a good one.

"Well, it... well... it asked me to."

"The bird asked to be released, so you did?"

"Oh for God's sake," I stammer.

"Answer my question," he says tersely.

"Yes, that's basically what happened… but it was just a fluke."

"Hardly a fluke dear boy, the bird tricked you into doing its bidding, admit to it." I'm awestruck. For some reason my rational mind fails –or is unwilling- to admit this basic fact, that in actuality, it had asked me to do this very thing, release it.

"But the dogs…" I stammer.

"The dogs?" Lucien asks.

"I was going to go for help, to get the bloody thing back in its cage but the dogs-" I quit mid-sentence as I bring the car to a stop before the old sun-bleached El Rey Motel. He stares at me fixedly, waiting for me to finish my sentence, but I know somehow it's pointless. "Yes, you're correct, it asked and I did it. This is absolutely crazy," I say exasperated.

"There's nothing crazy about it," he says. "*The sorcerer seduced you*. It's very real and very serious. You understand the village and the tribal elders are involved? The men you met today at Grey's, all very busy men who immediately came out."

"Yes, I suppose," I murmur.

"Let's check in and get some sleep," he says. "I'm very tired." Lucien doesn't say anything else nor does he have to.

Later that night in my room, I have an epiphany, or so what I thought at the time. I feel that I clearly see the entire thing is nothing but an extravagant hoax perpetrated by my mentor and his Indian companions. My mind fabricates the details of the whole elaborate scam; all designed as an enormous joke for their collective enjoyment. My mind keeps me awake until the early hours with all sorts of ideas as to why they would entertain such wild schemes. It isn't until the morning –after a fitful sleep- that somehow the reality of this strange and perplexing occurrence seems to place itself into the forefront of my attention. Try as I might to somehow dismiss it all as farce, I know as we retrace our journey back to the reservation –and Lucien's quiet brooding- that I have managed to place ourselves squarely into an odd sort of fate. I know within my heart that our situation is troubling him and what should have been a quick trip to the reservation and a flight back to San Francisco, has now become an open ended affair. I curse my carelessness, or was it carelessness? Lucien used the phrase *seduced by the sorcerer.* Is this in fact what had happened? In a momentary lapse of attention had I allowed myself to be used as an unwitting pawn? The latter thought is very disturbing to some aspect of my inner being.

Upon our arrival at the ranch, a rotund Indian woman with a beautifully smiling face emerges from the old house and informs us that Grey is already at the sweat lodge near the river. She instructs us how to get there and the rocky two-track is almost more than the rental vehicle can handle. When we arrive, Grey emerges from the sweat lodge clad in a loincloth. The lodge is nothing more than willow or cottonwood saplings lashed together and covered over with a few old tarps and blankets and barely large enough for four men. The fire pit is not centered, as I had experienced on sweats in California and South Dakota, but off to one side with tin plating up the side of the lodge wall to protect the fabric from burning. We strip to our briefs and join Grey inside where within the womb-like darkness of the lodge he sings beautiful songs in the Apache tongue and beats four-four time on a small deerskin drum. Despite the intense heat, the experience is rejuvenating. When we conclude the sweat we cool off in the river, which Grey tells us is completely dry mid-summer.

When we return to the ranch, I'm introduced to Grey's wife, the woman we had met that morning. I'm told she is a *seer* and can foretell things by use of ashes from a fire, built in conjunction with the person who's concerns she is addressing, and the careful placement of crystals within the ashes. Questions are asked and *the answers appear within the crystal's facet.*

We have a meal of beans and cornbread. Then Grey says it's time for he and I to *walk the desert.* We head south by southeast on foot. It isn't long before the heat begins to tax my constitution. He informs me that *the heat is my mind playing tricks* and not to pay attention to it. Although it is well over one hundred degrees Fahrenheit, this advice proves to be sound; I begin to notice the discomfort start to wane. He then begins to tell me what I'm up against. My *adversary* is a black sorcerer, very clever and cunning but prone to manipulation by means of his consistent desire to roam in the guise of a coyote.

"He likes that best," Grey mumbles as his boot heels crack the sun-bleached rock underfoot. "So the way you'll catch him is walking this same path here at night, he'll come."

"At night?" I ask somewhat alarmed.

"It's the only way to be sure. Coyote prefers night and is attracted by movement in the desert. He'll come."

"What then?" I ask.

"I'll rig a snare, when he tries to sneak up behind you, you snare him around the neck." This is a bit more than I've bargained for and voice my concern openly.

"Why don't we just set a trap, like hunter's do?" I question him, somewhat imploringly.

"It doesn't work," Grey says matter-of-factly. "He's not a coyote, he's a man. He thinks like a man, but acts like a coyote. He sees through it, just like any man would."

"How about if we just shoot him?"

"That would be murder," he says incredulous. "If he's shot, he'll turn back into a man, dead there on the ground."

"Well, wouldn't that be his just desserts?" I ask and Grey stops in his tracks and stares at me from behind his sunglasses.

"You'd shoot a man down in cold blood?" he asks pointedly. I stare at him. "He hasn't killed anyone... yet... just livestock... and scaring and frightening the women and children," he says returning to walk in the direction of several distant buttes golden in the afternoon sun.

"Why?" I ask. "Why does he do such things?"

"*The black sorcerer feeds on fear, making people afraid gives him energy.* He's an old man so no one's afraid of him when he's an old man... *so he changes into the coyote and stalks people at night as an animal.*" Something inside me knows this is correct and that I mustn't show fear if I am to engage in this pursuit. Another part of me is afraid of being afraid. Suddenly Grey stops and addresses me abruptly.

"You following this here path closely?" he asks. I look about not seeing anything like a path at all and say as much. "You better start paying attention. We'll walk this path every afternoon, next three days, then you'll walk it alone at night. This path is the warrior's path... your friend, if you heed it, probably your death if you don't."

"I thought you said he's not killed anyone?"

"When we caught him he tried to kill me. If my son hadn't been with me…" his voice trails off. "When he finds out what you're up to, well… you better not show any fear."

"Who will come with me?"

"No one… no one wants to do it."

"What if he kills me?"

"*We'll probably not find the bones*," he says and I'm left to ponder in silence. Grey stops briefly looking at me intently. "When it happens, trust your spirit guide, you're not really alone, *none of us are ever alone*. Lucien says your spirit guide is strong, when your personality doesn't get in the way. Trust it and don't show fear. Fear is your undoing if you let it. Make him afraid of you. *Fear can be as much a friend as an enemy*." With those words, he turns and we continue to walk the rest of the way in silence.

We sweat each morning and walk each afternoon for the next three days. The evening of the third day, he says I'm ready. We are eating on the old knotty pine table when the same white truck roars up and Grant and the thin man get out and join us at the table. They speak with Grey and his wife in Apache and whatever is said I do not know but their attitude towards me is the reverse of what I had experienced on their previous visit, a kind of quiet respect in their mannerisms. After approximately ten minutes of discussion, the thin man unfolds a cloth he is carrying. Inside is a large –and beautiful- spotted eagle feather. This feather is then presented to me.

"The tribe is presenting you with an eagle feather," Grey says to me. "That's pretty good, you're a warrior of the tribe now," he says and hands me the delicate object and a feeling unlike anything I have ever experienced before fills my chest. Both of the village elders shake my hand and nod, their dark eyes gleam beneath the brims of their round hats. Then as abruptly as they had arrived, they leave and Lucien and Grey look at my gift with a profound appreciation, Grey's wife smiles at me.

"They're gonna make you chief," she says and they all laugh together. She then goes back inside the house. Grey leads us to what I had thought was a haystack or large pile of sticks covered with a couple old blankets. I'm shocked when Grey throws one of the blankets to one side, revealing a door, and enters. Grey tells us the structure is a traditional Apache home called a *wickiup* and that it's referred to affectionately as *the old woman.*

He lights a fire in the center. We take places on the ground and smoke a tobacco mixture Grey has rolled into a cigarette paper. He corrects the way I hold the cigarette dissuading me from holding it outwardly between my middle and index fingers in lieu of cupping it inward by pinching it between the thumb and index digit. The flavor of the smoke is very pleasant, and it goes around repeatedly until the very stump at which point Grey throws it into the flame.

The fire softly burns on into twilight. One of Grey's sons sticks his head through the door and speaks softly in Apache. Grey nods to me.

"Time to go."

Outside, I'm surprised to find several of his family in attendance. I'm introduced to his two youngest sons and two daughters and their children. One of the daughters fastens the eagle feather to my hair and one of the sons presents me with a long wooden pole with a loop of buckskin strapping on the end that can be drawn in tight by a drawstring.

"What is this?" I ask.

"The snare," Grey says. "He'll think it's a walking stick. Jab at him a few times like this… then hook the noose around his neck and pull hard and cinch it. Don't let go until you get back here." I must admit I'm not very much impressed by this contraption nor its intended use, however I take it and thank him. The last person to talk to me is Lucien.

"Have faith… trust in your higher self." There is nothing more to say. As the sun dips below the distant desert horizon, I wave to the Indian family, shoulder my small pack of foodstuffs and water and with my makeshift coyote snare – crudely disguised as a walking stick- I head off into the desert alone.

I edge my way down the side of the ravine and dig my boot heels into the dry sandy gravel of the desert floor. I look back over my shoulder once and am surprised to see everyone lined along the top of the hillock watching my descent into the desert. *Strange* –I hear myself think sarcastically- *they're watching a dead man walking.*

Approximately an hour into the desert on my south by southeast course, I decide to pause and take a break from the constant trekking. I find a large rock and press my rump against it. Despite the coolness of the rapidly enveloping night, the rock is still warm from the day's heat. It feels good. I begin to drink from my canteen when a strange sound causes me to pause and take heed. It's an odd sound, like *the sound of laughter emanating from the arroyo. I* think perhaps some young people are out in the desert drinking and laughing.

I continue upon my trek toward the south. I haven't gone more than several hundred yards under the moonlight when the same sound issues forth from the desert night but this time much closer. What is it? Were some Indian kids actually this far out into the middle of the desert indulging in some illicit drinking? I continue on course, recognizing some of the familiar signs Grey has keyed me into, when the sound erupts so loudly and in such close proximity that I stop dead in my tracks and listen with all my attention from whence the sound has come. All becomes quiet and still. I begin to realize this is not the sound of human beings at all, *but something else.* I scan the area with the flashlight I have brought with me but see nothing except rock and cactus in shadow creating a strange almost alien landscape. I commence my journey south, quickening my pace.

My objective is Black Butte, a particular butte two hours southeast by foot from the ranch, the entire round trip just over four hours at a good pace. The first time I walked it with Grey it took nearly five hours. By the end of the third day, we returned just under four. It is my intention to accomplish the night's work as quickly as possible. The moon – regrettably- is nothing more than a sliver, a shard of illumination in the omnipresent darkness and the magical landscape, under the endless blanket of stars, stretches on into infinity.

I had made about another half hour at a good pace and could make out the silhouette of Black Butte rising in the distance when a peculiar feeling began to creep into my mind. Not a strong feeling initially, almost unnoticeable at first, however soon I become aware of *something shadowing my pace.* As I walk along, I can discern the sound of something behind me. However, whenever I halt my stride, only the sounds of the night insects can be heard. I continue along, the night getting darker, closing in around me. Suddenly the unmistakable sensation *that someone is right behind me,* grips me. I quickly turn and shine my light, half expecting Grey or someone has traced my steps but there is no one; only shadows dancing in the light emitted from the flashlight in my hand.

I turn and commence my gait in the direction of Black Butte, now a distinct looming shape in the near distance. I welcome its familiar outline and anticipate my arrival when I'm absolutely certain someone is immediately behind me. I instantly stop and turn switching on the light. Incredibly, nothing is there, nothing at all, only the eerie shapes cast by the light of the torch. I pan the beam yet nothing is there to account for the feeling. I switch off the light standing motionless in the dark for several moments listening, but all remains quiet. Commencing my trek toward Black Butte, no sooner do I resume my gait when the unmistakable sensation of something in very close proximity causes me to stop and turn, switching on the light, certain I will see something trailing me yet again there is nothing except the desolate barren landscape of the desert calmly contemplating my passage.

I scan the torch but the way the light's beam causes the shadows to jump and cavort, is unnerving. I switch off the light, let my eyes re-adjust to the night and use my ears. All is quiet only the sparse rattle of night insects. I glance about the omnipresent darkness and the eerie landscape of the desert is so stark and barren as to seem surreal, like another world. I ponder my nervous state of mind. Am I letting my imagination get the best of me? Actually, I thought the entire idea of the *Coyoteman* and human beings changing into the shape and form of animals so far-fetched as to seem ludicrous. My mind simply refused to embrace the concept. These Indians are full of wild tales and notions, I muse to myself. My mind reminds me this is the twenty first century not the eighteen hundreds. I turn and resolutely commence my journey through the scrub. I'm anxious now to make Black Butte and the cabin at its base as quickly as possible, take a break and get this over with.

The cabin is Grey's term for a beaten old den built with ragtag lumber years ago by rogue miners illegally digging for peridot stone. This makeshift structure served as the southern most terminus of this little charade I have so unwittingly stumbled into. The previous three days of sweating and walking was focused upon this spot. After our sweat, meal and desert trek, it was to this tiny shack we would travel, sit for a short period before returning to the ranch.

"Don't get attached to it," Grey had said on more than one occasion. "Rest and get moving again," he reiterated on the three previous trips. I push on.

The next twenty or so minutes of my sojourn is quieter, whatever my mind had conjured up was now relegated to imagination. The trepidation I had felt gives way to thirst and a gnawing sense of fatigue. I desire to sit someplace comfortable and regain my composure for the return trip.

Just as I start to ascend to where the cabin sits beneath the ebony shadow of the enormous butte, something darts across my path, a mere shadow in the meager moonlight, the faint sound of breathing punctuating the night. I stop dead in my tracks and switch on the torch and think I can make out –for a fraction of an instant- the retreating form of a large animal. I approach, carefully panning the entire area with the torch yet nothing is within sight of the flashlight's beam. I quicken my pace and walk perhaps two hundred yards when a disturbance from behind causes me to turn instantly and this time I catch a glimpse of *a low dark form disappearing into the scrub.* I hold the light fast upon the spot as if frozen. I'm of the distinct impression that *something is hiding within the shadows cast by the sagebrush, just out of reach of the torch's light.*

For some unexplainable reason, I cannot muster the courage —or desire- to retrace my steps and investigate the spot fixed within the radius of the beam. My mind reasons that there is nothing although *my gut* feels much differently about it. I bare down upon the spot for several moments with the light before turning and commencing to ascend the incline toward the hut, being careful to listen attentively to my rear but there is nothing for the remainder of the slow arduous ascent up the scrabble at the base of the monolith. Approximately ten minutes later I see the dim shape of the cabin standing like some solemn dark stranger under the moonlight.

As I near it, *a sudden terror seizes me.* I sense a kind of depredation lingering about the periphery of the bent and withered shack, as if *something evil* was positioning itself near the old structure. Again, as I cease my gait only the quietude of the desert can be heard. I resume my approach, cursing the noise created by the gravel and dried cactus under my boot soles. When I walk I feel my peripheral hearing is picking up the near imperceptible sound of something moving rapidly within the scrub.

At this point I'm walking with the torch alight —despite Grey's advice to the contrary- and in constant motion about my person. I cannot relinquish the fear arising within me that something malignant is within the shadows about me and it takes a stolid and resolute intent upon the cabin to get me there. Less than one hundred feet from the hut I hear a guttural sound emanating from the bush, a low growl, and it is quite obvious that some wild creature *is in fact shadowing me.* The revelation causes a sort of dread within my chest. I quicken my pace nearly to a trot and the frenetic action of the flashlight's beam sends a thrill through my stomach. It is with a kind of morbid elation that I make the blackened portal of the beaten wooden hut and enter its dark and ominous environ. I immediately close the door and for the briefest moment think I can hear *something claw at the jam on the other side of the door.* Or is it the loose floorboards swaying underfoot?

The ramshackle shed is so old and dry it creaks and groans at every step. It also seems to have the habit of moving of its own accord, the uprights and roof creaking and groaning sporadically. I realize that the advent of the cold desert night is playing its course upon the wooden structure swollen by the day's heat and contracting with the night's chill. I pan the room with the flashlight and the place sends a chill up the marrow of my back.

Striking a flame from the butane in my pocket, I light the kerosene lamp Grey keeps upon the table. It casts a weak pallid glow throughout the cabin and the effect is eerie. Outside I hear the sudden baying of a wild dog. It is a long solemn howl, almost a wailing and it causes the hair on my neck to bristle. I fasten the wooden latch and take a seat at the table and stare at the door. Whatever the commotion is outside, it quickly diminishes into a stagnant silence. It seems even the night insects have hushed to mere whispers outside. The placid moon shines a meager luminance through the window creating a dull glow within the window's frame.

The lamp's flickering light casts strange shadows across the dull ochre wood and the old hovel begins to show its familiar face. I drink from the canteen and slate the thirst that has been gnawing at me for the last hour. After a hearty drink I chew on some of the cornbread and the food and drink have a grounding effect on my wary frame of mind. Soon the emotions I had felt upon arrival begin to fade and I relegate it all to a tired and active imagination. I begin to relax and the old cabin takes on the familiarity it had shown me on previous visits.

Soon the relaxation I feel begins to give way to a gnawing sense of mission. Within my mind I am deciding to finish out the night inside the hut yet my heart keeps repeating my commitment to the tribe –and myself- pushing me to return; the mission concocted by the medicine man. Grey was adamant about my obligation to journey to Black Butte and return that same night. This was the *warrior's journey* I had agreed to undertake. I struggle with this duality for the better part of an hour as I eat and drink from my pack all the while being constantly harassed by that part of my mind that fears what is outside the door, waiting.

"Why are they insisting I do this silly thing?" I hear myself say. "Putting my life at risk over such a request is selfish and foolhardy. The desert is full of scorpions, snakes and predators of all sorts and kinds. It's only common sense to remain in the cabin for the night and return to the ranch in the morning. Everyone knows the dangers of walking about in such a barren and inhospitable place. Why is Grey being so stubborn about the whole affair? Because of one silly little bird! The whole thing is ludicrous, a joke being perpetrated upon me by the natives… and Lucien in collusion with them! This is just a trick being played for their personal enjoyment. After all, everyone knows a bird can't be a man nor a man be a wolf!" On and on my mind rambled *until I heard it.*

At first I think it might be the wood creaking, then it sounds again, a soft almost imperceptible *rasping on the wood*. I stare at the door in wonder. How is it possible this far out into the middle of the desert and at night that someone is tapping at the door? Again, I can discern an odd sort of feeling emerge within me about the scratching upon the old wooden door. I cannot take my eyes off the rough-hewn planks that compose it. "I must be exhausted," I hear myself say. "My mind is playing tricks." Several moments pass and all becomes strangely still. Just when I think it perhaps a product of an active imagination, again, I hear *an odd tapping upon the wood.*

"Who is it?" I ask through the door, rising to my feet. "Who's there?" I call out but all remains eerily silent, then again, *the same odd rasping*. I step near the door, afraid to move the wooden stop that locks out the immense unknown. "Who's out there?" I demand to know and this time a thin voice sounds in an unfamiliar tongue. My heart is beating and I can hear the blood rushing in my eardrums. I take up a split portion of a short plank in my hand, slide the peg aside and pull wide the door.

In the meager light being shed from the lantern, framed within the blackness of the doorway, stands a queer old man, humpbacked, with sharp beady eyes and an unnerving smile. His teeth are deplorably bad and his clothes torn and frayed, the old garb of the tribe. His hands are like gnarled root wood and his face is creased and weathered. His eyes shine like obsidian in the night and he speaks to me in his native tongue. I gesture that I fail to understand his words. He peers about in a rather queer manner attempting to take in the interior of the little cabin all the while his face possessing a strange smile. He gestures his desire to come into the cabin. I stare at this weird visage for a moment feeling the twin voices of reason and intuition both speaking their piece, all within the scope of a fraction of an instance.

Reason said otherwise, however something took hold –the thing called *civility* perhaps- and I hold wide the door, bidding the stranger enter. He carefully sticks his head through the portal and looks about in the oddest manner. His movements are quick yet pensive and strike me as strange for a man of his apparent age, which I discern to be seventy to possibly eighty years. He takes a bench at the table, looking about the cabin, studying the windows in detail.

The glow from the kerosene lamp flickers casting an odd pallor across his features, *shadows dancing within the gleaming pupils*. He finishes surveying the room as I re-fasten the door latch and take the bench across the table from him. He locks his gaze upon me and a gnawing discomfort accompanies his stare. There is distinctly a queer essence about the man. I watch as he eyes my pack, what he perceives is nourishment inside. I withdraw the full contents of my ruck and lay it upon the table. We are in compliance understanding each other despite the language barrier. He immediately takes to it, as if famished. All the while he eats and drinks, his stare is upon me. In the dull light of the kerosene lamp that flutters wildly, a strange glow seems to emanate from his eyes, a sort of wild anxious gleam. I begin to feel that same sort of revulsion I felt *upon the first sight of him*.

He constantly looks about. What is he searching for? As we stare at each other in the meager light a kind of dread begins to seep into my mind and some aspect of myself becomes aware *that he knows this*, that he is purposefully using his eyes and mannerisms to instill a feeling of uneasiness in my mind. I ask him his name. He fails –or feigns- understanding. I say my name aloud and point to myself and repeat this process for him again. Nothing. I ask if he lives nearby, again, nothing. I gesture toward the cabin over our heads. He then expounds about something, in the native tongue, at which point I'm forced to relay that I neither speak Apache nor understand him. He then begins to look about again, an incessant scouting of the premise. Suddenly his eyes lock upon something in the room. It's as if he has spied a ghost. I look to where his eyes fixate and see the object of his concern. It's the pole Grey has sent out with me, casually placed aside within a grouping of lumber boards. He catches my eye and points at it and in clear English he asks:

"Stick?"

"Yes," I say. He points to me.

"You... stick?" he asks and I nod.

"Yes, my stick." This produces a remarkable reaction. He begins to laugh in a weird unsettling manner, showing all the mottled teeth in his mouth, some missing, some rotting showing bits of metal fillings. The bread he is gorging on drips from them, the crumbs littering the tabletop.

"You stick!" he says again pointing and laughing. With intent, I control the alarm welling up inside me caused by this weird inexplicable behavior. He then becomes quiet, almost morose, looking at me in a queer way. I feel a gnawing fear begin to grip my heart that has a *distinct relation to the look in his eyes and the manner of which he acts*. Again a profound inner sense of calm tells me that this is premeditated behavior. I have the sudden inspiration to show him the thing.

"You like?" I ask him in pidgin English. "I show you?" I ask, not waiting for an answer but quickly take up the device and lay it upon the table between us. He seems in awe of it, touching it, loosening the pinch strap and rolling it in his fingers. I then begin to gesture its function, which seems a fascination to him for his eyes seem to glow more intensely. I gesture with my hands as to how the apparatus might work, he watches as if transfixed, the bad teeth smiling.

I then did something I am utterly unprepared for. As if watching a play upon a stage, I take up the device and carefully –but with intent- coach my ungainly visitor into allowing me to place it over his neck. He is certainly not inviting about it but something in my character is so completely at ease about the whole affair that he reluctantly is compelled to acquiesce and I place the device methodically about his neck. I pull the strap and it ratchets nicely into place; and there we sit seemingly without the slightest effort of my mind, his head in the noose and I at the other end of the pole.

He laughs, as if in awe of it, then gestures for me to release him, but something inside me –certainly separate from my mind- chooses to hold the fixture taut. The mocking grin rapidly disappears replaced with a dark look, the eyes dilating into black pools. He tugs at the strap sharply, then grabs at the pole and shakes it violently. I hold fast. Then, in the clearest English, a thin raspy voice emits from him:

"Let me go!" Again, the same tiny voice, "Let me go," more shrill, more alarmed in tone and this voice, its manner and inflection, sends a thrill through me. I brace myself.

Suddenly he raises up and with an explosion of animal-like fury attempts to rip the device from my grasp but amazingly, I hold on. The tempest doesn't subside. With a sudden herculean viciousness, he screams and lunges at me, his cracked and yellowed nails slicing the air; yet still I hold on, a strange vibrancy coursing my body that seems to energize my arms and legs. The weird old man howls, a jarring, chilling blood scream and sets us spinning knocking over the table and upsetting the lamp which spills its liquid across the floor and walls instantly setting the cabin ablaze.

In the wild light cast by the dancing flames, I watch in horror as the old man goes through a dreadful metamorphosis. The ugly mouth contorts into a gaping maw, the yellow teeth like daggers dripping a viscous liquid and the nails tear into the skin of the pole, ripping thin channels into the grain of the wood. To my utter fascination –as if watching a nightmare in silhouette- *the queer old man changes into the form of a howling screaming horror!* It shakes and bellows like hell set loose, it convulses and heaves as if to jump free of its bonds, but some unfathomable inner resolve within my chest *refuses* to relinquish my grip. He hisses and spits at me in a rage as if to shake my resolve and certainly some part of me wanted to release that pole and get out of there but a warmth, a heat from within the center of my stomach, holds on fast. It is as if my feet pull some kind of solidity from the floor beneath my feet, as a strong electric current locks something in its path.

The horror rages without respite as if certain it can break the bonds –or my resolve- and my mind frets that the leather strap can never hold under such strain but apparently the device is well designed and built of sterner materials than its outward appearance would belie. The *creature* tries to find the strap with its teeth but can only bite into the pole. It tears into the makeshift table that splinters and breaks under its voracity adding kindling to the growing fire. It actually attempts to flank me and we go around several rotations knocking the benches asunder.

Eventually a kind of rage surfaces within me. I begin to wrench the lead and amazingly the beast's fury begins to wane. It's at this point I become acutely aware that the hideous creature –the half man, half beast- I so feared at the end of my stick is in reality *nothing more than a mangy, coyote.*

It now grows quiescent, its head hanging between the fore legs, its tongue extended and dripping. I relax my grip but an instant, to reset my hold but something deep within my breast knows the creature is spent, at least for the moment. He stands unmoving, the mouth panting, saliva cascading onto the floor.

With care, I reach out one hand and pull open the door. The animal growls and gives two hearty tugs but I'm not about to lose hold of him now. I pull him toward the door, he attempts to hold his ground and for an instant my mind wants to lock him within the burning structure and burn him alive. Only after I yank hard upon the lead with all my might does he reluctantly resolve himself to his fate. Once outside I'm shocked by how quickly the cabin becomes engulfed in flame, lighting the rock face in a bizarre eerie glow. Within minutes the entire structure is a burning waste. I stare down at my charge heaving and panting. It slowly turns its head, the putrid yellow eyes looking into mine. I whisper to it softly, in a cajoling tone, as one whispers to a spooked horse. In the bright glow of the burning shack, I see it much more clearly. It stares unblinking, the eyes no longer demonic black pools but placid yellow eyes of the canine species.

We set off into the night, a very tenuous relationship indeed, I, pulling him in the direction of Grey's ranch, he constantly fighting and contradicting our path. Several times he storms violently and I'm forced to cease my stride and plant my feet until his fight wears out. After these episodes he's good for many yards, sometimes about a quarter of a mile before he rails violently again. He repeatedly attempts to lunge for my hands or legs. Twice he manages to gash me, once upon the knuckles of my right hand, which bleeds profusely and once catching me in the lower right leg ripping through the denim. I can feel blood slowly seeping into my boot.

After approximately two hours of consistent struggle, and primarily due the vile beast's incessant circumnavigating, I lose the path. I curse under my breath for not heeding Grey's adamant advice about paying attention to specific details along the path. It seems as if the beast is aware of my situation for he suddenly becomes nearly unmanageable. I'm fatiguing rapidly. I then recall Grey telling me of a peculiar procedure. At the time it seemed senseless, perhaps because I had no empirical reference for it. He had instructed me how to wedge the stick between two hearty rocks and by using my leg or the heel of my boot, toe the pole in tightly thus securing it without the necessity of using my hands. He then instructed me how to stand quietly, facing north, long enough to rest myself and see the mountain that will help guide me back. Desperately now I follow this advice. I find two formidable rocks in the darkness, with just enough of a gap between them to lodge the end of the pole holding my quarry. Having inserted nearly a foot of it within the crevice, I lock it tight with my boot heel and try to relax while I wrap my hand with the handkerchief from my back pocket.

This new situation seems to energize the damn beast for it begins to rail about from side to side as if attempting to bolt, or perhaps snap the stick. After three or four times, he's spent —or injured; the principal thing is it grows quiet, seemingly exhausted. Once the creature settles, I stand silently facing north and wishing with all my being to glimpse the stately mountain and adjust my bearings but the night is all-encompassing.

Some quality within me attempts to quiet myself, as if Grey's advice might still come to pass despite the darkness, if I can but quiet myself long enough. But my doubts and fears are getting the best of me. I labor to control my discontent. Then the worst begins to happen. As if sensing my dilemma the damnable beast begins gnawing at the pole. I realize with horror that if I don't wrench it away from him and commence my trek again he will eventually gnaw his way out of his tenuous prison. I also know that I'm terribly lost, lost within a vast and bizarre landscape and that to simply trek aimlessly will be the end of me. Before dawn break I would tire and the creature free himself and turn on me. I've no doubts whatsoever the evil intentions of the beast to do me harm. I not only sense it, I can feel it within its vicious mannerisms and actions. I begin to despair, profusely. I wish to the very center of my being that something, someone, somehow could aid me in this very critical moment of my life.

Does a person, every man, possess the inherent primordial ability to call upon a higher consciousness, a higher source in times of great physical or mental duress? I recall the concept, *lamenting*, used by the native peoples for guidance. Is this what I'm asking, praying for with all my heart? Do I deserve such accolades? In my self-centered perception of the world and its mysteries have I doomed myself to loss, self-injury and impending death? These questions have no immediate answers but truth be known it is a quiet and sincere calling of my heart and the earnestness of my mission –for by now I know the myth of the *Coyoteman* is all too real- that a most strange and incredible happening occurs.

At the point where I am afraid the devil at the end of the stick is soon to loose itself back onto the world a most profound thing happens. Silently, as if part of the night, *a living aspect of the desert comes to life.* I realize we are being watched by something from the darkness. Whatever it is, it catches the attention of my adversary for he begins to snarl and bite at the blackness surrounding us. Something has shaken him up. I can just make out sleek low forms in motion about us. *Something is circling us in the shadows.* The rascal now nips and snaps from side to side as if something were just outside its reach, when inexplicably, it begins to coil and whimper. What on earth is causing this caustic devil to recede so? I begin to fear something more diabolical is afoot. I then remember the butane in my pocket, the one I used to light the kerosene lantern in the cabin. I extract it and hold it aloft.

At first, I cannot see anything, the sheer magnitude of the ominous night is impenetrable by such a tiny and insignificant flame, but then slowly I begin to make out the forms of animals moving within the blanket of darkness that surrounds us. What is it? I ask myself this question when the most incredible thing occurs and *an enormous black wolf emerges just at the edge of the soft radiant glow.* It's an enormous beast with a deep intense stare. It slowly edges its way closer. I can just make out its features dimly in the dark. The eyes are intense predator's eyes that reflect the tiniest pinprick of light from the lighter in my hand. Its coat is darker than the night.

We sit staring at each other in the meager moonlight, this extraordinary creature and its host of companions. The coyote begins to growl low, then snarl at the alpha of the pack and the wolf addresses it likewise baring its mighty fangs and advancing upon the foul beast causing it great fear, the coyote whimpering and adopting a submissive posture.

The great wolf, snarling all the while, towers above the quaking body of the coyote. Then with an almost lightening-like movement, he lunges at the devil causing it to yelp violently and whine in a mortal dread. The wolf stands above it baring its striking fangs as if ready to deliver the death blow, but the reaction of the coyote, cowering, trying desperately to squeeze itself into the tiny crevices of the desert rocks beneath its body seems to quell the fury of the larger animal. The sudden intrusion of the pack diverts its attention. I watch mesmerized as it slowly retracts back into the darkness.

I immediately retrieve the foul creature at the end of my pole and move in the direction the pack has taken. They seem to be moving toward what appears to be higher ground in the distance. The coyote is now submissive to the extreme, as if innately willing to be lead in whatever direction I desire. I attempt to catch up with the swift movement of the pack but it proves useless, the further into the gloom I penetrate the more certain I am that they have gone. In my haste to follow have I scared them off? Were they even real? Obviously their strange inexplicable appearance has had a profound effect upon my captive for the mangy canine on the end of my stick is either wounded or in utter submission, neither diverting my tread nor contending my lead.

At the crest of this small hillock, as I look about in the gloom, I'm surprised to see the tiniest most insignificant of lights, almost imperceptible, as if watching a firefly perched upon a branch from afar. The tiny light seems nearly beyond sight. I immediately commence a renewed and steady pace in its direction. I can feel the thick viscous blood congealing within my boot and realize that the wound on my leg inflicted by the beast at the end of my pole is serious in nature and most likely accounting for my lack of focus and fortitude and the thought that I'm wasting valuable life energy in pursuit of a *phantom in the night* fails not to divert me from my objective, for with every step I take in the direction of this miniscule glow it becomes larger and more real.

The light so far into the depth of the desert slowly, inexorably begins to grow, from a pinprick eventually into a soft round glow, soon breaking into a long thin line and as I ascend a narrow ravine, I begin to discern a line of random spots of fire. To my amazement, as I crest the ridge, I realize that members of the tribe are aligned along the top of the ridge in single file holding aloft a series of torches, beacons within the absolute night. I have made it back to the ranch alive.

As I near them, emerging from the darkness I hear shouts, then howls emitting from the host, shadows run back and forth from the hacienda. As I step directly into the circle of light, the people encompass me. I vaguely discern their hoots and howls, not unlike Nature herself as the people stare in awe at what I have brought back from within the womb of night. At the end of the lead, the wild canine snaps and bites at the people who venture too close. It growls and rails anew, but it is the end of a very long road for him.

Suddenly everything grows eerily silent and the people slowly part. I watch as Grey appears from the direction of the house, flanked by his sons. He walks up to me his eyes –this time without the sunglasses- gleam in the firelight, a distinct look of joy, perhaps it is fascination. Whatever the emotion, he stands straight backed, his right leg forward the other and says in his deep resonant voice:

"Pretty good." His son, gingerly but firmly, takes the lead from my grip and the dog tries to bolt causing him to dig his boot heels into the gravel. The people howl and those with torches attempt to shoo him back into the circle of light. The coyote leaps and snaps with all his might but his vitality is taxed, he is only a shell of the vitriolic essence he was in the cabin and upon the long lonely path through the desert.

The animal is lead away and the last thing I remember is seeing Lucien standing beside me, his grip –like an iron vice- holding my upper arm. I seem to be stumbling. I try to put my foot forward to balance myself but it's as if I'm mired in quicksand and I feel myself slowly falling as they gently lower me to the ground. And the ground feels good, a feeling of lying upon soft beach sand. I recall a ring of brown faces with glittering eyes like obsidian all about me, then a soft enveloping blackness.

When I awaken, it's a bright morning, perhaps midday. I'm alone in the new house, lying upon a brand new bed with brand new sheets, pillows and blankets, just like a movie set. I instantly recall an old memory, a memory I had completely forgotten until that moment.

I had been hired as a production assistant working nights on a feature film that was dragging on and on. My assigned station, my *lock up* –in the parlance of the industry- was the rear door of an antiquated warehouse we were using as a soundstage at the time. The second AD (assistant director) stationed me at the door with a walkie-talkie and so there I sat hour after hour until a disheveled old janitor passed by me at about two in the morning and inquired what I was doing.

"They've stationed me at this door so no one walks in on the shoot," I told him.

"No one uses this door, you're wasting your time," the old man assured me.

"Are you certain?" I asked.

"Mister, no one ever uses this door, *it leads to nowhere*," he said zipping up his jacket and moving on. I was about to call this in on the second channel when I decided to look over the interior sets first. These were the house interiors, propped out and lit up when the schedule required their use. Here now in the quiet darkness they seemed strange and surreal as if life had come to an instantaneous halt.

I wandered through the darkened kitchen set, the refrigerator still stocked with fake foodstuffs, the stove and coffee maker were fake, everything, even the apples and bananas in the bowl upon the fake counter were plastic. I was always amazed by the surreal nature of working on film sets. Everything always looked so real but was not. There were no ceilings, only lighting grids filled with cables and lighting instruments. The walls looked real but were made of quarter inch luan wood and their backsides were bare, held in place with one by three inch pinewood jacks. The jacks were stabilized with sand bags. Thick rubber electrical cables were laced throughout the entire facade.

Eventually, after shooting a game of Nineball on the – surprisingly- real pool table in the *living room set,* I wandered to a far-recessed corner where *the bedroom set* had been built. It was very dark and quiet due its remoteness. I stretched my tired and aching body upon the enormous bed that, like the pool table, was also real and incredibly comfortable, the sheets, blankets and pillows all newly acquired and dressed in advance. I placed my walkie-talkie on the lamp stand and turned the volume low, just enough to hear a whisper of the commotion from *the shooting set.*

I lay there, exhausted by the intense nature and schedule of the project. I had never liked shooting nights. One was required to work from sundown to sunrise in a very pressing and intense manner before limping home during the morning commute, when the rest of the world was just waking and racing about on their way to work, or wherever.

The project had been assigned a particularly dour first assistant director whose personality traits included a negative perspective toward other human beings. It was obvious to us all this man despised people. He wouldn't hesitate to verbally assail anyone within his sphere of influence for the slightest infraction, however trivial. The coveted position –running the set for the director- was entirely an egotistical endeavor for him, not a professional one. It was grueling. Soon I felt my mind harping at me to get moving and report that my assigned position at the rear door was superfluous. However, something about the sound of the man's voice nagging and shouting over channel one at my raft of colleagues made me feel quite content to remain in the soft quiet solitude of the fake bedroom world of which I was now, a human prop. The more my mind insisted that it was in my professional interest to report in, the more belligerent –and repulsive- the voice became over the walkie-talkie near my head. Part of me had no interest whatsoever in offering any further assistance to this uncouth individual. This was in direct contrast to the production I had just concluded where the first assistant director had become such a precious person to us all that no request seemed unattainable. As the seconds ticked by into minutes, I became enraptured by the quiet womb-like atmosphere of this silent make believe world. It seemed to embrace me, refusing me to leave it, as if it had come into existence solely for my own wonderment. Before I realized what was happening, I was asleep.

When I awoke, the sun was peeking through the large glass dormers that proliferated the old warehouse turned sound stage. I sat up shocked that it was suddenly dawn and wondered if perhaps I had slept through the entire night's work when a voice on the walkie-talkie barked: *'That's a wrap!'*

I hurried down to the shooting set to witness the chaos as the exhausted and sagging grips and electricians were quickly wrapping out the floor mounted lighting and dolly equipment. The camera operator was talking to one side with the director of photography and the first camera assistant and the rest of the camera department were rapidly dismantling the camera and filling out their production reports. The sleepy –and crabby- old Teamster captain was barking at his drivers as the passenger vans were filling with talent, hair and make-up technicians, all very much anxious to get back to the hotel, their baths and their beds.

Jan Ivers, the script supervisor was finishing detailing her notes. (In an epiphany, I suddenly realize how much Jan reminds me of Beryl Collins, Karras and Corbeau's chief financial controller.) Jan eyed me curiously.

"What have you been up to?" she asked in a pointed manner.

"I was on a lockup in the back," I said, probably unconvincingly. She gave me that *particular* look. "Why? Were they calling for me?" I questioned nervously.

"Not in the least," she said closing her binder, placing her pen behind her ear. She leaned in close to me and at a whisper said: "If you were sleeping in the bedroom set make damn sure you dress it back properly. It's first up tomorrow and you know what a raging bitch Simone can be if she thinks anyone's been screwing with her 'immaculately' dressed sets." I looked at her and said nothing, her eyes glittered and she smiled broadly. "Do try to behave yourself... it's always the good ones that get chewed up in this madness." Then slinging her bag over her shoulder she jumped into the nearest van and I watched as it sped away into the New England mist.

These memories flash through my mind in an instant as if reliving them within the blink of an eye. I pull back the sheets and step from the bedroom out into the bright –and hot- Arizona showroom living space. The interior is immaculate, nothing out of place. In the corner sits the birdcage and inside what looks like the same bird flitting about and for the briefest moment I almost wonder if it had all been a weird inexplicable dream. However the bandages on my hand and leg are reminders that my nocturnal adventure had been all too very real.

I study the bird closely. It cocks its head and looks at me and I wonder if it might not be an entirely different animal than the bird that had duped me into releasing it into the wilds. We stare at each other a moment.

"Let me out," the rascal chirps aloud. I go back into the bedroom and dress.

Outside is blistering hot and I immediately seat myself upon one of the plastic milk crates under the big cottonwood tree and scan the rugged horizon. Everywhere is bare rock and cactus. I feel incredibly tired, as if nearly drained of my vital energy. One of the small Apache boys watching me runs into the old house and soon Lucien and Grey emerge and join me under the tree boughs.

"How are you feeling?" Lucien inquires. I nod absently.

"A little tired," I say looking at my bandages. Grey looks at me curiously.

"How did you do it?" he asks. "How'd you get his neck into the noose?" I tell him and Lucien the entire story.

"But how did you know the old man wasn't just some old miser on his way to his home?" Lucien asks and I contemplate the question for only a moment.

"I knew it when he knocked upon the door," I say and Lucien's eyebrow rises and he and Grey exchange a curious look.

"What do you mean?" Grey asks. I stare at him, through the dark sunglasses, remembering the look of his eyes.

"Well… the way he knocked. It wasn't the way a normal person knocks on someone's door." Grey looks at Lucien who leans back and extracts his deerskin pouch and silently begins filling his pipe.

"How did he knock?" Grey asks, pressing the issue.

"He didn't. It was more a… tapping, like a rasping… like a dog might." I say and shrug. Lucien lights his pipe with a cedar match and nods softly. Grey stands up, pats my shoulder then walks off in the direction of the corral where his sons are engaged with the black stallion. I watch as he joins them then look at Lucien who is quietly smoking and I can discern just the wisp of a smile hidden behind his shaggy beard and that is the last we speak about the whole entire episode.

"We've been invited to attend the Sunrise Ceremony being held for his granddaughter," Lucien says. "Truly an honor."

"What's a *Sunrise Ceremony*?" I ask.

"A rite of passage for all young Apache maidens who come of age," he says.

The Sunrise Ceremony turns out to be a three-day event commencing that Friday evening and finishing Sunday morning. The ceremony is a rite of passage for Apache maidens that pass from adolescence into womanhood. When the girl begins menstruation the family seeks out the medicine man to conduct the three-day festival. The ceremony brings into proximity the entire tribal community. The people arrive Friday morning and prepare a camp consisting of an enormous central bonfire that is lit Friday evening when the ceremony begins and will remain lit until the conclusion of the festivities Sunday morning. During this time, the Indian maiden –clad in her beautiful buckskin dress, adorned with feathers, beadwork and the conical tin bells upon the fringe- wields the crooked staff and dances in place to the beat of the giant drum that the men play in unison, their singing piercing the night. In this role, perhaps the most profound of her life to that point in time, she is the central conduit of the tribe's prayers. These prayers and wishes are channeled through the girl now an honored woman of the tribe.

Saturday night, as the medicine man and his singers are gathered about the great drum beating the steady heartbeat of the people to the rise and fall of the Apache song, *the Spirit Dancers emerge from the blackness of the surrounding desert*. These are the weird inexplicable *Thunder beings* spoken of in Apache legend, that descended from the sky, down the mountain two thousand years ago and helped to raise the Apache from the meager gatherer society living in dirt hovels to a tribal nation with a history, and spiritual calling. The long extended *lightening bolts* protruding from their ominous black cowls depict their origin and ancestry from the stars beyond. These are the *energy beings* of Thunder, Wind and Lightening and the three primary deities dance and sway about the fire casting ghost-like shadows about the desert floor mingling with the dust thrown up from their elk-skin moccasins. Their wailing and *willowing* through the course of the night is mystifying and enthralling and the experience is a deeply spiritual one.

The fourth member of the supernal entourage is *the joker* or so-called *trickster*. His headdress –and physical stature- is inferior to those of his three larger brothers. He swings a hemp rope about his head with a whistle tied to the end that screeches and howls and creates the most unnerving sensations. This fellow has the penchant of chasing after the children of the tribe. If he spies any of the little ones wandering too far from the large circle of villagers, locked arm and arm and rotating about the great fire, he will inevitably chase after them until they seek out the shelter of the nearest pair of legs and this goes on the entire night until the group tires and seeks out the shelter of their tents, some retiring to small modern trailers, others going back to their homes to return in the morning. Upon conclusion of the ceremony Sunday morning, the girl is transformed. The village exchanges its salutations and the community disperses. Soon nothing is left but a few discarded remains and the smoldering ashes of the large cottonwood trunks, once the great fire, now mere ashes smoldering down to nothing.

I hardly see anything of Lucien the entire three days, he, very much in close proximity with Grey and the immediate circle of singers and dancers. At the conclusion of each night, he retires with this retinue to some remote area of the reservation while I'm berthed in a small but comfortable tent near the fire circle and given food and water from various members of the girl's family, the immediate group governing the ceremony. It isn't until Sunday morning that I converse with him.

I wait off to one side as Grey, the principle curator of the occasion, wraps out the last of his ceremonial formalities. I'm tired and dirty from the three days of dancing about the raging fire and my leg is bleeding again. I found the previous night's slow arm-in-arm rotation about the fire strangely rejuvenating, but here now on this tired Sunday morning, the desert once again bare of its people and the beat of the large drum replaced by a dry hollow wind, I find myself again extremely tired and oddly disinterested, a kind of unexpected detachment from the entire occasion. It's only as I say goodbye to Grey's beautiful granddaughter that a sense of the magnitude of the previous day's events return to my wearied frame of mind for I see it clearly in her face, a knowing and emphatic look. Her eyes, although weary, are enhanced with a kind of knowing, a sense of responsibility, in the affairs of her tribe, her family and herself.

When we finally return to the ranch and I'm instructed to pack, I'm shocked when Lucien joins me at the car unladed, somehow looking younger, spryer than earlier in the week. He leans against the vehicle and stokes his pipe, his view engaged upon something down the valley.

"I've telephoned Beryl, she's arranged a flight for you from Sky Harbor to San Francisco. Leave the rental with the appropriate firm at the airport when you arrive in Phoenix."

"You're not returning with me?" I ask in a rather incredulous tone.

"I've become quite close with Grey and his family, they've invited me to stay on for awhile, I've accepted their invitation. You, of course are welcome to stay at the house in San Francisco, as long as you like, or return to London if you desire."

"How long will you remain here?"

"There's no way to tell at the moment, not long I imagine," he mutters. "Well, travel safely," and with that he turns and heads back toward the old house. I stare after him and watch as he enters the house without even a look back in my direction. There's nothing left to do but wheel the car west into the desert quietly awaiting my departure.

The French Witch

The journey from the ranch to San Francisco is surreal. I'm exhausted and have lost a fair amount of blood from the wound on my leg. The collective effect of these conditions coupled with the bizarre and traumatic episode within the desert creates a kind of trance-like state, not altogether unpleasant, but strange and dream-like. Or has my awareness changed somehow?

I recall driving from the reservation through the Superstition Mountains, the landscape alive and moving. Apparently my mind devoid of its usual inner dialogue leaves my attention free to roam. I feel an inordinate comprehension of detail about the desert unfolding across the periphery of my vision. What earlier in the week seemed to be a near lifeless landscape of rock and cactus now seemed vibrant and teeming with life; creatures of all sorts, flowers and green shades of plant life. How had it all escaped my perception earlier? What had seemed burnt brown and beige rock face now possessed a vibrant pink hue, almost lavender.

I don't remember the passage through Tempe or Mesa but do recall pulling into the rental station at Sky Harbor yet no clear memories as to how I managed to navigate to the terminal gate. I'm suddenly there, waiting for my flight to San Francisco. The rest is more or less a blur, the plane, the egresses all of it, *until I see Her.*

I had not expected her. It is a singular moment in time, captured in my mind like a still frame from a camera; her lone form standing in the distance like a shadow in the wing, awaiting my arrival. A soft dulcet joy arises within me upon seeing her image, then her eyes, then her touch, then her embrace; neither of us speaking. We stand there awash in humanity, holding each other and this sends me further into timelessness.

I don't remember talking at all. It's not until we are driving north on highway 101, toward the distant beautiful city, the sky a brilliant blue with white clouds like cotton, that she speaks the words that ground me and slowly the details of my life begin to stack together forming the bridges and walls of my life.

"I'm leaving, tonight," she says, a determined tone in her voice. She doesn't take her eyes from the road ahead. I look at her, the face turned northward, then the fingers clutching the steering wheel. She turns her face toward mine and the green eyes tell me silently of her worried state of mind. These eyes that only a week ago seemed filled with the wonderment and joy I had come to treasure, now possess a darker sense of this beautiful and mysterious woman.

"What do you mean?" I hear myself ask in a dry haggard voice and realize these are the first words I've spoken since leaving Grey's ranch. She splits her attention between me and the traffic for what seems an eternity of waiting, her words —especially the word *leaving*- too fraught with anxiety.

"I've been unable to speak with mother. I'm going down there, to New Orleans, tonight." I cannot process it in my mind. It's as if I have stepped from a dream world into a sudden quiet desperation.

"Morgan..." I whisper, "don't leave... not tonight." She looks at me, her eyes growing misty. "I thought you spoke with Lucien about all this? I thought everything was okay?" Tears begin to run the course of her cheek.

"You remember my premonition?"

"Yes, of course but-"

"I can't shake it. It's recurring again and again, over and over... something's wrong."

"Can't you call them?" I ask already knowing her response.

"They won't let me speak to her on the phone!" she nearly shouts. "I'm going down there. I have to," she says, a rigid fixation upon the road ahead. After an engulfing silence she says, nearly indiscernibly, "Come with me," her voice a mere whisper. "I know what you've been through. Uncle Lucien told me... but I want... I need, you to come with me," she says and her eyes lock with mine. There is nothing but those eyes. I take her hand and slowly fall into oblivion.

Louisiana. We are driving from New Orleans International airport. The atmosphere is heavy and gray, the trees and grass exceptionally green after the sparse brown fauna of Arizona. I crack the window of the rental car and breathe in the rain, the moisture creates a schism within me, compelling after the arid dryness of my days in the desert.

She looks over and although her expression is pensive it has none of the dark dilation of the eyes so evident in San Francisco. She even smiles, albeit a thin fragile one.

"We'll be there in an hour, go back to sleep," she says. I see her eyes fixed upon me as I fall back into a deep dreamless slumber.

When I awaken we are pulling onto a gravel two-track that pierces a tall iron gate pulled back on both sides. The gates mimic the black iron railings that extend into a mass of foliage; magnolia trees, dense with parasitic moss, like the wax of melting candles.

Ahead sits an enormous white manor home that anticipates our arrival, its large white columns are tarnished with a patina of mildew and the place seems to have lapsed into a lesser state than its original design. Above the expansive porch rests a large ornate placard of a golden rooster with the rays of a golden sun emanating from behind his statuesque head.

The car pulls up and stops. When we emerge from the insulated environment of the automobile a rich pungent aroma fills my lungs and ignites my senses. The air is heavy with humidity and the smell of fauna. It is absolutely quiet, as if the stately old home were somehow removed from the world.

I watch Morgan as she scans the estate. I actually sense her stepping back in time, something in her expression and the utter silence of the moment. Her eyes suddenly fixate in the direction of the house and I'm shocked to see a gaunt mongrel, something resembling an old or sick Rhodesian ridgeback –with bared teeth- methodically trotting directly at us. The visage of the dog sends a thrill up my back but my fears are allayed when Morgan sets down upon one knee and extends her hand.

"Majo," she says and the canine instantly acknowledges her. It wags its wiry tail and rubs itself upon her waist, licking at her jeweled earlobes. She strokes the beast lovingly, which in better health –or younger years- must have easily weighed seventy pounds. When she stands, the dog entreats me to a series of quick jabs and pokes of its nose against my leg and sneezes. There's a sharp whistle from the colonnaded porch above and the dog makes for an old white haired man well into his eighties, perhaps nineties.

"It's Granddad," she whispers, almost reverently, and strides in his direction, taking the wide stairs in twos. They embrace upon the porch. He kisses her affectionately upon both cheeks and the eyes beneath his enormously expressive eyebrows glisten and glow.

"Morgan child," he says in a deep southern drawl. "What's all this about you coming down here like Jackson? Ya'll got everyone in stitches."

"I'm worried about mom, Grandpa. They still won't let me talk with her on the phone," she says and he looks at me as I crest the top of the stairs. His eyes are solid beads of black under immense white brows fashioned into furls that give the impression of some tempestuous John Brown figure.

"You've a man friend," he says studying me.

"Grandpa, this is Willem Furey, he's accompanied me down." He extends a long gnarled hand. I notice a silver ring with a large black oval stone, similar to the ones Morgan and Emerald wear.

"Honored," he says.

"This is Colonel Emory Montaigne, my grandfather," Morgan says with a reverent tone in her voice and manner. His gaze is less a smile and more a deep study of my over-all appearance.

"You're making a real fuss granddaughter, your aunts are all about ready to spit! You know damn well your maw is amongst her kin."

"I told you on the phone Grandpa, I'm having premonitions and I want to speak with her. Why won't they let me talk to her?"

"What kind of premonitions?" he asks but before she can answer he interrupts. "Hold on, ya'll best come on inside and get out of the heat."

The ancient house is indeed cooler inside. There's a tangle of vines, ivy and dwarf trees growing from large pots at the base of every window, which are vast and numerous. There's an impressive array of antique furniture throughout the stately home and more old hardbound books than I recall seeing in one place at one time outside a public library.

"Sadie!" the old colonel shouts and pounds his cane upon the floor. "We've guests." He shows us into a large sitting room full of books, music and plants. There's a grand piano, a Steinway, in one corner laden with books and sheet music. He mutters under his breath showing impatience as a sleepy-eyed girl with dishpan blonde hair, perhaps twenty years old, enters the room yawning. "Sadie, get a move on... you're slower than sorghum. Here's my granddaughter from New York City with her man friend. Can you roust yourself enough to serve these folks a pitcher of sweet tea?"

"Yes Colonel... there's lemonade ready already."

"Then go fetch it," he gestures and she exits.

"Who is she?" Morgan inquires.

"Some young thing your aunt inherited from the city," he grumbles. "Another beaten child. I admire Monique's concern for the orphans and waifs of the world but I don't like strangers lurking about my house," he says and gives me a sideways glance. "Don't stand around, there's more than enough chairs." We take the white wickers near the large window surround, dominating the room. He studies Morgan for a moment.

"Morgan, by thunder, you're as lovely as ever," he says beaming. "Hell, I put up the necessary front but I'm damn glad you come down. It's been far too long. Where's that scallywag Lucien, is he coming?"

"No Grandpa, he's in Arizona. He's very busy with-"

"Always the same," the old man interjects. "You'd think we were beset with the plague down here."

"He's just very busy Grandfather," Morgan says and the old man scowls.

"No excuse... not to see an old soldier in the twilight of his life," he mutters extruding a thin black cheroot from a silver humidor. "Sadie!" he calls out. "Dammit! Why's she always off with my cigar lighter?" he shouts pounding on the floor with his cane.

"He's been in the twilight of his life, for the past decade," Morgan whispers to me and a smile curves the edges of her beautiful lips. I realize the old man is having a rejuvenating effect upon her demeanor. "I think he's too ornery to die," she says and I laugh softly which catches the old man's attention.

Sadie emerges from behind the mahogany panel door with a crystal pitcher of ice water mixed with lemon slices. Upon the silver tray with several matching glasses sits his lighter. She sets the service down upon the sideboard and proceeds to pour three tall glasses of lemonade, adding sugar with a long stemmed spoon. When she hands the first one to the Colonel, he scowls at her.

"Guests first, Sadie," he scolds and she begins to hand the beverage to me. "There's a lady present young-un," he says and she quickly hands the drink to Morgan.

"Thank you Sadie," she says graciously and they exchange a friendly smile. She then hands me a glass, and her smile, in fact her whole demeanor, seems genuine and pleasant.

"Thank you," I say. When she hands the third glass to Colonel Montaigne and starts to leave he knocks the handle of his cane against the chair arm.

"You've forgotten something child." She stares at him with a concerned look upon her face. He waits as long as he can tolerate it. "You damn well know that I take bourbon in my glass!" he shouts. I spy a grin in the corner of Morgan's mouth.

"Colonel, Miss Pearl says you're not to have liquor before-"

"Go fetch it!" he shouts and she hurries off. The old man simmers silently until she returns with a bottle of Kentucky Bourbon and carefully begins to trickle the amber liquid into his glass. The old man actually uses the handle of his cane to tip the bottle until enough of the elixir has been added before he nods and she quickly caps it and goes to leave. "Leave the bottle Sadie, it'll save all this traipsing back and forth," he says and she reluctantly does and exits. "Insolent child," the Colonel says once she's left.

"I think she's just looking out for you Granddad," Morgan says smiling.

"Depriving an old soldier of the one pleasure left him is hardly 'looking out for another' as you state it." He takes a long draught from his glass and exhales his content and looks directly at me. "I prefer my bourbon straight but my daughters all rail on me like harpies set a-loose." I smile holding his stare as he sizes me up. "You from New York too?" he questions me directly.

"No sir."

"Military?"

"No. No sir," I say and he lights his cigar.

"I'm a military man, my granddaughter tell you?" We all exchange looks and I immediately realize this is important to him and that Morgan failed to mention it.

"Of course sir, definitely." He relaxes into the wicker and crosses his gangly legs clothed in lightweight muslin pants. His shoes are white leather Hush-puppies.

"I've waged war across the globe son, world war two and Korea. I was a Major with the army when we put the screws to that rapscallion in Europe... and still stayed on with my unit, all the way into Asia. Been all over the world. Of course not that any of the women I'm *blessed with,* would ever even bother to mention it," he says eyeing Morgan. "Women hate warfare son... loathe it... any gal worth her salt, rightly so. War changes everything. Nothing's sacred anymore when you're in the crosshairs of another man's rifle."

"Grandfather... let's not talk about the war right now."

"See what I mean?" he says to me. "There you have it," he says gesturing toward Morgan. "I've been a military man my entire youth, my formidable years, and now look, living with a house full'a women. It's a cruel fate... my repentance for being a man of the world... and a soldier all my life."

"Grandpa..." Morgan says, a dramatic look upon her face. She turns toward me. "*Methinks he doth protest too much,*" she says quoting Shakespeare and we smile.

"Don't deny it Granddaughter, you're part of the conspiracy," he says and looks at me. "That vixen I married begot me daughters, all daughters, five of 'em all total, try as I would for a son... Pearl, Monique and Em, Angeline and my sweet, sweet baby Gilly, God rest her eternal soul."

"Grandpa, that was all a long time ago." He leans closer to Morgan.

"You know she done that, you know it."

"Who did what?" she asks a slight impatience in her voice.

"Your Grandmother! Her and that... Choctaw priestess." She gives me a pensive look.

"Grandpa, please..."

"You can turn off your ears if you want but I'll go to my grave sayin' it… them and their potions…" turning toward me again, *they can change a boy child to a girl child in the womb*," he says intensely. "They wanted this bloodline all women."

"Grandpa, please don't talk about this right now," Morgan says. I can see her gesturing toward me with her eyes.

"He might as well hear it," the old man presses on relentlessly, "Lord knows he'll be getting a belly full of it soon enough."

"Audrey asked me to send her love," Morgan interjects gallantly trying to change the topic.

"And there's another one," he says re-addressing me directly. "Em's other girl, her sister… from Los Angeles no less!"

Suddenly the door bursts open and a copper-skinned Creole woman, who looks to be in her late forties, enters and squeals. The women immediately embrace and I'm struck by the moment, their obvious affection for one another.

"Oh my lord girl, look at you! You've become so lovely," the Creole woman says holding her at arm's length and looking her over, head to toe. Her black eyes glitter and her thin face can barely contain her beautiful smile.

"This is Magdalena, my… my childhood nanny," Morgan says and the Creole maid extends a lean hand in my direction; her grip is like a vice. Her face beams and her teeth are perfect and white. She wears a thin gauze dress with a tarnished apron.

"Lord, baby," she says holding Morgan's waist. "Your aunts are all gonna to be so pleased." She pinches her ribs. "You're getting thin girl."

"I've been working a lot lately."

"Lord and haven't I heard all about that! Why do you worry your aunts and your maw so?" Morgan's countenance instantly changes.

"Where is mom, Magda? I want to see her... right away." This question creates a distinct change in Magdalena's beaming demeanor. I notice the quick furtive eye contact with the old Colonel before she reverts back to her effusive state.

"She's fine Morgan, just fine. You'll see her soon enough. You'll see all your family soon enough. Meanwhile I'll have Sadie take your things upstairs."

"We're traveling light Magda, there's no need," Morgan says and there is a moment's silent exchange between the women.

"Your room still hasn't changed... not at all," she says to Morgan then looks at me. "Will your man be comfortable in one of the guest chambers?" she asks and Morgan stares at her.

"I'm sure that'll be fine," she says and Magdalena beams.

"I'll have Sadie change the linens and I'll get lunch ready right now. Pearl is on her way over with Angeline as we speak," she says and Morgan seems surprised.

"They are?"

"Your aunts... they been planning since yesterday." Morgan's expression is one of deep thought and Magda seems to sense it. "Just relax now, take a stroll around the garden, explore a bit... before this old bone bores you to tears," she says addressing the Colonel. He huffs indignantly and she glares at him placing her hands firmly upon her hips. "And you... quit ordering Sadie about like she's your personal servant, ordering her to fetch your devil juice! You know she's under the strictest orders not to give you that wretched stuff. That's the poison that ruined that child's home!" The old man waves his cigar at her.

"Go make lunch old woman," he huffs and looks at me. "The hired help... hum!" he snorts and she scowls then seems to fixate upon me, her dark eyes burning into mine, Morgan glancing between us.

"What is it Magda?" she asks.

"Your man... he's been wounded," she says not removing her gaze.

"Oh, it's nothing... I was bitten by a dog," I say and she turns squarely before me.

"*You weren't bitten by no dog,*" she says with an intensity that tingles the hair on my neck. "Show me the wound." I reluctantly pull up my pant leg and she studies the bandage, a smatter of blood seeping through the gauze. "Ya'll go upstairs. I'll be up in a minute to tend to that," she says then turns and disappears behind the door.

The young girl shows us upstairs ascending an enormous curving staircase leading to a large ornate common. Two hallways split from the common leading to a series of bedrooms. Mine is a luxuriant room filled with antiques, every piece of furniture at least ninety to one hundred years old. Several minutes later Magda returns with a woven basket.

"Strip," she says and I look to Morgan. "You heard what I told you boy, drop your pants," Magda says extruding a roll of gauze bandage and an old vial of lemon colored salve. "I can't work on that with your pant leg all cocked up." I look to Morgan once more and she sighs aloud.

"Just do it," she says shrugging. I reluctantly remove my jeans. Magda raises an eyebrow in Morgan's direction then unwinds the bandage carefully removing the poultice Grey's wife had applied to the wound.

"This here was done by a real professional," Magda mutters discarding it into a mason jar and sealing the lid. She then wrenches the wound open nearly causing me to cry out and pours a small vile of scarlet colored liquid directly into the gash and I nearly tear the wooden ball off the bedpost. "That hurt?" she asks.

"A little bit," I say through my clenched teeth and Morgan covers her grin with her fist. Magda then commences to clean the wound with a wad of gauze and I nearly blackout.

After an eternity of this cleaning, she rubs a generous amount of the salve into the wound and an immediate cool sensation saturates the bite. She then wraps my leg snuggly with a large gauze bandage and secures the end with tape.

"There, that wound will be nearly healed by tomorrow night. Whoever dressed this before me knew what they were doing. The poultice pulled the poison," she says holding up the jar and studying it closely. "I'll go burn this in the fire."

Morgan shows me her room, which is apparently very near how it looked when she left years ago. I ask her how old she was at the time and she tells me sixteen.

"Did you start college when you were sixteen?" I ask and she looks at me long and hard, the pupils dilating slightly.

"No… that was the year my father died." I immediately feel stupid.

"I'm sorry." She senses my state of mind.

"Don't be ashamed of death," she says. I study her a moment then the environment. I see her as a much younger person. There is an old Nikon F2 film camera with a few lenses and a hand-winding Bolex 16mm movie camera. There are several oil canvasses and I'm shocked when I learn the artist is Morgan herself. They are darker canvasses, one of an old black woman near the side of a road, just after a rainstorm, the wet road receding off into a gray stormy horizon. One of the other canvasses is a portrait of a black Cajun man playing a guitar.

"That's Robert Anthony..." she says over my shoulder, "and this one... is Carter Rollins. They both still live on the estate," she says and I wonder a moment what she means. "The woman is Tallulah... Magda's mother."

"These are quite good," I say and she looks them over.

"I wanted to paint, when I was younger... not sure what happened."

There is a sudden commotion at the front portal downstairs. Morgan immediately heads across the large wooden landing and races down the stairs. I witness from the landing above as she lovingly embraces two women, the elder with white hair and a cane and a younger, thinner woman with straight black hair in a rather plain blue dress. I join them.

The elder aunt wears a beautiful mauve dress with a gossamer knit shawl. She prods along with a thin black cane fashioned from a stick of hardwood. I'm introduced to Aunt Pearl, and am astonished by her eyes and their *completely white irises*. I'm also introduced to Aunt Angeline who is exceptionally thin, her facial characteristics rather long and bland but the eyes keen and intense. She escorts Pearl, leading her by the forearm. Morgan whispers in my ear.

"Aunt Pearl is completely blind, and aunt Angeline won't speak a word in public." The women pause before me, and the blind aunt –as if she could sense me- addresses Morgan.

"Niece, is this Lucien's assistant I've heard tell of?" she asks and Morgan acknowledges her. "May I... be so bold?" She extends her hand toward me. Morgan takes my arm.

"She wants to touch you... your face." I smile at the old woman and her pale white irises staring directly at me, gives off a queer sensation. Morgan gently takes her hand and places it upon my cheek. She gently fathoms the contours of my face. She's careful, using only the tips of her fingers. The white eyes seem to glow –or are they reflecting sunlight from the windows?

"He's handsome, niece," she says and I think I see Morgan blush slightly. "I'm very pleased to meet you young man."

"Likewise," I say. She immediately sets about tapping her way toward the Colonel's chair, intrinsically knowing the way. She bends down, kissing him.

"How are you father?"

"Above ground," he mumbles.

"Well blessed be the angels for that," she states in her eloquent southern drawl and taps her way to one of the wicker chairs near the window. "Morgan dear, would you raise the blind a bit? I want to feel the sunshine." Morgan raises the blind that separates the sun, peeking through the foliage and the chair Pearl has chosen. She rests her cane neatly against the arm. Angeline helps remove her shawl and drapes it across her own arm before taking a bentwood chair near the Colonel's. "How was your trip dear, was it pleasant?"

"Yes aunt Pearl, it was. How have you been?" Pearl turns her face into the tiny frame of sunshine and it's as if I can feel the warmth upon her face, so lovely is her response to the radiance, like a flower turning to the setting sun.

"I've been well," she says and I notice her nose twitch. "Are ya'll having lemonade?" she inquires and Morgan jumps up.

"Yes, would you like some Aunt Pearl? Aunt Angeline?"

"Oh indeed," Pearl says. "Magda makes the most splendid lemonade." I can see her nose still in action. "Father, are you drinking at this hour? Surely you're not partaking of drink at such an early-"

"Are we going to start in with this again?" he bellows. "The chair's not even warm and here it comes."

"But father, you know what doctor Harmon said about-"

"What would that damn quack know about a man's health?" He looks directly at me. "A new young doctor. All he's good for is dispensing drugs. The old one kept me tickin' with vinegar and bourbon and I outlived him!" the old man declares to the host.

"But when you start in so early..." He pounds his cane on the floor, startling her.

"Blast it Pearl! Between you and Magda a soul can't think straight." He slowly, rather loudly, rises retrieving his straw hat. "C'mon Majo!" he shouts poking the dog with the end of his stick. The dog seems less enthusiastic about relocating but faithfully follows his master out the door.

"Why, he's getting so durn grumpy, a person can hardly be in the same room anymore," she says flustered.

"Aunt Pearl, where's mother? I want to see her, right away," Morgan interjects and Pearl becomes rigid as if deep in thought. "Aunt Pearl did you hear me?"

"Of course I heard you Morgan."

"Well?"

"You left here a long time ago child, when you were still very, very young."

"I know that Aunt Pearl, that's not what I'm asking you." There's a sudden, and unexpected, tension that emerges between the two women, aunt Angeline gazing intently back and forth between them as if watching a tennis match. The two women stare at each other, the modern contemporary photographer and the blind southern heiress.

"Wait until Monique gets back dear, we can all talk together then."

"I'm not asking Monique Aunt Pearl, I'm asking you," Morgan says and you could hear a pin drop.

"I think your tone is disturbing," the old gal declares.

"My tone?" Morgan asks incredulous.

"You act as if you were amongst strangers niece, as if your darling mother were not firmly within the body of her family." Morgan places her fingertips to her temple. I can see she is struggling.

"Is there a reason I can't see her... or talk to her? Why won't you let me talk with her?"

"Morgan, you were always an impatient child, I see you've not changed into womanhood... young man?" she suddenly says *looking* to where I sit.

"Yes Ma'am?"

"Lunch will be ready in half an hour. Would you be kind enough to escort my niece about the property? She needs to relax after such a long and difficult trip." Morgan stares at her aunts and I know she is seething.

"Certainly," I respond slowly rising. I hold out my hand to her and whisper, "c'mon." *Her eyes suddenly change* and she takes my hand and we exit the old house to walk the gardens but she jerks my arm in the direction of the car.

"Get in." Instantly we're heading down the drive and back onto the old asphalt road that brought us.

"Where are we going?" I ask.

"Away from there." I can see her eyes are black. She withdraws a box of Marlboro cigarettes and unwraps it, pulling one, before tossing the pack on the console between us.

"I think there's a fine for smoking in a rental." She lights it anyway. I'm about to speak when I see the tears forming in her eyes and I remain silent. It's only after a dozen or so miles through the Louisiana countryside before she says:

"They'll never let me forget it, never forgive me." I look at her, the beautiful green eyes filled with sadness.

"Forgive you for what?"

"For leaving." I think this over a few moments.

"Everyone leaves Morgan, sooner or later." She shakes her head.

"No... they don't, not everyone. Not everyone has the privilege." I silently ponder this remark.

A dozen miles further down the road, she pulls the car off to the side of a small glade and kills the engine, then turns squarely toward me in her seat. Her eyes although wet are intense and dilated.

"Tell me what you know. I know uncle Lucien spoke to you about me."

"About you?" I ask sincerely.

"About us, about this family, about... my youth." Our eyes lock, then as if listening to someone else, I hear myself say:

"Maybe, *you* should tell me." This has a sudden and profound effect. She turns back in her seat and silently stares at the windshield for several minutes. Then slowly she turns over the engine and pulls away.

We drive in silence for a long time. I won't be the one to break it and fight the desire to do so. Morgan becomes lost in her thoughts. There's no more tears, no more anger, no emotions at all really. We simply drive. By the time twilight comes, we are pulling up the two-track toward the old house that seems to anticipate our arrival.

When we enter the front door, it's like walking into a family gathering. In the dining room to the right of the great hall, seated at the head of the enormous wooden table is the old Colonel flanked on the sides by Pearl and Angeline while Magda and Sadie are placing dishes of wonderfully smelling foods amid the center of the table. There are seven stations of fine china and ornate silverware.

I'm shocked to see Emerald in the sitting room across from two finely dressed women –one a brunette the other gray haired. I'm excited to see her but alarmed when she turns and looks at us. Her eyes no longer are their tranquil blue but seem dark and intense. *In fact the right eye has become completely black as if the color has left it!* The hair is not its radiant wavy fullness but has become much longer, straight and pure black with two thin streaks of white. Her fingers no longer possess their fullness but are more svelte, the nails longer, and she's changed the décor of her jewelry to very old design and craftsmanship. This sudden abrupt change in her appearance shocks me and I feel my skin tingle. She rises slowly and is clad entirely in black.

"What's happened to Emerald?" I whisper to Morgan. "She looks…" I stop, words suddenly failing me.

"That's not mother," Morgan whispers. "That's my aunt Monique… *her twin*." I can hardly believe my eyes. She's an exact version of Emerald, nearly identical except the long black hair and the eyes, their dark intensity reflecting the flame of the candles upon the table. The twin gazes at us in silence for several heartbeats.

"Mon Dieu… Morgan," she whispers as the distance between aunt and niece slowly closes. They embrace, and kiss each other on both cheeks.

"How are you aunt Monique?" Morgan asks, her voice now seeming frail. She doesn't answer, simply stares with eyes that gleam like two coals at midnight.

"Look at you dear," she says. "You've become a beautiful woman... a very beautiful woman..." Monique says to her, turning to the ladies, "Look Alma, Morgan has come to visit." They nod and the brunette embraces her.

"Hello Morgan, what a pleasure to see you, my word how long has it been? Why, Aldee's all grown up now with two boys and a girl. I bet she'll want to make the trip over from Kenner to see you. How long are you staying on?"

"Not very long Mrs. Richardson. How is Aldee these days?"

"Just grand," she says turning toward the other woman. "Morgan is Monique's niece, Emerald's daughter, she went to school with Aldee, right through their junior year of high school. You remember Aldee, Monique, my youngest?"

"Of course Alma," Monique says smiling before she returns her attention to Morgan, her eyes move to mine and it's as if I'm looking into Emerald's face but the eyes are not a soft azure hue, one is green, the other completely black, possessing no color whatsoever. "And this... *this is Lucien's apprentice?*" she asks mysteriously, gently taking up my hand. Her eyes gleam, searching mine. Her choice of the word *apprentice* strikes me as rather odd. "Please sit children, this will take but a moment." Morgan and I retire to the wicker chairs near the window.

"Mrs. Keyes, I do apologize that you've made such a long trip for naught. I do wish I could help, however, Alma should have informed you that I rarely engage in problems of this sort."

"This sort?" the gray haired woman asks.

"Personal relationships, especially between couples." Monique turns and looks at her friend. "Alma is an Ursuline... a member of the sisterhood, thus our work together on behalf of young women such as your granddaughter." She returns her dark penetrating gaze upon the octogenarian. "However, Alma doesn't share my belief in the Eastern concept of Karma. To interfere in the relations of others is inviting the upheaval of their Karmic destinies."

"Miss Montaigne, is it terrible Karma, as you call it, to love one's granddaughter so... so fervently that I'd do anything to preserve her?" She looks at Alma, despair etched upon her tawny colored face. Alma reaches out, placing her hand upon her friend's.

"Monique's right Gail, I'm a firm Catholic heart and soul, but I know good deeds when they're done. Monique and her sisters have done a lot of very good things for a lot many folks," she looks across the table. "Monique, this time it's different... this boy's a bad seed... a bad seed Monique... something has to be done before-" she catches herself and exchanges a grave look with Mrs. Keyes.

"Go ahead and say it Alma... before he kills her! Our minds are the same on the matter. Miss Montaigne, this boy is leading my Elizabeth astray. Everything we've tried is of no avail. The harder we try the worse things become, the more distant she grows. Can't you help us before something terrible occurs?" All becomes quiet and still, then Monique reaches out her hands.

"Take my hands Abigail," she says to the stranger and the old woman does as requested. "Grip them hard dear, as hard as you can and close your eyes," she whispers and the old gal does so with earnestness. "Quiet your thoughts... concentrate only upon the face of your granddaughter. Visualize her in your mind, just as if she were sitting here before you instead of myself." There's a quiet pause. "Oh yes... I see her... clearly... a lovely girl, perhaps twenty years of age... auburn haired... spirited... she's driving a small blue car."

"Yes, that's exactly her... and she has a blue Chevrolet."

"Fine. Now I want you to visualize the young man… see him in your mind's eye…" another long pause. "Yes, I see him… I see…" she suddenly breaks off their grasp and seems to subtly recoil.

"What is it?" Mrs. Keyes inquires intensely. "What did you see?" There's a moment as all present wait for an answer to the question. Monique shakes her head, her hand across her throat.

"I've… spells, when… my heart flutters for a moment… that's all, my apologies."

"No Miss Montaigne… you saw something… what did you see? Please tell me. I'm right aren't I? He is going to do something," turning toward Alma, "something dreadful! Alma… help me, whatever shall we do?" Alma Richardson, trying to calm her, looks to Morgan's aunt.

"Monique… what can be done, surely you've insight?" The aunt studies her friend and her companion before once more reaching across the table.

"Take my hands again," she says and Mrs. Keyes reaches out and the process repeats. "I see something… something about you," Monique says and the old woman stutters.

"Me?"

"It's been your long desire, your dream, to travel abroad."

"Oh yes, I've always wanted to see Europe… and England. I've relations in England on Jack's side, Jack was my husband of sixty years."

"And you've never once ventured forth? Why have you not done so?"

"Oh, there's always too much to do around the house. There's always better things to spend such money on than… than…" She drifts, caught up in the reverie.

"Listen to me Abigail. You've come to me for help. You've asked me to intercede upon your behalf for the benefit of your granddaughter. Are you prepared to align yourself with my instructions implicitly?"

"Yes Miss Montaigne, I am."

"It's imperative you follow my instructions to the letter… to the letter Abigail."

"I will, I promise," she says and the three go silent.

"Upon your return to Monroe, phone the airline… purchase two tickets abroad to leave in exactly a month's time. Chose the destination yourself, the exact place is unimportant. The duration abroad must be for at least one month, no less. You must be strong… be prepared to take this journey by yourself, alone… do you understand me?"

"But… if Elizabeth might come with me, perhaps…"

"Under no circumstances whatsoever are you to instigate asking your granddaughter to join you on this trip. It must come from her. *That, which has hold of her mind, will build an empire of subterfuge, and despite her higher self, the personality will rebel.* If you do this… if you fall to the temptation to ask her, you will undo everything and the enterprise will fail."

"But… but how will…"

"If she comes to you Abigail, of her own volition… guided by those energies of her better nature… it was meant to be… if she does so… *the issue will resolve itself.* Now, if you don't object, my niece is here to visit… we're about to sit down together for dinner."

"Of course Monique," Alma blusters getting to her feet and helping the old woman. "I'm so very sorry for the intrusion,"

"It is not an intrusion Alma, I treasure your visits, and you," she says and the two old friends embrace lovingly.

"Thank you Miss Montaigne, how much do I owe you for your time?" Mrs. Keyes asks holding out her purse but the aunt places her hand atop hers.

"The fee is your promise."

"My promise?"

"That you will not fall to the temptation to ask your granddaughter to join you. This effort is contrary to your own nature Abigail."

"Yes, yes I know it… it is."

"Then the fee is your promise."

"I promise."

"Abigail… the Holy Muse has two daughters, do you know them?" The old woman shakes her head. "The fair one's name is Faith, she is golden and radiant and jubilant, her sister is the darker, quieter one… her name is Patience. Patience has hidden herself away from the world, yet she comes to those willing to seek her. *Her touch is the velvet hand of knowing*. Ask Faith and Patience to help you succeed in your desire. Your wish is a noble one," she says and the old woman takes up her hand.

"Thank you," she says effusively. "I will, I surely will do it," she says and beams toward her friend, "Alma, I'm going to go to Europe… I'm going to do it. Visit Edna, Jack's sister in England. I know this is exactly the right path to take. Why hadn't I thought of it?" The old woman rambles on as Alma Richardson steers her toward the front door.

"Gail, wait for me in the car, I'll be right out," Alma says and the old woman leaves. "Monique, forgive this one more thing," she turns toward Morgan. "I'm sorry Morgan this will only take a second."

"No, please Mrs. Richardson, go right ahead."

"Monique, Everett's boy has returned from the war in Afghanistan. He was an Army Ranger, you may recall? Anyway, to be short, his… group, were all killed, Tommy was the only survivor. He's in a terrible way Monique. Everett thinks he's considering suicide. He won't talk about

it with his dad, the pastor or anyone. We're all beside
ourselves with worry. Everett fears the worst."

After a moment's pause, Monique takes up Alma's hands
and they stand together silently this way until a most
remarkable thing occurs. Tears begin to stream down the
aunt's face.

"Goodness Monique! What in heaven's name is it?" Alma
asks stunned by this incredible sight.

"It… it's the same as with my Shelly… when he returned
from war," she says. "He blames himself for what happened.
Oh Alma, if I knew then what I know now… Shelton would
never have taken his own life." The two friends embrace
each other and Morgan holds a hand over her mouth.

"Shel was a good man Monique… it's tragic, just tragic. If
he had lived you would have never married Harl- oh, I can't
even say that man's name in this house!" There's a drawn out
moment as the two friends collect themselves. Alma hands
Monique her handkerchief to dry her eyes.

"Alma, when will it end? We take our young men and send
them to the devil… off into these man-made hells…"
Monique whispers, "…mere boys Alma… filled with dreams
and hopes… God bless their souls."

"I'm sorry, forgive me for bringing it up," Alma says
wiping tears from her eyes with her sleeve.

"Don't apologize Alma, for caring about him. Tell Tommy
he is deeply loved and to expect our visit next week. He
needs to *speak with his friends again*. They'll set it right.
Everything will be alright." Alma embraces her companion
for several heartbeats before she pats her cheek.

"Bless you Monique, my regards to the rest of the family…
and to you Morgan," she says and exits quietly through the
front door. Monique stands as if lost in memories of the past.
Morgan gently touches her sleeve.

"Aunt Monique, are you alright?" she whispers and the aunt looks upon her niece with wounded eyes.

"Yes Morgan, I'm alright. It's just... when I saw the young man... I saw Shelly," she whispers and Morgan lovingly strokes her back while the aunt dries her eyes. "Don't dwell on it dear, let's go sit with the family." She takes Morgan by the arm and leads us into the dining room. "You missed lunch, you both must be famished," she says pointing us to our seats.

Magda takes a place with us at the table. We partake in what is an entirely vegetarian meal. There is a delicious tomato and rice soup with a hint of cayenne, an eggplant ratatouille and a rich salad full of a variety of fresh greens including mint. The bread is fresh baked with fennel seed and delicious. Magda pours a robust red wine from a decanter so I'm unsure of the vintage but it is exceptional. A variety of topics permeate the festive air. I notice Monique seems nearly transfixed upon Morgan, her gaze continually returning. Colonel Montaigne is talking about the Battle of Pavia in 1525.

"The French knights were decimated... what good is a man draped in armor against the arquebus? Once again the art of warfare changed for all time. And I'm not ramblin' on about just technology... you saw a change in the professional soldier. Any man taught to wield a musket could knock out a heavily trained fully armored knight, and on horseback no less. It was revolutionary. Exact same thing repeated in Japan fifty years later. The most skilled Samurai swordsman... ineffective against a pauper with a flintlock... except maybe in the rain." Morgan suddenly addresses her aunts.

"Will mother be joining us anytime soon?" The question has a remarkable effect as the discussion rapidly dies down to nil. There's a spate of French amongst the family. "Please answer my question Aunt Monique. I'd appreciate seeing mother, right now." The two exchange long and intense eye contact. Pearl huffs something in French and Morgan – incredibly- seems to go mad. "I've phoned you for over two weeks! Why can't you put her on the phone with me? I want to see her now, right now!" This sudden and unexpected outburst has the entire table at odds. Pearl immediately interjects.

"I've told you Morgan, I dislike your tone of voice. You're crossing a very thin margin niece!" she shouts. Monique says something to her in French and Pearl reacts indignantly, growing quiet.

"Morgan dear… why do you persist so?" Monique asks calmly. "Surely you know our dear sister's health is of the utmost concern to us all."

"I want to see her."

"But you can't see her dear. Not at this time."

"Why Aunt Monique? Why is that?"

"Because she's in healing. You were most certainly told this as well."

"What sort of healing?"

"Morgan, my child, you wouldn't understand. You've been away much too long to understand something so-"

"And *that's* what's at the heart of all this drama… isn't it?"

"What on earth do you mean?"

"You've never forgiven me for leaving… leaving my, *my calling* as you refer to it. This is your way of getting even." Monique's eyes turn to fire, her back going rigid.

"You'd think me capable of such ridiculous games?"

"Yes, yes I would." Morgan rebuffs and this seems to shock the family. There's a spirited conversation in French that abruptly comes to a halt when the old man slams his palm upon the table.

"That's enough! That's all I intend to hear. That's my grand daughter sitting at my table! My dear mother's great granddaughter," he shouts. A sudden and intense silence permeates the room and the old man looks at them all one by one. "You women! So damn involved with that Choctaw witch, ya'll would shun your very own kin. This girl is your blood! She's her mother's daughter," he says staring hard at Monique. "Ya'll tell her what she's come here to know... and in the tongue of this nation. You want her man friend to leave the room, I'm certain he'll oblige you but this here has gone on long enough!"

A silence fills the room and eyes dart back and forth as the family collectively takes in this sudden expostulation. I watch as the old man and Morgan exchange a deep heartfelt gaze and Morgan's eyes well up with tears. He shakes his white mane.

"Don't cry little one," he says lovingly, "you're with your kin. Everyone here loves ya. You'll know soon enough. Tell her Monique... go on." He pushes back his tall mahogany chair and withdraws another of his crooked black cigars and clips the end into an ashtray with a cutter. Finally Monique breaks the ice.

"Magda, bring the tea to the sitting room, we'll have it in there."

"Yes Monique," she says rising and they all slowly follow as if in unison and make for the sitting room, all except the old Colonel. I pause.

"Are you coming sir?" I ask quietly. He waves his cigar at me.

"No son, there's no use for a worn out old soldier in that room... go on." I stare at him for a moment, his head low upon his breast and I realize how much this has pained him.

In the sitting room are a number of kerosene lamps with crystal chimneys and several large candles that shed a soft amber glow. Monique and Angeline re-enter from an antechamber just off the room where they have sequestered themselves for several minutes and take seats within the circle of chairs that line the room. Magda serves us tea and I choose coffee that proves to have a unique flavor. Monique is studying me from her chair.

"Do you like the flavor?" she asks.

"It's different," I say and she smiles.

"The coffee's made with chicory... from the French quarter." I nod approvingly.

"I like it," I say and she smiles then immediately turns to Magda.

"Magda... did you see Sadie to bed? I don't want her listening in on what we have to say. She's incessantly poking about the keyhole."

"I've that girl under wing Monique... she's sound asleep."

"And Montara?"

"Off into the Astral," she says. There's a quick furtive glance in my direction. "She's been asleep well over an hour," she responds, taking a seat with the group and I begin to realize she is much more than just a maid or a cook. Everything is as quiet as a graveyard, except for the dog.

"Majo must have tree'd a coon," Pearl says staring blankly into space.

"I best tend to him," Magda says beginning to rise from her chair when Monique gestures.

"Don't bother sister," she says staring into the room. "*Gillian has arrived.* Let's get started." I look about but see that no one has entered the room at all. Morgan is staring at me. I gesture inquisitively and she takes my hand tightly.

"Aunt Gillian is here," she whispers low. I stare dumbfounded, again glancing behind me but Morgan yanks my attention back. *"Aunt Gillian died years ago."* We exchange a long intense look and I can see that she is absolutely serious.

"Sisters, let's welcome our beloved Gillian who was asked to be present tonight," Monique says and they all bow their heads. "Dearest Gillian, our apologies to you beloved sister for asking you to revisit us upon this dense mortal plane but our endeavor is dire. We seek your guidance and forgiveness." They collectively sit motionless for a moment, some genuflecting. "Let's get started," Monique says turning directly toward Morgan. "Morgan Laurel MacIntyre..." she says firmly, "nobody in this house disdains you, or wishes you ill in any way. The blood that flows in our veins and that of our beloved sister is the same that flows within you. *You were chosen* to carry on the line but you made your own choices in life as your mother and your father made theirs. No one begrudges you for following in their path and that of your own making. If there's ill will growing betwixt us it's of your errant assumption that our dear Emerald has fallen into a bad state whilst under our care. Your mother came to us of her own free will... for healing... *she's with Aphelia now.*" There's another bowing of heads and muttering of prayer as if a kind of supplication were set in motion.

"Who is Aphelia?" I whisper under my breath to Morgan.

"The Choctaw medicine-woman," she whispers not removing her attention from her aunts. "Where?" Morgan asks Monique directly. "Where are they?"

"Where?" Monique answers her. "Why... out there," she points. *"Deep within the Silence."* There's a mood change in the room as the others fall into a sense of reverence.

"The Silence? What are you talking about?" Morgan asks and Magda, Angeline and Monique exchange looks.

"You'd know child if you'd remember your heritage," Pearl says and the women all stare at us.

"What is it? Where is it?" Morgan insists.

"A daughter of the Montaigne line asking this question," Pearl says with spite. "It's a travesty," and Morgan flares.

"I'm asking Aunt Monique! Answer me!" Morgan shouts and a sudden wildness erupts within the room. The flames in the lamps jump, casting strange ominous shadows across the walls and ceiling; then, an intense wind from nowhere whips through the room and the candle flames are all instantly extinguished. Morgan, in fact everyone except Pearl, looks about the room in awe. Suddenly, it's as if a shadow has entered the room, a thin diaphanous silhouette against the kerosene lamp's wild flickering glow.

"Aunt Gillian…" I hear Morgan say under her breath. The shadow slowly approaches and *enters into Angeline's seated body and she goes rigid as if stunned.* Her fingers grasp the arms of the chair and a subtle but amazing transformation occurs as Angeline's eyes, her countenance, changes in a most discreet way. We watch as Angeline slowly gazes about the room and in a strange quiet voice says:

"Good evening sisters." Everyone except Morgan and I say:

"Good evening Gillian, welcome sister." A keen focus to this incredible thing ensues. I take the moment to whisper to Morgan.

"What's going on?" She looks at me, her eyes wide.

"Aunt Gillian's come," she whispers and quiets me with a gesture of her hand.

We all sit in silence as Angeline looks at her arms and fingers, moving them as one tries out a new garment. After surveying the room –a strange grimace upon her face, very unlike Angeline's stark blandness- she stares directly at Morgan and the look in her eyes makes the hair at the base of my skull tingle. Ever so slowly she rises from the chair and takes the center of the circle never removing her eyes from her niece. Then in the most unnerving voice says:

"Restrain thy angry heart niece... draw back from the mouth of the abyss." All eyes shift to Morgan who stares in wonderment. Or is it fear? Whether fear or wonder, she remains steadfastly silent. Angeline slowly points outside, her long thin arm and finger pointing the way. *"Thou hear? The bay of the hound."* We all take pause to listen to the low sonorous wail. *"Hear with thine ear. It is She."* The room is in abject silence, only the strange soft wail of the dog in the distance. *"The great Silence that is She... where our beloved lies within Her healing embrace, locked in mortal contention with the demon mind."* No one utters a sound. Her voice suddenly rises in intensity. *"Look not upon your sisters askance niece, it is thy world that instills such wickedness within the divine body of our beloved."*

"What are you talking about Aunt Gillian? What... what *wickedness* do you mean?" Morgan stammers.

"Thou ask this question yet thy hast the answer with thineself," she says mysteriously and Morgan is noticeably confused.

"Answer? What answer?" I feel an icy cold grip my heart as Angeline slowly turns and points her long finger accusingly at me.

"He." I watch Morgan turn her head and look at me in horror. I'm shocked to my core.

"What?" I ask and Morgan cannot remove her eyes from me. "What is she talking about?" I ask, but Morgan only stares at me as if I were some unfathomable thing. Then, as if on a wind, a calm serene feeling washes over me and I turn to Angeline. "What is it you mean?" I ask her.

"Twas thee... upon the alter of the temple... the olden land, cross't the great sea. T'was thee bear witness the wicked befallen our loved. Why doth thou remain here without the words of thy mouth?" There is a profound silence as all eyes are upon me. The frantic side of my being wants to claw to dominance, but the calm serenity, like a guardian angel, stays with me this time as I fathom the puzzle. When the epiphany hits me, a kind of knowing overcomes me.

"I think I understand," I say softly and no one even breathes let alone speaks. "It was something Lucien said to me when we returned to San Francisco from Prague."

"What did he say?" Monique queries.

"Yes, I think I have it, he said... 'They are wrong, the scientists of the world,' he too included himself, he said, 'Energy *can* be destroyed, it can seep into the morass of the unconscious, be dissolved into nothingness,' something along those lines." I study their faces looking at me in the dim light. "Don't you see? It wasn't destroyed, not at all. It's transmuted itself into Emerald, it's this thing that makes her sick," I proclaim and this has an alarming effect upon the host.

"What is it?" Pearl asks from the darkness of the room.

"The Burning Man," I say with dread in my voice. It's as if time stops. I can only hear the clicking of the old clock; nothing moves. Angeline slowly extends her arm toward me and holds open the palm of her hand.

"Return what was bequeathed thee," she says and I'm completely in awe. I look to Morgan and shake my head slowly.

"What does she mean?" Morgan whispers and Pearl shushes her. We all watch and wait and wonder.

"*Return the star... we beseech thee.*" Again, there is the rocking of breeze within the room and the second kerosene lamp is extinguished. Within the meager light of the lone lamp we all watch as suddenly the gossamer image of a beautiful young girl, of perhaps sixteen years of age, steps from Angeline's body. Her dress although not ancient is neither contemporary in design and she is very thin in substance, nearly a wisp. The apparition stands squarely before me and holds out its hand, palm open. Although I'm shocked by this unexpected and unnerving sight, I also know that it wants the small silver crucifix I still wear around my neck, the one given to me by Emerald just before the fateful encounter with the Burning Man entity.

I withdraw the chain from around my neck but when I place the bauble into the spirit's hand it is actually Angeline's that receives it. The moment I place it within her palm she falters. I manage to catch her and help her to a chair. When she slowly collects herself she presents the jewel to Monique. This immediately creates an astonishing reaction from the women, the Creole maid gasps and cries out.

"What is it?" Aunt Pearl asks from her chair. "What is there?"

"It's Emerald's crucifix, the one presented her at Basilica Saint Louis at seven years," Monique says and an encompassing sadness permeates the room. "Where did you get this?" she asks me. "How is it possible that you have it?" and Morgan's eyes are wide and scrutinizing me closely.

"The night before confronting the demon... in Bratislava. She gave it to me to wear, to protect me." There is a sudden intense mourning, a low moaning from within the collective group, words of regret and disillusionment.

"Be still of heart!" Monique says sharply and the room falls into silence. All eyes except the blind are fixed upon her and her look is unnerving. "Out of love she lent it sisters. What might have befallen him without such a gift?" she says and everyone present falls into a kind of stupor, the silence broken only by the stifled cries of the maid.

Monique holds the tiny talisman, her eyes burning into its feeble silver light.

"Fear beset her... doubt... *the small infinitesimal door into the heart*... yet it's not this that concerns us now... but how? How was it done?" she queries the host. "How was it done sisters? This hideous and remarkable deed?" she asks and stares at me again. "Kind sir, the last... bit... of the quandary," she says queerly but I've no idea what she's getting at. You could hear a pin drop. Morgan, her eyes wide with concern and confusion, gently touches my arm.

"What else was there?" she whispers. I can only shrug.

"I don't know. There isn't anything else... that's all," I say and think the episode finished when I'm suddenly confronted by a memory. "Wait... there was one thing else," I say and all eyes and ears are upon me. "It may be completely insignificant... but I do remember she was cut," I mutter low and the group stares. "Emerald, after the tempest. She had a small tiny cut here... on her right cheek. I remember... it bled." There's a silent exchange shared by all the women.

"What does it mean?" Magda asks solemnly.

"Is it significant sister?" Pearl queries as Monique paces deep in thought. She stops abruptly and stares into the void.

"Indeed... indeed it is as he says, the Holy Muse help us," she whispers as if to some invisible person.

"Sister?"

"Mon Dieu, how clever!" Monique says turning. "The gorgon resides still... within the physical realm," she whispers. Angeline suddenly falters and Magda reaches out for her. "Don't fret over her sister, Gillian leaves us," she says and slowly resumes pacing the room. "The imp is wise sisters… ancient and resourceful… how clever. As it was dying it hid a shard of itself within the wound it created. This fragment is growing within our dear sister."

"Diabolical!" Pearl hisses. There's a soft muted crying and I realize Magda is deep in sorrow. Angeline holds her eyes hidden behind her long gangly fingers and Morgan stares fixedly at Monique.

"What does this mean, Aunt Monique? What will happen now?" she asks nearly frantic in her tone and the woman reaches out to her niece and their hands clench together.

"We know now with what we do battle. We've a finger on the devil m'love… be strong for us all. How could we have ever guessed? Aphelia failed to divine it, even Lucien, the wise old wizard was remiss. Mon Dieu! Do you realize the strength… *the will* involved? It's a devil. It must be annihilated from this world," she says an unworldly intent in her eyes and words. "But how? How to do it?" She turns suddenly. "Aphelia must know sisters, at first light," she says and Morgan pulls Monique's hand to her.

"I'm coming," she says and the aunt looks deep into her eyes.

"You cannot my child… this is not for you. It will be far too dangerous. The thing is insidious, we must be ever alert, anything could happen. *This will be a fight to the death*," she says and her eyes are like fire.

"I'm going Aunt Monique!" The women exchange glances culminating with Monique brushing Morgan's hair from her eyes and in that moment I'm taken by their affinity. I can't shake the notion they are intrinsically connected.

"Oui," she whispers taking Morgan's face within both of her hands. "Oui c'est bon," she says gently kissing her cheek.

I'm struck by the tenderness of the moment. Monique slowly rises and exits the room still carrying the crucifix.

The following morning is raining. The water drips from the foliage and saturates the green earth. It is a solemn procession as the women prepare to leave. I'm packing my small bag I've brought from San Francisco when Morgan knocks on my door. Although she engages me in idle conversation, I know deep in my heart what she has come to say. Before she says it, we take a walk in the garden under the rain. I note how the gardens seem in disrepair. The stone, the walkways, are cracked and choked by moss. There's an old marble fountain, long disused that clamors with vines and brambles and it's before this very lonely place, lost deep within the world that *she breaks my heart.*

She asks me not to join them on this sojourn, but her eyes cannot hide what her heart already knows, that we are both deeply in love with one another.

"Just until we get back," I hear her voice, but something so deep and original inside me knows *this is the end for us.* How do I know this? My mind fights with this notion but the same calm serenity I had felt the previous evening knows that I have already lost her, lost her to inexorable circumstances.

She begins to weep, her tears mixing with the rain. She knows too that something beyond our ability is taking hold, a relentless gravity pulling us apart. She buries her head into my shoulder and the finer laces of her chocolate colored hair catch upon my lips and I breathe her in deeply, fill my lungs with her.

"I'll be back soon," she whispers clenching my jacket in her hands. She knows as I do, we are being torn apart, not by a person or a thing, but by the very nature of our lives. "I can't bear this," she cries and I hold her with all my might, as if I would never let go. But I do let go. I look upon her. Her eyes are there, locked forever in the moment.

"When you come back, you'll no longer be the person I know," I whisper to her. *"You'll be the French witch you left behind twenty years ago."* She hides her precious face within the folds of my jacket forcing something into my hand and seals it.

When we return, they are waiting, dark and solemn in the rain, like a funeral. With barely a glance, she gets into the black Mercedes and the door closes. I can see her in the window, *but it is through the glass and darkly.*

It feels as if something has ripped out my heart by the roots and I fight the fear that would cause me to break. Monique stands beneath the black umbrella and turns toward me. She too knows. The fierce dark eyes that so recently put me on edge are now soft and utterly sad. She kisses me on both cheeks and when she touches my breast with her gloved hand she whispers:

"My heart cries for you." She slowly turns getting behind the wheel and the car slowly pulls away and is gone.

I look back over my shoulder, up at the porch. The aged old Colonel stands watching, his faithful brown mongrel at his boot. His shoulders droop, more than I recall. We look at each other, a long and solemn exchange, before he turns away, a weary old man with a limp, and disappears into the darkness of the house. The faithful old hound takes one last look, a solemn wayward glance at me over his shoulder and slowly retires within. I look about the great yard, not a soul, not a sound except the pervasive rain.

I realize I'm still holding something in my hand and stare at my fist for the longest time but I can't seem to force it to open. How odd, I think to myself, considering I know what it hides. I can clearly discern the long slender shaft of the keys, like knife blades against my palm. For some inexplicable reason I cannot unclench my fist and for the first time during the whole morning's business, I realize the water across my cheek isn't from the heavens but my own eyes, my own heart.

Epilogue.

'Dearest Love,
How are you? Where are you? Are you traveling once again? I miss you, I miss you more than these words can convey. On nights like this I think of you, and when sleep comes I feel we are together again, but always from afar. How I fight the desire to fly to you, wherever you are.

'Things are well Willem. Mother heals steadily. Our time together is the most meaningful I've ever spent with her. The aunts are all quite insane, and I adore them! Grandfather insists I send his regards. He was very impressed with you. Consider that a real badge of honor my love, he is extremely wary of anyone. I know he talks on and on about being a man of the world but Grandpapa could never leave Magenta. He talks about her incessantly. In the same breath he curses her for her wild ways he speaks in adoration. Every time he complains of her witchery he speaks into the distance as if he were with her again. I treasure him, but alas, I fear he is very much in the twilight of his life. What will happen when the patriarch dies? I shan't think of it.

'Aunt Monique inquires about you, they all do. I tell them I write but each letter fails me, except this one, this one will find you, it must, you must know you are in my thoughts everyday, every night. Oh, dearest love, how is it that we are apart so? Please forgive me for what's happened. I know we will be together again, I know it, do you believe? You must believe it. Hold this thought, this wish, to your breast my love as if you're holding me, as I hold you to mine.

'Our work here progresses steadily. It is very alive with me. I feel it throughout my body, a soft fluid motion. Oh Willem, what will become of my life in New York left behind, like grapes dying on the vine? I speak with my friends on the phone but it pains me deeply. Aunt Monique will not allow more than a few minutes of it, and this is how it has to be, but I still cry over it, and you. Would you do me something, if you can? Will you go to New York and tell them? Tell them what's happened. I simply cannot. I'm incapable of it, yet they are my dearest friends. Why should they not know? The key is on the ring I gave you upon our parting.

'What have you been doing dearest? I sit at the fountain and wonder. Aunt Monique has a flock of ravens, five of them, that visit the garden daily. It's a fascination to watch them, their personalities. Aunt Monique raised Lila from a chick, Astrid was her mother, the flock her children. Lila sits upon her wrist and actually allows Monique to stroke her plumage. It's quite magical. You'd marvel at the way they interact, the way they take turns taking bread from her hand. There's also a barn owl with a broken wing and a blue macaw you never saw named Samisen that's the twin of Kiki, the one on Sutter Street. I study the birds. It's part of the regimen.

*'I'm not supposed to tell you but, sometimes I come to you
on the wing and it is just as if I truly see you. Can such a
thing be true? When I hold your hand to my heart, is it
yours?*

*'Please don't phone here my love. If I hear your voice I'll
go mad. I simply cannot bear our parting. Can you write me,
if you've time? Could you send a picture, a photograph?
How is it possible that I have not a single photograph of
you? This was the insanity of my life at that time. That of the
thousand things I photographed during our time together, I
failed to capture that which was most precious to me.*

*'Audrey will send my cameras before she leaves for Europe.
They felt it was a good idea. I want to photograph the house
and gardens. I wander the bayou from time to time, so I want
to capture it with the lens. Deep in the swamp there's a
mangrove that reminds me of you.*

*'I've been spending time with my niece Montara whom I
don't believe you had the opportunity to meet. Oh Willem,
what a precious child! I just love her dearly. She is uniquely
special. I'm also becoming quite close to Sadie. Aunt
Monique runs a charity for abused girls, called Magenta's
Daughters. Sadie is the forty ninth girl they've spared from
broken and abusive homes. I'll be photographing their future
events and helping with their fundraising efforts. The
Women's League has awarded Aunt Monique a lifetime
achievement award. Monique's Foundation has raised over
twelve million dollars in assistance to single parent families
and the elderly that were displaced by Katrina. She won't
speak at the upcoming ceremony. I'll have to do it for her.*

'I must close, so dream my darling one, dream and come alive again. I am more alive now than I have been in years. I see things Love, hear things that before were as if through a veil. You know in your heart this is true. You feel it too don't you, that coming to life?
Yours, Morgan'

Concrete and Steel

South of Soho, east of TriBeCa, near the west end of Chinatown sits an indiscreet, narrow warehouse that has somehow escaped the advent of New York City's renaissance of modernization. Rather out of place yet nearly invisible, this tall thin innocuous building coincides with the address on the piece of paper in my hand.

As I tip the cabbie, I look up at the building, a somewhat gothic front façade entirely in dark-gray. Two small gargoyles complete with wings and bared teeth sit atop each extreme placidly staring down at me. Is this the correct address? Recessed near what looks to be more a small loading dock than an entrance to a residence, I find an elevator with the letters, *MINC* next to the fourth floor button. Inserting the key, I'm amazed that it works. The door opens and I step into a long service elevator and punch the button to 4F. The lift jerks and rises, groaning to beat the devil.

When I disembark, I see one lone door on the facing wall. In brushed aluminum lettering it reads: *M.MacIntyre Inc.* I stare at the door. I realize that behind this portal is Morgan's life in New York. I insert the key, the latch clicks and I enter into the darkness, the noise of the outside world immediately dying out to nothing but a distant hum; only small sounds… the banging of metal… someone shouting downstairs. I *feel* the ensuing silence, an anticipation of something. I pull back the heavy black drapes that cover the wall of glass overlooking the street below and New York steps into the room.

With the light comes the realization that her extended departure from New York was not anticipated, things left lying about as if she were merely down the street; the kitchen in disarray, half a bagel and a cup of coffee congealing on the counter.

Cameras and flash equipment are everywhere; several camera bodies lying on a large worktable with scores of lenses and filters stacked about. There's a large Apple computer with tandem twenty-eight inch monitors, hundreds of magazines and thousands of photo prints.

As I begin to stroll about the old warehouse studio, I become enthralled by the plethora of artwork. Several large canvasses and a few dozen smaller paintings are in various stages of display, some already hung, others sitting off to the side. On a large expanse of brick wall, there are two enormous black and white prints of a woman's face easily eight foot by ten foot in size. Above her bed hang several large black and white prints of children at play around the Eiffel Tower. There is a series on another wall of Parisians in the rain beneath umbrellas, French businessmen and women on a boulevard, a barefooted woman in a raincoat in a slip, an emaciated junkie smoking a cigarette. I feel I can actually see her in Paris, in my mind, shooting these photographs.

As I survey the tables and desktops I'm overwhelmed by the excessive amount of photography and printed imagery. One of the tables is littered with fashion prints cut from magazines with blue pencil and sharpie lines drawn about the edges of the ads. Everywhere there are photos of mostly women, in natural and aesthetic contexts.

I become lost in the study of all this work, when I'm startled by the rattling of the door, as if someone outside in the hall were fumbling with the lock. I'm astounded when an amazingly tall woman with a shock of black stringy hair and a grotesquely pronounced hump on her right shoulder enters the apartment and looks about. It's nearly surreal. She wears dark round sunglasses that give her pale complexion a somewhat skeletal appearance. Her hunchback looks massive. I feel as if I'm witnessing an apparition. I hope this isn't the person I'm supposed to meet. The very second I think this she spies me.

"Are you the guy from London?"

"Yes," I say trying hard not to stare at her deformity. She walks over, her boot heels sounding on the floor and juts a long boney hand at me. Her shake feels like sandpaper.

"Georgiana Snipes... how's it goin'?" She gazes about the warehouse. "You just get here?" she asks and I nod. "Cool. I thought I was late. You're on your way to Europe or somewhere?" She unbuttons her long black coat and I'm astonished that her deformity is in reality a cat, a large gray feline with brilliant green eyes.

"Oh my word, a cat," I say. She pulls the shades from her face and looks me over. I'm amazed, her eyes are two different colors; one has a deep brown iris, the other a brilliant blue. They give her a kind of wild look that is accented by the heavy mascara. Her lipstick is black and the fingernails too.

"This pain-in-the-ass is Maud, Morgan's little bitch," she says kissing the cat's face and placing it on the nearest tabletop. The animal scans the interior and cries out. "Oh, he's crying for his mama again. Poor baby." She hovers over the cat. "Your old lady's not here man… yer gonna have to wait it out." The cat jumps to the floor and wanders.

"He?" I ask questioning her use of gender. "A male cat named Maude?"

"Not *Maude* with an *E*, like a chick's name," she says, "*Maud* with an *L-I-N*," she says. I'm lost. "His name is Maudlin… because he's such a crabby ass!" she shouts to the cat then points at the refrigerator behind me. "Hey, does she got a beer in there?" I check the refrigerator and am shocked. It is nearly deplete of any kind of foodstuffs; mostly just old film stock, bulk reels of 35mm Kodak Kodachrome 64 and Ilford black and white stocks.

"Sorry… just film."

"Yeah, I think the girls cleaned her out last time we were here. I gotta get going anyway, I'm having my bass re-harmonized for the gig tonight. What's your name man?" I introduce myself to her. She looks at me closely. "Wait, say your name again," and I repeat it for her. She points a finger at me. "You been hanging with her in Frisco?" I nod reluctantly. "Oh yeah…" she says a bent smile curling at the edges of her thin mouth. "She told me about you man. I didn't get you were the guy she told me about… coming from England and all," she says folding her gangly forearms across her stomach, tattooed from the wrists up.

I look her over. She must be at least six foot in her boots and is wearing black leather pants and a frayed black t-shirt that reads: *Zildjian,* printed in cursive. Upon her long fingers are several silver rings that all seem to be skulls and one sharp pointed *talon* ring on the left index finger. Her belt is made from used bullet shell casings, some with full metal jackets. She looks very thin and gothic.

"What do you do for a living?" I question her.

"For a living?" she asks raising one eyebrow. "I'm the bassist and lead songwriter for *Concrete and Steel*," she says. "Heard of us?"

"No, I'm sorry," I mutter and she shrugs.

"We're a pretty little girl band," she says through her crooked grin.

"Oh…" I say. "How do you know Morgan?" She scratches at her ear that dangles a silver crucifix.

"Morgue's kinda like, our photographer… she shoots all our stuff." She suddenly breaks away to check on the cat crying out at the top of his lungs. "Maud! What're you doing you little shit?!" The cat cries out, walking through the apartment, searching for his master. "She ain't here Romeo, get it through your frickin' cranium!" She suddenly turns. "Hey, ya think I can leave him here for a little while, maybe overnight? He's goin' nuts over at our place," she says picking him back up and nuzzling him affectionately. "Aren't ya? Ya little fucker!" She strokes his coat but the cat wants to continue his search of the apartment. She rejoins me at the kitchen area. "The other cats and him are at each other's throats. It's pretty much feline hell over there." She looks me over silently. "How long you in town?"

"I'm not sure. Morgan asked me to speak with you all about…" I fall silent.

"Well, you're in luck. We're playing in town tonight, at the Netherworld."

"What is that?"

"A night club," she says laughing. "You get to meet all the girls at once. I'll put you on the guest list. You staying here?"

"For a day perhaps. I have to get back to England."

"Well, have at it. She's got a cool crib," she says. "Although… she should'a kept the bottom floor instead of renting it out to the Chinese. It's bigger and has a loading dock off the alley… and street frontage."

"She's the landlord?" I ask as she scans the beams.

"Yeah. I was here when she bought it. I thought she was nuts. Now the thing is worth ten times as much."

"Why not the main floor?" She grows quiet a moment, reflective.

"She wouldn't take the lower floor… *cuz it's haunted*… or so she says. Apparently something hideous went on down there at some point."

"What happened?" I inquire and she shrugs.

"Don't know, every time she starts to tell us, she gets a weird look on her face and changes the subject. One of these days I'll tie her to a chair and make her tell me." She begins donning her coat to leave.

"Hey wait… um… how do I reach you? In case… I don't know, the cat or whatever," I stammer.

"Nah, don't worry about him, he's got all his shit in the back. I'll grab him tomorrow. He just needs a break from the bitches," she says and I must look lost for she continues, "I live with my guitar player. She's got two cats that think they own the place, whaddya gonna do?" At the door she turns. "Hey, if you get to the club before nine, tell Kirby the club guy you're our friend, he'll let you in backstage. Thanks for watching the pussy," she shouts loudly, closing the door and I hear the lift engage.

From the bank of windows overlooking the street below I see her exit the building and start across the street. A cab driving too fast has to brake and honks at her. She reciprocates by showing him her middle finger in a very meaningful way. The cab honks again and speeds off. I watch as she saunters down the block like a *scarecrow in a crowd* and disappears around the corner.

I need a cup of coffee, luckily the kitchen is full of it, several varieties and an old Krupps bean grinder. When I open the refrigerator to see if there might be cream the cat is instantly beside me purring loudly. I find a quart of half and half, that's rancid and dump it in the sink, the cat jumping up on the counter and following my actions closely.

"Sorry bud," I say and rub his head. "We're out of luck." He *talks* to me all the while, carrying on a rather one-sided conversation, his eyes wide and he never stops purring. He cries out several times not relinquishing his place on the counter until I realize he's waiting for me to open the cupboard above him. When I do, I see this is where she stores his food. He whips his tail in anticipation –perhaps its impatience. I take one of the cans and peel it open and place it on the floor. He immediately sets to work devouring the contents, purring loudly as he eats. "Well at least she has food for you," I say as I toss a bag of spinach –completely black- and dump out what I believe to be a pasta salad and a moldy package of grapes. When his can is empty and he's licked the entirety of his paws and face, he reluctantly leaves and resumes his search for his master, his voice cracking in the solitude and I share his loss. The black coffee is good and soon the pain I've been feeling in my head subsides.

Later that evening I'm standing outside the nightclub Netherworld trying to get past the doorman. He's looking over my license and comparing it with the band's guest list. He shakes his head.

"Nope, sorry, no Willem Furey… you're not on the list."

"She must have forgotten." He just stares at me. "Can't you call backstage?"

"We don't do that," he says a blank expression on his face. I pull out my wallet.

"How much?"

"Fifty bucks," he says and I look at him. "*Concrete and Steel* is playing tonight."

"Yeah I know, I'm on the guest list," I say sarcastically and pull two twenties and a ten from my wallet. He smudges my hand with an ugly black dot and I enter the club. The opening band on stage is terrible. I work my way through the small crowd to the door leading backstage. A guy in a black t-shirt that reads: *Klub Netherworld* in phosphorescent green lettering holds up his hand.

"No access," he says over the din. I shout in his ear and he gestures for me to wait as he slips behind the door for a minute. When he reemerges, he waves me in and I pass the barrier into the Netherworld backstage area. It's a long cement hallway going both directions. I take the right because it leads toward a series of doors all painted a bland beige color. The walls are covered with messages and signatures written with crayons and Sharpies and there's hundreds of adhesive passes stuck about. Half way down the hall, Georgiana emerges from one of these doors clad head to toe in black leather, and whistles like an ironworker, waving me over and I enter the door she's left ajar.

The room is filled with beer, liquor, and Perrier. There's a fruit and vegetable tray with some cheeses and a large bag of beef jerky.

"Hey gang, this is Morgan's pal, from Cali," Georgiana says loudly. A thin black haired woman, with dark expressive eyes, clad in a blood-red leather suit extends her hand.

"Yeah, I remember you," she says. "How ya been?" she asks but I've no answer for her since we've never met before. Georgiana looks at me strangely. She's an amazing sight in her black leather stage costume. An Asian girl is applying make-up to the face of a woman sitting in a canvass chair and Georgiana borrows her mirror and checks the wisp of fake blood down the side of her mouth, winking at her own reflection.

"Oh yeah, by the way ladies..." Georgiana says to the group, "this guy is *the* guy..." she says emphasizing the word *the* and they all look at her blankly. "From Frisco," she says, same blank stares. A heavyset woman with tattoos on her large forearms –who's eating the beef jerky- snorts:

"We can see he's a guy G, whooptie fuckin' shit." Georgiana shakes her head.

"No, no, this is *the guy*," she says using her long boney fingers as quote markers. "From Frisco... Morgan's *guy*..." There are sudden knowing expressions on the faces of the women and the one just shaking my hand stares, her eyes lighting up.

"Oh... this is *the guy*," she mimics and they all stare. Georgiana takes my shoulder.

"Here, let me introduce you to the band man. This lovely thing here is VD, our bitchin' guitar player," she says pointing to the woman I've just met. Although she's probably about five foot six she looks like she weighs perhaps one hundred and fifteen pounds –in the leather.

"I'm sorry," I interject, "your name is Edie?" and Georgiana laughs.

"Nah, it's V-D... Victoria Denise Stockton in person," she gestures, "but we call her VD, for other reasons..." The woman shakes my hand again and seems to be looking me over. Georgiana twists my shoulders in the direction of the heavyset woman. "And this is Tiny, our bad-ass drummer." She must easily weigh two hundred and forty pounds and wears a plain black t-shirt and black jeans. She basically ignores me. The Asian girl has finished primping the woman in the chair and Georgiana strokes her long wavy black hair. "And this little number... is our lead singer Bambi Giordano." She's a very attractive woman. She wears black leather pants with a spider web blouse and lots of rings, at least one on every finger and a large silver cross dangles from her neck. She's tall in her four-inch heels, not quite head to head with Georgiana. Her lips and fingernails are scarlet red and her eyes are full of mischief.

"So... you're Morgan's boyfriend? From San Francisco?" she asks point blank.

"Um..." is all I seem capable of saying. She laughs and turns to her mates.

"Well, that answers that question." She places her hand on my shoulder as if to whisper in my ear but says aloud for everyone to hear: "Hey man, if you got into *that* chick's pants then mister you're a better man than any woman in this room." Everyone seems amused. She takes up a bottle of Glenlivet scotch from the table and tops off her glass. "No, I'm serious, that's a hell of an accomplishment. Am I right girls?" They all laugh and the conversation banters back and forth until Georgiana whistles.

"Okay, be nice..." then to me, "you want a beer... or a glass of scotch?" I shake my head. "Glad you came down. Any hassle getting in?" I stare at her for just a fraction.

"No, no problem."

"Right on," she says, a crooked smile on her face. "Hey, we've some sushi if you like that. Bambi likes it, right Bam? But not as much as she likes her scotch and rocks." The two women look at each other.

"You try'n to say something G?" Bambi asks and there's immediately tension between them.

"What possibly might that be Babs?" Georgiana says in a droll manner. "Let me think a minute…"

"Oh, like *you* never drink before show?" Bambi says tapping at the bottle of Pabst Blue Ribbon in Georgiana's hand. The guitar player immediate defuses the situation.

"Don't get on her Bam-Bam, yell at Dominic… you know the new rules."

"Fuck Dominic! Who died and made him prince?" she says and takes a long drink. The other three exchange looks.

Suddenly the door bursts open and a young Italian looking guy, with a slew of earrings, in a Mario Bros t-shirt enters.

"Dammit Dominic, can't you ever knock? This is a girl's dressing room!" Bambi shouts but he's completely unfazed by her.

"That shit band is finally off the stage," he proclaims loudly. "You guys ready?" There are four different responses to this question all spoken simultaneously. He holds up his palm. "Jesus, one at a time," he says and all four speak non-stop. He whistles loudly and immediately interrupts them. "The club wants to stay on schedule, we go on in fifteen minutes." Again, there are four different reactions to this news and an onslaught of expletives. "Whatever!" he shouts over their collective disdain. "Rickey's setting our back-line now, just be ready to rock in fifteen." He goes to leave when Georgiana stops him.

"Hey Dom, this is Morgan's buddy from California. You got room for him at the boards?" she asks and he sticks his hand out and we shake.

"Sure, you can hang front-of-house if ya want. We've a couple chairs, or you can stand, whatever."

"Sounds good, thanks," I say as he heads out shouting:
"Fifteen minutes to rock and roll ladies, fifteen!" The girls all stand simultaneously and converge in the center of the room placing their right hands atop each other's and in a unified voice they all chant as one:
"With more guts than brains, rock on!" then one by one they disappear through a side door into another room. Georgiana finishes her beer and looks at me a moment.
"We're gonna get fixed up for the gig. Come back after the set is over, we'll talk then… okay?"
"Sure," I say and she smiles, an odd bent grin.
"Enjoy the show," she says, her different colored irises creating a remarkable sensation with the thin wisps of fake blood. She disappears into the adjoining room closing the door behind her.
I gaze at the chaotic state of the room before heading back down the dull beige-colored hallway. The *opening act* is moving about the hall talking at the top of their voices. I notice how sophomoric they seem compared to Georgiana's band. I suppose the proof will be in the performance, I think to myself, and exit back into the club.

The crowd has swollen remarkably. There's barely any more sitting or even standing room. The place is suddenly full of leather and black clad partisans. I watch as the band's roadies, and a club stagehand, are rapidly wiring microphones and Marshall amplifiers. I work my way through the crowd to the front-of-house area at the sound and lighting boards. The security guard stops me.
"No one's allowed in here," he says. I lean into his ear.
"I'm with the band, Dom invited me." He glances over at Dominic who is preoccupied with setting sound levels for the

microphones. The guard pulls back the little rope and I step into this *sacred* area.

I watch as a skinny tattooed guy in a New York Mets hat tests each microphone while Dominic sets the levels on his board and tweaks the ranges.

"Check, one, two… check, one, two… check, one, two," the guy repeats over and over like a mantra into the three microphones situated on stands across the stage. Then he plugs in Georgiana's black Fender bass and plays several notes and a snippet of a tune before he gets the okay from Dom and moves on to VD's cherry red Gibson Les Paul. She also has a dark-red Gibson SG and he tests this too. He then tests a keyboard.

"I didn't know they had a keyboard player," I say to Dominic.

"They don't, Bambi plays it once in awhile… not very good either." When they finish he gives the okay and the guy begins taping down cables. Dominic picks up a hand mic and tests it by tapping on it, punching a button on his soundboard you can now hear the tap-tap of his finger. "Hey Rick… Rickey," he says into the mic and the guy pops up from the floor. "Drums… I need to hear the drums yet," he says and Rickey signals okay; turns and shouts at the other roadie who jumps up from behind the stage and takes the seat at the drum kit. "Start with the bass," Dominic says into the mic and the guy begins stomping on the bass drum pedal. I can hear the guy beating on the drum but it sounds dull and distant. I watch as Dom pours over his channels until he locates the right one and as he brings the level up the drum booms loudly until he finds the right level for the room. Suddenly two guys drinking beer amble up in front of him blocking his view of the stage.

"Hey dude, who's playing tonight?" they ask already inebriated.

"Your frickin' dead uncle. Get the hell outta my way!" Dominic explodes, waving them aside and they immediately recede. The roadie at the drums is not paying attention, he's just pounding away on the bass drum and Dom swears out loud then grabs up the hand microphone again and turns it on. "Move on man!" he shouts, his voice booming over the PA. "Next, please!" and the guy signals okay. "You gotta be listening to me bro, turn up your headset!" he shouts and the guy signals okay. I watch as they go through the entire kit until Dominic is happy with the mix and says into his headset: "Cool, thanks," and they exit the stage.

The lighting guy at the board beside him asks something about the show's lighting.

"Reds and yellows, orange, think fire... and no pinks, the girls don't like it... and nothing pastel. Blues and purples, reds, yellows and orange." He pulls a cigarette out of his breast pocket and lights it. "Just keep your shit moving man, and when the song peaks make it look like explosions and shit. What are you using for movers?"

"I got Martins, they're a little old but still look good." The guy activates several moving lights shooting bright beams of orange and gold into the ceiling and crowd.

"Awesome, that's exactly what I want. Give me everything on those moves. Don't stress over the front fill too much, backlight the chicks, they look really good backlit."

"Yeah, I saw you guys at the Epsilon awhile back."

"Cool," Dom says puffing on his smoke. I see one of the security guards milling behind him.

"How long you been with them?" the lighting guy asks but before he can answer the security guard interrupts.

"Excuse me, you can't smoke inside the building, fire code."

"Know what dude?" Dominic says in an irritated tone. "You guys have been on my shit all day… I'm having a smoke, deal with it."

"You have to take it outside," the guard informs him.

"You gonna op my board while I'm standing around outside with my hands in my crotch?"

"Look, you can't-"

"Know what dude? Go somewhere else and it ain't a problem," he says taking a puff and exhaling it into the ceiling. The guy leaves grumbling and Dom taps the lighting guy on the shoulder and says: "Just have fun. Stay away from pastel colors, stay with your primaries and we'll be alright." The lighting guy gives him the thumbs up.

An older gray haired man in a brown leather jacket over a black Tommy Bahama shirt is let into the area, his hands in his jean pockets and nods at me. Dominic immediately shakes his hand and is smiling broadly as they converse. I can tell by the change in Dominic's behavior this is a special person. Right in the middle of their conversation a muscular guy with a salt and pepper beard and long hair stands before them on the other side of the soundboard.

"Dom, what the hell?" he shouts and Dom immediately drops his cigarette crushing it underfoot and holds his hands aloft.

"It's done Tony…" The guy glares at him shaking his head.

"Not that easy buddy boy," he says and an animated conversation quickly ensues. The older guy standing next me rolls his eyes. I laugh silently by his reaction. He sticks his hand out to me and in a staunch British accent asks:

"Sorry mate, do I know you? You look familiar." I tell him my name. "You tour?" I mention several of the tours I've traveled with in the past years including a very prominent British guitar player. "Lucky bastard, great tour, except for all the bloody Welshmen," he jests. "Nyle," he says, shaking my hand. "I'm sure we know a few of the same people," he says. "What do you do?"

"Video... camera," I say and he nods.

"Interesting... we may need video if this tour takes off," he says. I've no idea what *tour* he's referring to. "Who you with?" he inquires.

"No one, I came alone," I say and he laughs.

"No, I mean the band, you friends with one of the girls, or Dominic's chum?"

"Georgiana invited me."

"Ah... the boss," he says. "She's a damn good bass guitarist... good songwriter too. I need more out of her, but good." Eventually Tony leaves and Dominic complains about what he terms *the smoke Nazis* but Nyle gives him a hard time about smoking inside the club.

"You're a bloody twat Dominic... never stir up trouble with security. Sooner or later you'll need 'em." Suddenly the crowd roars and Dom jumps, sliding on a headset. A short little man has entered from stage right and is at the center mic. He silently talks into it until there's a sudden burst of his voice that fills the club.

"Testing, testing... this thing on? You can hear me?" he asks and the crowd answers his question. "Cool, cool, alright. We're running a little behind so let's get to it. What you've all been waiting for, from our very own New York... get your hands in the air for *Concrete and Steel!*"

The crowd erupts as the girls enter from upstage. Except for Tiny, they all look like lean black shadows as they take their places on stage. I watch as Georgiana dons her all-black Fender bass. VD's red *Les Paul* reflects light back into the crowd as she tests her monitor. I can hear Dominic shouting over the crowd into his headset. As the band settles in, Bambi takes the center microphone.

"How ya all doing tonight New York?" The crowd roars. "Right on. Hey, it's really great to be back in town again… after our West Coast thing." Whistles and catcalls. "Hey, I gotta tell you guys… I got alotta friends out there but LA pretty much sucks compared to New York man," she says and the crowd loves it. She laughs, then turning toward the band I can hear from her microphone as she asks: "You guys ready?" That apparently is a cue to go as Tiny knocks out four beats on her sticks and the band cuts loose a tsunami-like wall of sound that floods the club with a heavy driving beat.

As Dominic suggested, the lighting guy is backlighting the band in solid red and the three *frontwomen* are now in silhouette. When Bambi starts to sing, he brings in the front lights in solid purple and blues and the effect is striking. Her voice is deep and resonant. I listen to the poetry of the song over its heavy beat. A song about a girl named Lucy who falls from grace, and life, a song about self-loathing and desire, the power of the beat energizing the words. When the tune finishes the crowd is very vocal and the band good-naturedly jokes with them.

"This next tune was written by G, it's called *Shine In Your Eyes*, Bambi says and several of the crowd react as they start a steady driving beat, the song referring to self reflection, higher thought within a sea of self-absorbed humanity and self-debased thinking. Georgiana and Bambi move about, shaking their long black manes to the beat while VD seems frozen, focusing all her attention on her guitar and the mic set on the stand before her; Tiny tears into the drums.

"I like this tune, what'd she say it was called?" I shout in Nyle's ear and he immediately grabs the set-list from Dom's console and hands it to me. It reads:

1. Lucyfer: Denton, Giordano, Snipes, Stockton
2. Shine In Your Eyes: Snipes
3. Sister Double: Snipes
4. Back On The Street: Moreno, Snipes
5. Infected: Snipes
6. Sugar Pill: Giordano, Stockton
7. Hell On Your Doorstep: Denton, Giordano, Snipes, Stockton
8. Dumb & Fun: Snipes (acoustic)
9. Hallowed: Snipes, Stockton (acoustic)
10. East Coast On The Skids: Snipes
11. No Room For You (In My Head): Snipes
12. Is It My Body: Alice Cooper
13. No Tomorrow: Moreno
14. Lock & Load: Snipes
15. Coming In Hot: Giordano, Snipes
16. Black Again: Moreno, Snipes (opt)
17. The World's A Mess It's In My Kiss: X (opt)
18. Gloria-Fangoria: Snipes (opt)

"This is a really good band. You hear that?" Nyle shouts into my ear. "That's rock and roll mate, and from an all female band," he says, his fingers moving to the beat. I nod.

There's something very alluring, very appealing about these women and the intense music they play together.

The second song finishes as abruptly as it started and the crowd is in a festive mood, the room getting louder. Bambi shouts into the mic.

"Wanna thank the Netherworld for having us over, always a pleasure." The crowd is completely on its feet and loud. It's obviously a good start. Bambi takes the mic again. "Thanks a lot, really appreciate that. This next song's another by G, about girls who like girls," she says and some of the women in the crowd shout. Something takes place just in front of the stage and Bambi says into the microphone: "There's a guy up here who needs his teeth kicked in." She tries to ready herself when there's more shouting. "Yeah I'm talking about you!" More heckling. "Go screw yourself. I'm sure you're the only one willing to do it." The crowd laughs. There's more heckling. Georgiana doesn't wait for it to escalate. She starts the song with a heavy bass riff. VD and Tiny both come in on the next measure and the wall of sound buries whatever was being said, a rocking number about a woman who is misunderstood in the eyes of her significant other. Dominic shouts at the security guard nearest us. I can just make out what he says.

"Better find out what's going on in the pit before that prick gets kicked in the face." The guard nods and heads off. When the song finishes the guy in the front row is again shouting something vulgar. Before Bambi can say anything, two of the Netherworld security guards are on either side to reason with him but apparently it doesn't go well. I can see the tops of their heads as a scuffle ensues and the guy is forcefully escorted out between them, the crowd cheering. Bambi takes the mic sipping her scotch.

"Some guys just don't know how to have fun, ya know?" and the crowd agrees. "Unless you call that shit fun?" she says and downs her drink. "You guys wanna have some fun?" The crowd roars. "This is an old number we still do called *Back On The Street.*" The band instantly launches into a piece about homelessness. When it finishes they immediately jump into *Infected* a love song with deep haunting overtones, the lyrics tragic, about loss of love and the desire for its return. The song immediately after this, *Sugar Pill,* is loud and raucous and difficult to understand, the crowd dimming in enthusiasm.

When this tune ends they take a moment to catch their breath and VD plugs in and re-tunes her SG. There's some calls and whistles from the audience. When VD gives her the nod, Bambi takes the center microphone.

"You out there ladies?" she shouts shading her eyes from the overhead lights and many of the women in the crowd shout and whistle. "This one's for you guys, called *Hell On Your Doorstep.*" The crowd reacts loudly and Bambi seems delighted. "Yeah. This is a song about a chick who just won't take *no* for an answer, you know the type," Bambi says as VD busts into a guitar solo followed closely by Georgiana and Tiny's heavy back rhythms. I assume this is one of their hits by the way the crowd reacts and the room begins to fill with cigarette and herbal smoke. The lyrics are humorous and make me smile. Nyle, beside me, catches my eye.

"Great tune," he shouts over the tempest of sound.

At the mid point the band is sweating and takes a minute to towel off. VD drinks Perrier while Georgiana and Tiny both crack Pabst Blue Ribbons. Bambi tops off her scotch.

The band sets up for the acoustic set taking tall stools. Rickey is helping Georgiana plug in an acoustic bass guitar. I watch as he helps place an earbud in her left ear and she seems to be happy with the patch. VD has a beautiful Martin acoustic guitar and the other roadie helps her get squared away. Bambi has a mouth harp and tests it out.

"Thank you guys. We really appreciate it. We're gonna slow it down for a coupla tunes," she says and they start into a really lovely acoustic set.

"You've seen them before?" Nyle asks. I shake my head and he places his mouth near my ear. "Get a load of the way Georgiana and Victoria play together... solid. Victoria attended Julliard," he says. I'm surprised by this news and show it. He nods. "This is a really rare band, the bass drives it. Usually the bass is backing. You hear it?" he asks and I realize what he means. Georgiana is so steady and full that Victoria is free to improvise and expand the melody. "Georgiana's been playing with Tina for years." He looks at them admiringly. "And Barbara's stage presence is very good don't you think? I mean the way she engages the audience. She's comfortable, so the audience is comfortable... great voice... and a great body. These girls could make it." He holds up his index finger between us. "If... they can keep it together, that's the question." The girls have a rocking rhythm going on the acoustics. Georgiana keeps a steady bass line going with VD's fretwork and it's a really invigorating sound. The second in the acoustic set, *Hallowed,* is a quieter more haunted tune about the dark sacredness of life.

When the song finishes, Rickey walks off with the acoustics in each hand and the ladies don their electric axes and immediately launch into *East Coast On The Skids* a fast and raunchy tune about the state of affairs on the eastern seaboard.

Nyle excuses himself. I watch as he makes his way through the crowd to the backstage door, the guy in the black t-shirt recognizing him immediately and letting him in.

"Who's the guy I've been talking to?" I ask Dominic.

"That's Nyle, our new producer, slash, tour manager. He's putting together a new disc and a European and Domestic tour to promote it."

"That's great," I say but Dominic's reaction is less effusive.

"I don't know... this band dude..." he shakes his head and gives me an odd look. "Sometimes it's like that Ozzie song, you know, *going off the rails on the crazy train...*" he says and I'm not exactly certain what he means. When I return my attention to the stage, the meaning begins to creep in; the little details, the breaks and mistakes, the singer now inebriated, starting to slur her words. On *No Room For You (In My Head)* they seem to lag, however, the Alice Cooper cover is livelier and I can see why they cover it. Bambi plays with the subject matter and the effect is a good one and sets up the existential angst of *No Tomorrow* where the band returns to a heavy metal wall of sound. At the end of this song they seem exhausted and wave to the crowd that's on their feet and extremely loud.

"Thanks you guys... wow, really appreciate the noise!" Bambi says and the other band members wave as they mop their sweaty brows. "You've been a really swell audience tonight, really awesome," she says. "Wanna thank Netherworld for havin' us. Everybody, rock on! Goodnight!" and they exit upstage.

After several minutes of non-stop applause and shouting the band returns on stage and I can hear Dominic on his headset.

"Copy, closing on *Lock and Load* and *Hot*... passing on the rest, copy that. I'm good to go." I realize he's talking to Georgiana over a small headset that she tosses aside and strokes her guitar and the dark bass responds like a black cat purring loudly, and with those tones the band syncs and the next to final tune is pure rock, like the beat of an enormous heart, a song about two lovers torn apart by continuous attacks on each other's personalities. Ten seconds after the tune is over they bust into *Coming In Hot* –obviously their closer- a fast moving tune with very provocative lyrics. The song ends abruptly and the entire crowd is on their feet. Bambi points.

"From Brooklyn New York, Miss Georgiana Snipes on bass! Outta Newark New Jersey, Tina Denton on the drums! Manhattan –via Los Angeles- Victoria Stockton on the guitar, yeah!" Then Georgiana takes the microphone.

"And from Brooklyn NYC, Ms. Bambi Giordano on the Vox." The crowd is deafening, wanting more. "Goodnight New York. Be good to yourselves!" Georgiana shouts as the band waves and heads backstage and like that it's over.

It takes twenty minutes before the crowd thins enough to get backstage. I knock softly and can hear voices from behind the closed door when it's suddenly wrenched open. I'm face to face with Georgiana, sans makeup. She pauses a moment and I wonder if she's forgotten her invitation earlier. She takes one look back over her shoulder then holds open the door and asks me to sit to one side and be quiet with two simple gestures. Nyle seems to have the floor.

"It'd give you a fuller sound and eliminate all this muckin' about which might really bite you in the arse, especially on tour. Bambi didn't even cover the keys on *Skids,* not at all. No offense sweetheart but the synth sounded like crap tonight," he says and the women are exchanging questionable looks. After a pause Georgiana says:

"I think I can speak for everybody in the band Nyle. There won't be any addition of personnel on this group. We're more of a… *a pack,* than a band. We can't just add somebody into the mix, it won't work that way with us." There's a lull in the room. Nyle rubs his chin and sighs.

"I'm not suggesting an addition to the band, just someone to cover keys during the tour. Think of it more like… an extended studio sessionist."

"No keyboard player," Tiny says flatly. "Bambi and G cover the keys, we're a foursome," she says and Nyle grows quiet.

"We'll work on it," Georgiana says to him. He scratches at the back of his head.

"I guess I can appreciate that, let it lie for now, but as far as sound, I'm fixed on my front-of-house and monitor mixers. Essential personnel. Non-negotiable. I've got exactly the right boys for the job." He walks to the table behind them speaking to a woman who seems to be waiting for him and pours more red wine. The girls look at each other.

"What's he sayin' exactly?" Bambi asks below her breath and the band has a sudden impromptu huddle. I listen in as Georgiana spells it out.

"He wants a dedicated guy, his guy, to mix the venues, another guy, a monitor mixer, to just mix our monitor feeds."

"That's really cool," VD interjects, "I'm liking that part."

"But what's all the bullshit about Dominic then?" Bambi asks and Georgiana stares at her with an incredulous expression.

"That's what Dom does for us Bam, house and monitors."

"Meaning what?"

"Use your brain dumbo," Tiny says, "we have to fire Dominic." Bambi is visibly shocked.

"Whaaat? No way. He's a squirrel, but he's *our* squirrel!" There's a general consensus and when Nyle rejoins them Georgiana says:

"Okay, we'll roll with your sound team Nyle," and the girls look at her dumbfounded. She stares back at them. "What?" she says in reaction to their stares. "You're gonna say no? Go ahead, say no… see what happens." Everyone mulls over this for a moment. "So… what about Dominic?" Georgiana asks Nyle. "He's been with us for three years."

"I dig it. I'll offer him lights. We need somebody and he's been doing it anyway. You've actually got a reasonably good look. He'll get a raise." Bambi looks at Georgiana.

"Shit man… that sounds pretty reasonable," she states and Georgiana gives her a droll look.

"I'm so glad you approve."

"We'll also need a tour manager to manage the tour and a stage manager to manage the set up… the load-in and load-outs," Nyle says. "And I'm seriously considering carrying video. You'd look damn good up on the big screens every night. I'm thinking, if we carry a *head-end rig* and a video director, we could sub out camera and projection locally, if we have it in the budget. It'll depend on where the numbers drop on hotel and transportation and the rest. Giles wants the JBL line-array for Europe and the States both, the big columns with full front fill and delay towers for the larger venues. It won't be bloody cheap. I want a shit load of low end on this tour. That's where the money is baby. You're a heavy low-end band… let's go with our strengths… so we may have to carry additional floor cabinets as well. That all said, it has to be four-star accommodations wherever we go,

The Man Who Would Be Coyote

only way to do it. I might be able to scrimp a little from lights and if we put Production on the same bus as the band and the rest of the crew on number two, we won't need to rent a third bus. It's like bloody Tetris," he says and there's immediate excitement about all this, all except Georgiana, she's staring at Nyle.

"Why do we need a tour manager? I thought you'd be our tour manager?" she asks and he laughs softly and waves a finger at her.

"No, no. No way. I'm only interested in getting this up and running," he says finishing his wine. "We'll make some bread on the road girls but it'll be no pissin' around. This is strictly business. We can talk this all out tomorrow when you come down to the plant, you're all coming yes?" he says looking squarely at Bambi.

"Two o'clock, right?" Georgiana says.

"One o'clock, right after lunch, and don't be late." He heads out the door with the woman in tow and no sooner is the door closed than Bambi is blaring.

"Is that joker insinuating I can't play keys?!" she shouts and everyone seems to avoid this question from her. "Well?!" she says to VD and Georgiana directly.

"No…" Georgiana mumbles and Bambi cocks her head.

"No what?"

"I'll say it Bam-Bam," Tiny interjects, "you need to practice." Bambi glares then explodes.

"This is bullshit! I don't like this dick prancing in here barking orders… screw him, he's a creep!"

"That *creep* Bambi is our ticket to a new record contract and a European tour," Georgiana states flatly and Bambi instantly changes her demeanor.

"You really think so? You don't think he's just another bullshit artist?"

"Of course he's for real, I told you who he is. It's all connections."

"Shit man, Europe sounds pretty damn good right about now. I could use a vacation," she says topping off her scotch.

"It won't be *a vacation* Bambi. It'll be an ass load'a hard work," Georgiana says.

"Screw that about adding a keyboard player," Tiny blurts out, "we're a foursome."

"Yeah, and all that BS earlier about adding more covers," VD interjects. "Let's just do our own stuff. I'm really burning out on covers you guys."

"Can we please discuss all this at a later date... like, tonight?" Georgiana says and everyone suddenly seems hyper-cognizant of my presence. I realize I'm actually being surrounded. There's a round of eye contact before Georgiana says: "As you know, we were all very curious about Morgan. She doesn't say much on the phone. We were hoping you might be able to shed some light on that situation."

"Alright. Like what?" I ask.

"Like where the hell is she dude, and what the hell's going on?" Bambi shouts loudly, "...just for starters."

"That's our own special way of saying... we're her friends," Georgiana interjects, "and that we're concerned about her."

I look around, at the four faces that delve me and I realize that indeed, these people are her friends and they care about her. I contemplate the answer deeply then remember Morgan's words and decide to tell them.

"Yes, you should all know," I say aloud and the women all stare at me. I look at each face. I see what makes them similar and what makes them unique.

"Morgan has gone back to her familial roots. More specifically, into the study of Nature, nature religion, what

140

some people might call... authentic witchcraft," I say and you could hear a pin drop. There is utter silence yet also, stillness. I watch Bambi move slightly to get a better look at my eyes.

"What did you just say?" she asks and I study her a moment before repeating my statement. I marvel at the utter quietude of the moment, the sound of ice settling in her glass. No one says a thing until Bambi says: "Wait... you're saying... the reason Morgan's... that she's... she's become *a witch*?" she asks incredulous and I nod.

"Becoming... yes," I say. "As I understand it." The moment extends itself for several heartbeats of silence. Then, Bambi abruptly sets her scotch and melting ice loudly upon the table and proclaims she's leaving and that she'll see the band *at the crib* later. She's obviously at odds with what I've told them and doesn't attempt to disguise her feelings.

"Hey Bambi, can I get a ride?" VD asks.

"Hurry up!" is all she says and exits the room. VD grabs her coat and hovers over Georgiana a moment speaking to her softly then kissing her on the lips. As she goes to leave she smiles at me.

"Nice to meet you," she says. I say the same back to her and she's gone; it's just Georgiana and Tiny sitting in silence. Tiny gets up and downs the rest of her beer.

"I'm gonna help Dominic and Rickey take down our shit, you know, like the good old days," she says sardonically. As she goes to leave she belches loudly, looks at me and laughs, perhaps it's more a sneer. "Morgan's a witch huh? That's a scream," she says and slams the door behind her.

I'm feeling uncomfortable. I'd not expected this reaction from them. I prepare myself for the worst when Georgiana stands and glares down at me. Her bi-colored eyes are piercing.

"Are you fucking with us? Is this some kinda gag? Cuz if it is… say so now." I stare into her wolf-like eyes.

"It's no gag, it's very real," I say holding her gaze. An understanding passes between us and she knows what I'm saying is in fact truth.

I watch as she quietly detunes her bass and places it into its hard shell case. She dons her long black coat pulling the collar up around her ears.

"You just lost the band man. They all think you're a nutcase." I shrug.

"They deserved to know."

"Oh yeah… they deserved it alright." She laughs. "Your delivery was superlative by the way," she quips taking up the guitar case, laughing under her breath. "That was the one answer none of them were prepared for, ya know? They were ready for… family this, or career that… *but a witch*… ha!" She laughs, obviously amused by the reactions of her mates. She places her hand on my shoulder and gives me a shake. "Don't worry man, they'll quit knocking you in a month or two."

"I don't know… I don't think so."

"Yeah, *they will*." We exchange a knowing look. "Hey… you cool with walking me home? It's just a coupla blocks, no big deal if ya don't." I readily agree. We take one look back into the chaotic room with its mix of liquor bottles and she shakes her head. "I think our little musical band has a drinking problem."

Outside, as we stroll down the avenue, she becomes preoccupied with her own thoughts. I feel a need to talk but don't want to address the topic of Morgan so I ask:

"*Concrete and Steel*… strange name for an all girl band."

"Not necessarily... once you get to know us. Except we're more concrete than steel these days." She's silent for a moment. "Although, there was *steel... once upon a time... Nicci*," she says as if suddenly somewhere far away.

"Who is Nicci?" I ask and it snaps her back into the present.

"Nicci Moreno started this band originally. They lost their bass and rhythm guitarists in a head-on one night coming back from a gig on Long Island. I was playing in a chick band called *The Vestals* that was going nowhere fast. When Nicci and Tiny asked me to try out, I jumped. They liked my sound but we couldn't find the right rhythm player and we had gigs lining up so... Nicci taught me how to cheat some of the rhythm parts, some of the melody-line. It was tough at first, but if ya stick with something long enough..." She looks at me. "You a musician?"

"No, not really, not much."

"Gotcha," she says and grows quiet.

"Who was he?" I ask and she seems torn.

"*He*... was an incredibly accomplished guitar player, songwriter, is what *he* was. Destined for fame. When Nic died, it all crumbled man. Our whole world fell apart."

"What happened?" I ask and her expression grows severe.

"Don't ask. Anyway, Tiny wanted to keep going. I didn't have much of a choice ya know. This is all I know how to do." The bent grin emerges on her face. "You may have figured out by now, I'm not the kinda person who can sling drinks at the local bar... or flip burgers or whatever," she says. "Let's just say I'm not good with the general public... as a rule."

"How did this particular group come together?" I wait for her to continue. "We'd met VD on a gig in Los Angeles. By sheer coincidence she was in New York studying, of all things, classical guitar at Julliard. Since there's not alotta demand for dyke classical guitarists she decided to join. Bambi... Bambi and I go way back, back to my youth. Actually, how could you even know? Bambi's mom, my aunt Barbara, basically raised me... pretty much saved my life when ya get right down to it."

"Oh?" She looks at me darkly.

"It's a long story man. Some other time maybe."

"I've got time," I say and she looks away, exhales loudly.

"Ray Snipes was a mean drunk. My brothers got the TLC... I got the belt... mom just sorta... stood around. One night when Bambi was sleeping over, think we were... twelve... maybe thirteen... ol' Ray got loaded as usual, yanked me outta bed and whipped me stupid. Bambi freaked out and ran home. Half an hour later aunt Babs is pounding on our front door in her pajamas. She came in and went after Ray with a spatula. Gashed his head open, lacerated an arm, the whole nine yards. Then... then she took me by the hand and without saying a word drove me back to Bensonhurst and that was pretty much the last time I ever stepped foot in that house."

She slows her pace and in the darkness I realize she's in fact reliving the pain of these childhood memories. She stops and gazes up at the buildings that tower above us taking in a deep breath then suddenly shoves her guitar toward me.

"Hold Babe for me, willya?" I take the instrument and wait as she pulls a beat pack of Camels from her coat, takes out a crumpled cigarette and lights it. "What a mook. Listen to me... blah, blah, blah." She curses under her breath. "You ask me a simple question and I talk about this shit." She reaches back for her guitar. When I tell her I don't mind carrying it she takes it anyway and we continue on.

"To answer your question, we never changed the name of the band. Why? Everyone knows you by that name why change it?" We walk on but the silence is suddenly oppressive. I decide to ask her about the band's reaction to my news regarding Morgan, and question her why she's taken a different perspective on it.

"They don't know Morgan. They only know her as this big-shot photographer. I know her from the early days... as a down-and-outer," she says but I'm uncertain her meaning and say so. "You know, the trucks parked along Park Avenue... beautiful models and expensive equipment sitting around... hair and make-up and catering and all that crap." She looks at me in the darkness, the blue iris catching the streetlight.

"What do you mean by *down-and-outer*?" I ask and she laughs quietly.

"I used to call her *the barefoot Countessa*. She used to run around the lower east village photographing orphans, junkies, the homeless... there's a part of her I know that they don't." I press her about it. "Well, okay, here's a good one. Just after Bams joined the band, she brought over some stud, the long hair and all that... Morgue freaked."

"Freaked?"

"She didn't like him, not at all, and told Bam to leave him alone. Well, Bambi being Bambi... no one tells *her* what to do. Sure enough, the guy goes ape-shit one night, beats the crap outta her and splits with all of grandma's jewelry. I asked her... what was it? *What did she know*? She told me that when they were introduced *she saw his real face*. That's just one little story out of another couple dozen examples I could give you." She stops and crushes the cigarette under her boot heel. "Like the night mom died. Morgue calls and says, 'Hey, is your mom okay?' I'm like, 'What do you mean?' She's like, 'You better call her, right away.'" She stares at me and I immediately sense her meaning.

"She died?"

"Yeah... right then. She wasn't even sick. Well... not in the conventional way," she says and grows silent.

"Did you get a chance to... to say goodbye?"

"We talked a little... that was it. If it hadn't been for that call from Morgan, Myrna Snipes would have died without my telling her... that I didn't blame her, for my *shattered youth*." She pauses and I sense a rush of emotion in the darkness. "I could actually feel it... over the phone. It was like all this weight was lifted off her... and she just... split." She begins to stroll and I sense she's struggling with an inner turmoil. She stops again and looks into me, her eyes in shadow. "What the hell man? I'm talking about this... *stuff*... again. I never talk about my personal stuff... ever."

"I didn't mean to make you uncomfortable."

"You missed your calling dude. You should'a been a shrink," she says and we slowly continue our pace. "You're a lot like Morgan... did you know that? You're a damn good listener. That's a dying art man... listening. Everyone I know... just talks." She kicks an empty soda can into the gutter. "Is that what a witch does?" she asks oddly. "Someone who listens instead of talks?" I'm not certain if she's being serious or suddenly sarcastic.

"I don't know," I say. We walk on silently for half a block before turning into a darkened alleyway, the wind picking up slightly.

"There was a moment when it all came home for me, about her," she says and I wait. "We had gone through a really tough time, her and I. She had that same invisible insight into someone I was messed up on... but I had to learn my lesson the hard way... just like the rest of my life. Anyway, after Nicci died and the band went to shit... so did I and... *this person*. I mean, I'm not a rock star any more, so what's the big attraction right? The combination of those things, along with everything else... I was pretty much on the fuckin' ledge man. Morgan and I had a little... heart to heart." She flashes me a strange solemn look. "Dig this... she takes both my hands and tells me to close my eyes right? So I do. Then she tells me to feel my eyes behind my eyelids, put my consciousness there, right? So I do. Then she tells me to follow the optic nerve from the eye straight back into the center of my brain... she's talking me through this. So now I'm in the very center of my brain. Then she tells me to follow the... oblagata mondata... mondula... whatever you call that, down the spinal cord to the center of my chest, to where the heart is, so I do this. Then she says, I remember her exact words: *'Step into your heart, feel it, feel it beating. Now be there, be it.'*" She looks at me again, the eyes in shadow under the overhead streetlamp. "Then she said, *'Think about us, you and I. See us together at the center of your heart. Do you see us?'*"

She suddenly stops before the door of a dark shabby warehouse and stares at me. I patiently wait for her to continue as the wind swirls a discarded plastic shopping bag about us.

"I did, I *saw* us... her and me... can you wrap your head around that?" I gaze at her tall lean shadow-like image standing in the night, the hum of the city in the background. Somewhere a dog is barking.

"Yes, I think I can." I sense her fathoming me in the dark, an odd mixture of time and space, or a lack of it perhaps, permeating the moment.

"She taught me this... this beautiful aspect about my shitty life, despite the rough and tumble... the knocks... the scars, all of it." As she quietly looks at me I unmistakably sense her meaning. "I've tried to hide from it my entire life... but without it, we're nothing... *shadows walking around in twilight*... and it all begins here," she says tapping the center of her chest. "Until a person opens their heart, they'll never know it, never feel it." There's a long pause. "Ya know... I know I'm kinda scraggly... you know, *'a little rough around the edges'* as they say... but I've not always been like this. *There were other lives*." We stand and stare at each other in the dark.

"You're not scraggly," I hear myself say and she laughs.

"Are you blind? Look at me man. I'm flat as a board. I was six foot tall by eighth grade. I was born left-handed and learned to play the bass upside down. My hair is stringy and unmanageable and to top it off, God or Universe or whoever, whatever it is, thought it'd be funny to give me two different colored eyes. I was born into a family of boys with a weak mother and a mean drunk for a father. I'm a mess. But, ever since that... *talk*, with Morgan, I'm okay with who this life has turned me into this time around. Morgan showed me these things. If you call that being a witch... well... then so be it." She nods at the beaten old warehouse. "This is it," she says quietly, "*home*." I look at its bleak lonely façade, staring at us in the dark. She juts out her lanky hand and we shake for several moments. "Nice getting to know ya." I wait for her to continue but there's nothing more. "See ya around," she says turning toward the dark vacant door with her guitar in hand like some strange, silent, companion.

"Yeah, I hope so," I call out and she pauses for a moment, her odd bent grin behind all that stringy black hair.

"Thanks for walking me home," she says and disappears inside.

"Yeah," I say quietly under my breath as I turn back toward the empty street. I pull my collar up around my ears. It's gotten colder.

Woman in Blue

I had flown into Heathrow from New York and taken the public transit into Soho. I had scarcely been in my flat forty minutes when the phone rang. It was Lucien calling from America.

"How was your flight?"

"Fine," I stammer. "How did you know I was flying?"

"Beryl," he says succinctly. "She noted the charge and informed me that you were leaving the States."

"Oh, of course."

"How was your visit to New Orleans?" he asks and I immediately wish he hadn't.

"I'd rather not go into it at the moment." There's a pause on the other end of the line. "Perhaps if I phone you tomorrow?"

"Quite unnecessary, I understand," he says and in the brief moment of silence that follows I thank him.

"No thanks are needed, I do have a question," he adds and I pray it isn't regarding Morgan. "Are you fit to travel?" he inquires. "I realize you've only just arrived, however, something's up."

"What is it?"

"The wife of a man very dear to us has been in contact and is requesting my presence in Amsterdam. I'm wondering if you might go in my stead?" I pause to think. It had been my hope to relax and reacquaint myself with London, I'd been away and the old capital seemed quite distant to me, nearly a stranger again.

"Lucien, I'm certain I'd be a very poor substitute for yourself. Perhaps Mr. Corbeau would be the better choice?"

"I've contacted Anton, he's somewhat indisposed at the present. However, the situation is demanding an immediate response from us. I'm hoping that you're able to travel to the home in Amsterdam and speak with the client, feel out the situation, at least until we might arrange to have Anton travel."

"Will you be arriving later?"

"Not at all. I'm extending my stay in Arizona by two more weeks." I'm startled by the news.

"You're still at Grey's ranch?"

"Indeed, a most singular experience. I'm quite excited to tell you about it the next time we see each other," he says followed by a long pause. "Well, how about this trip to the Netherlands?"

"I'm sure I could be ready by tomorrow. Would that be acceptable?"

"Quite acceptable," he says. "I'll have Beryl contact you with the details. Welcome back."

"Thank you, and please send my regards to Grey and his family."

"I shall do that," he says and the line goes dead. I hang up the receiver and stare at the phone for several minutes deep in thought concerning Lucien's extended stay in Arizona. For some reason it shocks me that he's still there. What was he doing there, in the middle of the desert? I puzzle over it staring blankly at the phone. The second I take my eyes from the bloody thing it rings, making me jump. I pick it up certain Lucien has forgotten some detail.

"Yes Lucien?"

"Willem, it's Beryl Collins," says the thin voice from the other end of the line.

"Yes Beryl, how are y-"

"Lucien has informed me you're available to take the assignment in Amsterdam."

"Well... yes... I'm-"

"Can you travel this evening?"

"Well, I told Lucien-"

"That you could travel tomorrow, I know, but in all sincerity, Mrs. Van Teegan is fit to be tied. The woman is at her wit's end. I'd very much appreciate your prompt attention to this... if you're able."

"What's going on?"

"Something to do with her husband's increasingly odd behaviour. The woman rambles on to exhaustion. Can you make a later flight?"

"Well... I suppose I-"

"Smashing. I've arranged a flight to Schipol leaving Gatwick at seven forty nine this evening. I'd be indebted if you were on that plane."

"Of course Beryl... um... Lucien said Anton would most likely be joining me shortly. Do you know when he'll fly?" There is a protracted silence on the other end of the phone. "Hello?" I say into the receiver.

"Anton is being his usual difficult self. Getting that old badger out of his hole is becoming more difficult by the year. He's being rather obstinate."

"But... what am I supposed to do exactly?"

"With all due respect dear boy, what you're paid to do," another pregnant pause. "Interface with the client... take notes and report in. What's changed in that equation?"

"Alright Beryl, fine."

"You've your passport upon you?"

"Of course, I've just-"

"That's all you'll need, everything will be waiting for you at Gatwick and the hostel in Amsterdam. I've got to hang up."

"One thing Beryl-" but she hangs up anyway. Again I find myself frowning at the infernal device.

Several hours later I'm on the shuttle from Schipol to Amsterdam Central Station. The twilight enfolds me as I exit into the expansive environment of the ancient city's centre. It's filled with all sorts of people, from travellers to clowns juggling for farthings, musicians plying their craft, junkies begging for coins. I follow the thoroughfare into the heart of the Jordan district and eventually to the Oberon Bed and Breakfast. It's a tall narrow four-story structure with a pronounced lean. In fact the entire row of neighbours all seem at odds with the perpendicular.

I check in with Mrs. Van Doorn, the rotund, round faced proprietor and follow her lean frail looking husband to my room on the third level –which seems like a bedroom in a private house. I drop my things and immediately journey out into the city. The streets are lined with people and bicyclists of every description. I pass over a number of narrow footbridges that span the many canals permeating the city. Each canal is lined with old wooden barges turned residences, many set with mailboxes near the land's end of their planks, some adorned with small trees and flowers.

The night's air is festive and filled with fragrances. All the cafes and bars advertise either Heineken or Amstel beer. I find a bar that serves food and watch as people come and go speaking in Dutch until I wander back to the comfort of my little room and fall asleep on a bed too short for my height.

The next morning I'm standing before an address in the Jordan district; another narrow four-story building sandwiched between a row of others receding down the course of a meandering cobblestone street. It's a cool misty morning full of anticipation.

I press the button and introduce myself to the nervous woman who answers the door. She seems excited at my arrival beckoning me inside and we partake in a morning tea. We sip coffee with cream and honey in fine delicate china cups upon saucers. Mrs. Van Teegan is friendly but noticeably pensive. Her white hair is in disrepair and her gray eyes seem full of worry. Eventually she gets around to the reason for my visit. Apparently her husband has begun to behave strangely.

Over the course of the past few months it had been his habit after arriving home and having dinner to repair to the sitting room to relax. Within the past several weeks this habit had begun to take on rather monstrous attributes. Upon his arrival home he would bypass dinner, salutations altogether and immediately shut himself within the parlour, of late requesting not to be disturbed. On those occasions she might crack the door to check on him, she was shocked to find him utterly transfixed, staring off blankly into space and unresponsive as if somewhere else altogether. When she confronted him increasingly for explanations regarding this odd behaviour he had begun to rage at her to the point she was afraid to speak to him while inside the room. Recently it had become so bad that he rarely spoke to her nor ate his dinner but immediately enclosed himself within the parlour imbibing in drink often into the very wee morning hours before the call to work would wrench him from the darkness back out into the world. She had become fraught with the notion that he was rapidly becoming a stranger to her.

As I sat listening, writing down snippets of her discourse in my notebook I was struck by a feeling of foreboding in the things she was revealing about her husband who six months prior, she described as a loving and caring man full of life and laughter. The man she now described to me was nearly the opposite of the man she once knew. What was at first a diversion was now an all-encompassing obsession. She had no idea why this chronic change had occurred or what might possibly be causing it.

When we conclude our conversation I ask if I might look over the room in question. She readily agrees and unlocks the doors and entreats me to enter. When I question her about why she would lock an inner door, such as it was, she informs me that it was the wish of her husband that the door always remained locked. Also, amazingly, she asks that I not reveal to her husband that I had been within the room. I agree and enter the rather stagnant environ of the parlour and look about taking care not to disturb anything.

There is really nothing of much import about the chamber. It is rather ordinary in fact; a smattering of books and trivial objects-du-art, several large upholstered chairs with small end tables. An escritoire sat in one corner gathering dust; in fact the entire room seems dressed in it. When I ask Mrs. Van Teegan about this observation she tells me she no longer cleans in the room, another strange request from her husband of late.

I scratch my head as I gaze about. There just isn't anything special about the room. It's what I perceive as a typical

Dutch parlour, decent, somewhat modern, a few older antique tables with white hand-knit doilies beneath small electric lamps. In fact the only object that struck my attention was a large oil painting on the north wall, a portrait of an orange haired woman in black evening attire.

The painting was large, too large for the room in my opinion, approximately six feet in height by nearly four at its width and hung ostentatiously above a hearth no longer in use. I question her about the piece of art. She indicates it had been acquired through an estate sale approximately eight or nine months prior. It had caught the couple's eye and the artist was unknown. It had been their interest, initially, to have the painting appraised for a possible resale but nothing had become of it.

I tour the remainder of the home before shaking Mrs. Van Teegan's hand at the main entrance and setting our meeting with Mr. Van Teegan for later that evening. Due to the sensitive nature of the situation and Mr. Van Teegan's growing disassociation with the outside world, I agree to return that evening for dinner under the guise of a guest, an associate of Lucien's who happened to be in the city on other matters. I dislike *putting on airs* but understand and respect her wishes that we approach the matter cautiously.

When I return to the Oberon, I secure the use of their telephone and immediately check in with Beryl to report on my visit to the property and my interview with Mrs. Van Teegan. After my *report,* Beryl asks me about my impressions. I ask her to elucidate.

"Your impressions dear boy," she says resolutely. "Lucien is hoping you're able to get to the bottom of this and spare us the necessity of dragging Anton out of his hovel." I admit my impressions are very much as I had reported. There is a momentary pause on the line. "You had no impressions regarding the house whatsoever?" she asks.

"No, not really," I say and it's as if the line has suddenly gone dead. I think we have been disconnected. She indicates otherwise and requests I *report* back that evening, however late, after concluding the meeting with Mr. Van Teegan and hangs up. I puzzle over the phone call for several minutes. I realize that this is a peculiar line of work.

With nothing left to do for the remainder of the afternoon, I decide to have a look at the old city. Having never been to Amsterdam before I find meandering about its narrow winding streets replete with pedestrians and bicyclists intoxicating. I lunch at a tiny cafe then poke about several of the shops and coffeehouses.

I traverse a good portion of the Jordan district and walk several of the bridges and canals eventually loitering in a large expansive park somewhere near the heart of the city. Several young Britons advise me to visit the Riksmuseum and the Van Gogh. Having only enough time for one, I choose the Van Gogh museum and it is a splendid experience to see first hand the remarkable works of this great –but tortured- master.

I return to the Van Teegan residence just prior Mr. Van Teegan's arrival and watch carefully as he lays his briefcase and coat to one side and extrudes the tie from around his neck. He's friendly but I sense an odd sort of inner tension, a distinct feeling that my presence is not particularly appreciated, and throughout the wonderful dinner that's provided I feel the impression that he wished to be somewhere else than engaged at the table with his wife and guest. Even before the dessert is concluded, he retires to the parlour, the room that's become the focus of his reveries. As I depart, I shake her hand and can clearly see the wondering look in her expression. I realize the gravity of our work. She is counting on us to help with this deleterious occurrence in their otherwise impeccable marriage. I feel a deep empathy for her.

Back at the hostel, I phone in my report to Beryl at her flat as instructed. Stella, her daughter, takes the call. I can hear the sounds of what I perceive is a party in progress.

"I don't know Willem…" Stella says, "she's getting *pissed*, it might be best to phone back tomorrow… better make it the afternoon." I explain I'm *under orders* to report in. "Doesn't *that* sound like mum. Why not stop in, you can blather away over the hors d'oeuvres."

"Stella, I'm in Amsterdam… on company business." She exhales loudly into the receiver requesting that I *hold the line*. I listen to a variety of voices, primarily Stella's, talking and laughing while I wait for Beryl to pick up the receiver. After several minutes she finally answers.

"Am I calling at an inopportune time?" I ask.

"I've a few friends over," she says, "not to worry. How was your meeting with Mr. Van Teegan?" I tell her about the details including my impressions regarding his pensive disposition. "That's all? Nothing more conclusive?" she inquires.

"Conclusive?" I echo. There's a long pause on the line.

"Willem love, when are you going to fully realize your connection with other people?" she asks and actually waits for a response to this rather oblique question. "Lucien is far too easy going with you, you know that?" she states.

"What do you mean?" I ask somewhat abruptly.

"Regarding your development," she continues.

"My development?"

"Oh bloody hell!" she blurts out. "I've not the time for this nonsense. Expect Anton's arrival at some point tomorrow," she says and immediately hangs up. Again I find myself staring at the telephone receiver in my hand as Mr. Van Doorn watches me blandly from behind his countertop.

"Will you be dining in sir?" he inquires. I slam the phone down.

"No, I'm going out and getting drunk!" I declare and the old man merely shrugs and disappears into the back room.

Anton Corbeau arrives midday the following afternoon and his deportment is far less than cordial. I greet his arrival at Schipol. He gazes at me with those vitreous eyes and huffs his salutations with little to no formality before sending me off to baggage claim to collect his tote. Once we've *run the gauntlet*, he scolds me fiercely for suggesting the shuttle in lieu of a private cab. The man loathes public transportation, being in public altogether, and indeed he seems oddly out of place amongst the throng. He wears a rather old-fashioned suit, very much out of place.

We secure a taxi back to the Oberon B&B and once he's settled in, it isn't the Van Teegan residence we are off to but one of the drinking establishments plentiful throughout the Jordan district. He quickly consumes a respectable quantity of alcohol while I sip on espresso. He barely speaks a word the entire time. I tell him what I have discovered about the Van Teegan situation to date, which frankly isn't much. It isn't long before we are knocking upon the door of the aforementioned home.

Mrs. Van Teegan greets us cheerily but I notice a nervous tone in her voice upon meeting Anton. When Mr. Corbeau excuses himself to use the bathroom, she quickly inquires as to who exactly he is. I tell her he is Lucien's partner and she seems aghast.

"This is Lucien's partner?"

"Yes."

"Oh my..." she says and absently inquires if I'd like more coffee.

When Mr. Corbeau rejoins us he immediately sets about pacing the domicile, taking in its atmosphere. As he walks the entirety of the four levels I'm acutely aware of his eyes darting about and his nose subtly in motion. He returns and stands before the parlour a moment in silence then turns toward me.

"This is the sitting room you spoke of?"

"Yes, it is," I answer. He nods and enters directly. As I reach to turn on the light, he holds out his hand.

"Don't touch that," he says. I quietly stand to one side as he paces the room. Eventually he ends up squarely before me. He gazes into me with his narrow jaundiced eyes and the look is quite unbecoming. "Have a seat," he says oddly. I reluctantly comply attempting to take one of the lounge chairs when he beckons me to one of the two high backed leather affairs placed before the fireplace. "Sit here," he directs me as he takes the adjacent.

We sit in silence. I stare at the large painting of the red haired woman while he extracts a Gitane cigarette from a silver case in his breast pocket and places it in an ivory cigarette holder clenching it between his teeth. I watch passively while he lights the thing with a stainless steel Zippo lighter. He puffs several times on his cigarette and seems to be calmly contemplating the painting above us.

"This is the room the old bugger is dreaming his life away?"

"Yes. He apparently-"

"You sat here earlier? In contemplation?" he interjects.

"Well... yes, I-"

"And you felt nothing?" I look at the man and shake my head.

"No, not really." He leans in closely and snarls as quietly as he can contain himself to do so.

"You're a dunderhead! A blithering fool, do you know that?" I look at him with surprise.

"I'm sorry?"

"You most certainly are!" he states resolutely his wolf-like eyes burning into mine. "I've met my share of clods in my day but you are by far the most ignorant, addle-brained miscreant I'm yet to be burdened with. *It's astounding the depth of your shallowness!*"

"What do you mean?"

"That!" he shouts pointing at the painting above the hearth. "You drag me all the way here to rub your nose in the obvious?"

"The obvious?"

"The painting! The man's obsessed with the woman in the painting you imbecile. The solution to the problem is to get rid of it so the man can sleep at night, return to his family and his life." I gaze at the aquiline features of the red tressed beauty. "Any man knows women are vain by nature, obsessed with themselves... by beauty or the antithesis of it. I admit some age gracefully but not all, not every one. Occasionally one of them attempts this, that sits before you... *the immortalization of their ego prime.*"

"I'm at a loss to understand you," I say and he stares in utter surprise.

"Did you not sit here before this painting and not sense her presence?" I admit that I did not.

"You wretch! She sits before you like a sign on a roadway. A blind man could see it. Only a self-absorbed numbskull such as yourself would miss it." I stare at him in disbelief.

"I beg your pardon?"

"The painting you dolt, it's possessed!" I gaze up at the painting of the woman depicted in oils, her reddish complexion on the pallid skin offset by the dark wondering eyes. "It's obvious the piece is haunted. The previous owners undoubtedly inherited it from the poor soul who was trapped by it until his demise, *most likely consumed by it*. With a modicum of research you'll likely discover it the work of a master, French in fact, toward the end of the nineteenth century. This would be one of those mysterious canvasses that seep through the cracks, the one that *walks in unannounced one evening out of the rain*, so to say. Undoubtedly the anonymous work of a master or an accomplished neophyte who probably drank himself into obscurity but had the magnificent touch to capture in paint the essence of a beautiful woman." He stands abruptly and nears the painting scrutinizing it closely. "How could she resist... the sight of herself immortalized, like the image in a mirror gazing back upon itself... magnificent!"

"Who is she?" I ask.

"Fool! How could I possibly know?" he shouts. "Who she is or was is secondary, what's of import is to get it out of the house and into one of the museums of the world so she can't cause any additional grief. If it should befall another private owner it's inevitable she'll work her subtle magic and another weak-natured man will fall prey to her. *The succubus nurtures itself upon the energies of the beguiled...* the ignorant." He studies me intently a moment. "You in fact would be a perfect subject for her. I wager if you sat quietly for two consecutive evenings she'd swallow you whole."

"What makes you such the expert?" I ask and he chuckles in a most disconcerting manner.

"You'd like an answer to that question wouldn't you my arrogant young friend?" he hisses and I feel a shiver down my spine. "Alright then I'll oblige you. Go ask the old woman if she's any brandy about and leave the bottle on the table. I'll tell you the whole sordid little tale."

Mrs. Van Teegan did have cognac in the house. I did as he instructed, securing the bottle for his consumption and a large snifter. With these in hand Mr. Corbeau set about telling me this tale:

"There was a young man once... not much different in age as yourself. This fellow journeyed one day from the bawdy environs of Paris to the rural areas that lie to the south. The man secured employment on an estate near the village of Levant. Soon after his arrival the man witnessed a masterful painting within the residence of a beautiful *woman in blue*. Her hair was the colour of the raven and her eyes painted in those same hues as the sky on a clear day. The slender neck was adorned with a single strand of pearls and only the one golden band anointed the slender hands for she had been the wife of the master of the estate.

"It was shortly after his arrival that he began to notice a peculiar feeling whenever he was in proximity of the painting. At first it was whimsical, more fancy than anything real but soon he began to realize he was becoming infatuated by the image contained upon the canvas. Although he knew very well she was pigment and oil, he began to fancy her as a living breathing woman, in fact a sense of... *personality*, began to envelope his young mind and the woman's *presence* began to occupy an inordinate amount of his attention. Even his thoughts during his daily endeavours became haunted by her beautiful countenance and it became his habit to sit with her for longer and longer periods of time, his mind completely absorbed, to the point where the inhabitants, in particular the old dotard who was master of the estate, began to take heed.

"Soon it became an obsession, nearly as if engaged in some illicit affair, that he spent time with her outside the attentions of the master and his trove of servants and stewards. He would steal down during the wee hours of the night and sit and silently converse with her image until daylight would once again chase him back to his private chamber. As the charade continued, his composure, in fact his overall health, began to suffer for he had become so enamoured by the painting on the wall –*the woman in blue*- that he could not sleep at night, his thoughts filled with her lovely face, her form gracing his dreams. As days became weeks became months, his obsession became a strange kind of love and this love occupied his thoughts and dreaming.

"It was only a matter of time before his behaviour betrayed his inner most feelings and became a subject of controversy throughout the estate and a confrontation with the old man inevitable. A stranger set of circumstances I could hardly imagine, the two men, the elder and the youth, quarrelling over the painting of a woman. But truth be known, the old lascivious murderer knew the disenfranchised soul of his wife had taken to the facsimile, for he had murdered her in a fit of jealous rage, prematurely ended her life in the prime of her womanly youth *and buried her in a shallow unmarked grave behind the stable under a thorny blanket of framboise bushes.*

"It was for these reasons –perhaps others- that she refuted the pull of *the other kingdom.* Whatever the reasons –base mortal or supernal- she held fast to that which was *she* subject to the whims of the human mind and its infernal machinations. Perhaps she chose to haunt the old devil –for indeed he now feared her- alas the answer is beyond my capacity. What I can tell you is the subsequent years have shown me this phenomenon is not unique but a repetitive occurrence in many cultures and in many diverse places."

He finishes off the snifter and doubled the amount in the next pour. I sat mesmerized, gazing at the rusty haired beauty gazing down at us from above and knew intrinsically that he was correct. There *was* a presence in the painting and the presence was indeed *she.* What had previously been a whim or a notion now was an almost unmistakable feeling that the sharp eyes and slender face was watching, listening to our conversation and an odd feeling crept the marrow of my backbone.

Suddenly the door burst open and the severe countenance of Mr. Van Teegan is framed in the soft light of the parlour.

"Who are you?" he queries us directly. "What business do you have sitting here? Please leave this room immediately!" he says tersely. I begin to rise to my feet but Mr. Corbeau gestures that I remain seated.

"Come in Mr. Van Teegan, have a seat," he says calmly as he takes another long draught of cognac. Van Teegan seems in shock, as if caught in a quandary. He slowly approaches and stares.

"Who are you? Why are you sitting in here? I told you to leave and I-"

"We need to discuss *her* Van Teegan, now sit down!"

"Her? You mean my wife?" Van Teegan says in response to Mr. Corbeau's demand.

"Your lover," Anton says and points at the painting on the wall. Van Teegan is aghast. He steals one quick look at the picture and stutters:

"Wha-what are you talking about? Who are you? I demand an explanation."

"And you shall have it," Anton says turning toward me. "Close the doors will you old boy it's best if Mrs. Van Teegan not overhear our conversation," then looking back at Mr. Van Teegan, "wouldn't you agree?"

There is a long extended pause and the man seems as if struck. I quickly do as I'm instructed and secure the doors before returning to my chair. Van Teegan seems mesmerized, absently lowering himself into an adjacent chair, staring at Mr. Corbeau as if transfixed. "Van Teegan... Corbeau is my name. You recognize it? Lucien Karras is my partner. You'll recall he was instrumental in solving... eradicating, would be the better word... a rather dour situation suffered by a family member, a brother on your wife's side. This was two, possibly three years ago. You remember the incident, a haunting?"

"I remember!" Van Teegan snarls. "There's no reason to hash it all out again. It's done. Your company was compensated in full was it not?"

"It was, generously so, if I recall correctly."

"Then you're welcome to leave, good day to you sir."

"That's hardly the reason for our visit, as you damn well know."

"What do you mean? State your business sir or get out!" Corbeau studies him hard, sipping on the amber liquid in the snifter and the silent tension between the two men could be cut with a knife.

"Who is she Van Teegan? Has she shared her name?"

"What are you babbling about Corbeau?

"Her, the woman in the painting."

"You're insane. How would I know that woman's name? It was painted over a century ago."

"How did you come about acquiring it?"

"An estate sale in Den Hague."

"How much did you pay for it? If you don't object to my asking."

"Not very much really. What does it matter?"

"Indulge me… how much?"

"Oh for God's sake… several hundred euros… what does this have to do with my brother in law?"

"You secured a bill of sale, undoubtedly?"

"This is preposterous!"

"Procure the bill of sale and I'll double the amount on the ticket right here and now."

"You're mad!"

"Alright then, I'll quadruple the total."

"Get out! Get out now!"

"I'll wager you Van Teegan if I offered you ten, twenty times the purchase price you'd refuse it." Mr. Corbeau withdraws his checkbook from an inner pocket of his overcoat and cracks it open. "Go ahead Van Teegan name your price, I'll write you a check here and now."

"Get out sir!" Van Teegan shouts rising to his feet and Corbeau looks at me laughing. His sinister laugh seems to freeze Van Teegan to the spot.

"Of course not," he says in my direction. "No amount of money in the world could take that painting off that wall." He turns toward Mr. Van Teegan. "Only the most ardent use of inner will could wrench that wicked whore off that nail," he says and Van Teegan goes mad.

"How dare you address her in so repulsive a way!" and the man actually lunges for Corbeau's throat as if in a sudden wild fit. Mr. Corbeau is on his feet in a flash and has Van Teegan's wrists clenched firmly in his hairy fists, snarling in his face.

"But that's what she is Van Teegan. She's doing to you what she's done to the last poor bastard who had her… slowly sucking you dry, like squeezing the liquid from a dishrag. She's got you good aye! You'd kill for her, what! Just look at yourself. At another man's throat!" and like that it's over. I watch in awe as Van Teegan seems to melt lowering himself into the nearest chair and burying his face in his hands and sobbing in a most pitiful way. Mr. Corbeau shoots me a glance. "Get another glass," he says.

I quickly procure another brandy glass from the sideboard and pour a modest sum of liquor into it and hand it to Anton.

"Van Teegan, drink this," he says thrusting the vessel into his hands and the man gulps at it.

"I must be losing my mind," he whimpers from his down-turned face and when he looks up at us a more desperate look I've yet to see on another's face. "I can't sleep. I just sit here and… and…"

"We'll take care of it Van Teegan, all you need do now is let go."

The next day while Mr. Van Teegan is at work two men and a woman from the British Museum arrive in a lorry and collect the painting. Anton and I loiter about while the men wrap the painting and Mrs. Van Teegan signs away the donation. As Anton sips on a glass of cognac I chance to hear the men talk.

"Why, she's a beauty, a real genuine beauty she is."

"What, the painting?" the foreman asks.

"The woman... I wonder who she is?"

"Come on, get on with it," the foreman barks and a clean packing tarp is laid across where they have secured the frame and *she* is lifted and taken from the premise.

"We can't thank you enough for your generosity Mrs. Van Teegan," the young woman in a tight navy blue dress says snapping her case with the signed release and shaking her donor's hand.

"It's quite alright," Mrs. Van Teegan says with alacrity. "I'm pleased that you have it."

"Would you like me to contact you after our research is complete? There's no doubt about the painting's qualities."

"That won't be necessary," Mrs. Van Teegan says as she ushers the young woman to the door.

"Interesting about there being no signature."

"Yes very interesting... well, good day then."

"Oh... well... very best to you and Mr. Van Teegan-" she says as Mrs. Van Teegan gently but firmly closes the door in her face.

"And to you!" she says and quickly joins us in the parlour where she immediately withdraws a glass and pours herself a dandy. "Thank heavens that dreadful thing is out of the house!" she states and Anton looks at me. She then tops off his glass with a generous amount of liquor. "I know it's early but this calls for a drink! I can't thank you enough Mr. Corbeau for resolving the issue in such a manly way."

"I apologize if I was somewhat direct in my approach, Madame," he says and Mrs. Van Teegan laughs aloud and sits back in her chair.

"Hardly!" she laughs. "I doubt your gentlemanly partner would have had such an immediate result. I'm ecstatic," she announces broadly and partakes of her drink anew. "How did you surmise the problem so quickly?" she asks and Anton shoots me another furtive glance.

"Let us say I've something of a personal experience in such matters and leave it at that."

"Well, as I've said, I'm indebted. I'm doubling the payment. It's the least I can do, thank you," she says in the most genuine way and Mr. Corbeau bows his head ever so slightly.

"The thanks is ours, merci beaucoup Madame."

"Tell me though," she says deep in thought. "Are we just passing our problem onto someone else? Creating misfortune for some other poor soul?"

"Not in the least. The British Museum was the perfect choice. It takes her out of Amsterdam. With her nailed to a wall of a museum, she hardly has the time to weave her magics." Suddenly Corbeau tilts his head. "However… I suppose a night watchman could possibly become enmeshed. Well, it's rather a long shot." He pulls his shoulders to his ears and the look is rather comical. Mrs. Van Teegan laughs and I realize the woman's smile is a cheery and engrossing one.

"Who was she Mr. Corbeau? Don't you wonder?"

"Not in the least… and does it matter anyway?"

"I suppose not, but I do have pity for her. How long will this continue?" she asks and his eyes grow dark and intense.

"Not very much longer," he says quietly and they exchange a silent stare.

"Yes... I understand. Now gentlemen, there's a smart little cafe just off the Jordan I'd like to visit. I don't suppose you fine gentlemen would care to entertain a silly old woman for another hour?"

"A marvellous invitation Madame but untenable. We must return to Paris forthwith, we've matters to attend in the Sud du France," he says looking at me in a most odd manner. "Perhaps a rain check," he says and the two engage in an animated conversation while I ponder the meaning of his last statement and the nature of that dark look.

As we sit conversing, I'm intrigued by the realization that despite Mr. Corbeau's deformities, his eccentricities, Mrs. Van Teegan is distinctly taken with him. Despite the man's anomalous attributes –his sallow complexion, the narrow predator eyes and the stooped hunchbacked look of the man- I begin to realize I possess an aversion for him not necessarily shared by others. Here is a very proper Dutch woman that seems to have no reservations about the man in the least. In fact, a kind of affection for him permeated her manner and the conversation they shared. I began to realize what Lucien had tried to teach me on several occasions regarding what he referred to as *the dual nature of Love. The light and dark side of it, where universal thought bears no distinctions*. I recall him using the analogy of the sun.

We were standing on the quay on a surprisingly clear day and he pointed his briar cane up at the exquisite golden ball.

"You see that? The radiant orb of light up there?" I remember squinting at it and nodding. "That my friend is Love. It gives of itself endlessly, uniformly, without preference toward anyone or any thing, great or small alike. Without it, there is nothing except the boundless empty solitude of eternity. It's always with you, even at night, *its dark nature*. Without both aspects you'd surely go mad." He then pointed his old stick at the ground behind me. I looked but saw nothing but my shadow on the cement. "And that thing there," he said pointing directly at it, "your constant companion throughout the course of your life… always by your side. That too is Love."

I recall at the time not being exactly sure about the point he was trying to make but it proved superfluous as he turned and continued his stroll along the old river and nothing more was said about it.

The Schizophrenic Daughter

The party in Nice never happened. Instead I follow Audrey and her cousin Noelle to a small apartment just off the Place Garibaldi and wait around while the two women converse in Italian. I page through some magazines, mostly current women's fashion and a copy of Le Monde.

At a certain point Audrey asks if I would like to spend the night at *the family's villa*. I had just arrived by train, the TGV, and hadn't made arrangements for a room. She commences to discuss this, or so I assume, with Noelle and soon once again they are shouting and gesturing back and forth in Italian, broken only by moments of quiet fuming.

"Apparently we don't have a car," she says sitting beside me on the floor, thumbing through a catalogue from the Ecole des Beaux-Arts in Paris. "We could phone a taxi… but I'd rather walk." I readily consent and within a matter of minutes we are out the door walking the festive streets of Nice.

She carries only a small bag over her shoulder, insignificant compared to the knapsack I have dragged with me from Paris after the call from Emerald. I was elated to hear her voice again. She sounded weak but very much herself, and all too painfully succinct. She had asked if I could check upon Audrey in Nice.

"I had the feeling she didn't like me," I say to break the silence, "your cousin Noelle."

"She doesn't like anyone, she's a sociopath, and a misanthrope," Audrey murmurs as we cut through a small shaded park and she goes over an iron railing. "Don't worry about it. It has nothing to do with you," she says when we're back on the thoroughfare.

We stop for a moment at a small Marche and buy a baguette, cheese, some fruit and tomatoes. I offer a few euros, which she takes without a word. Back outside, she ducks into a tabac shop and adds a couple packs of Gitane Blonde cigarettes and —oddly- some candles. We begin walking a slow and winding road, constantly moving uphill until she gets tired and hitches a ride with two young men in a late model Citroen. They drive us just beyond the Nice city limits before they turn off, talking with her in French the entire time. I'm amazed at her ability to shift between the three languages. I realize that Audrey is the kind of person that engages people easily, an innate ability of accepting people on their own terms. I think about my impressions of her back in the States, in San Francisco; her constant coming and going from the house on Sutter Street; the collection of dark strangers in the park at midnight.

As we continue our walk, another steady incline uphill, she speaks about the previous few weeks, about her time in Italy and France and about Noelle. Apparently the apartment we were in earlier belonged to a male acquaintance Noelle had developed an attraction to. I inquire about the villa. She tells me it had been purchased by Emerald and that it was *slightly in need of repair.*

"Who currently lives there?" I ask. She looks at me rather strangely.

"No one," she murmurs.

After walking another twenty minutes, continuously uphill, the road begins to finally level and it's then I see off in the distance set like an enormous gloomy shadow against the rapidly darkening sky the silhouette of an enormous house, some three stories high with many dark foreboding windows and terraces flanked by cypress and cherry. Wild cascading brambles envelope the grounds and even from the distance its bleak chaotic appearance is all too evident. Audrey, I take care to notice, slows her pace staring as if transfixed. She looks at me, her eyes dark in the fading light.

"We're here," she whispers. "*Villa Santana.*"

I'm immediately struck, some tiny place in my midsection. An uneasy discomfort seeps into my being at the thought that this is the evening's destination; the Xanadu we have journeyed to from the crowded and lavish seaside city filled with shops and people; its raucous events and ebullient air. Had I misunderstood, somehow misjudged my handsome companion, *the girl on the magazine cover?* As we approach, I imagine I see shadows dart past the broken windows; their ragged shutters hanging limp and sullen. I question her as we draw nearer and the house grows larger more portentous.

"This is it? This is *the family villa*?"

"Yes, beautiful isn't it? It's over a century old," she says, a strange serenity in her face and voice.

We halt before it on the shoulder of the Rue de Fabron. *Beautiful* is not the word I would have chosen. The main gate is fallen and the grounds completely enveloped in weeds. The old house seems to contemplate us. I feel a chill bristle the hair on the back of my scalp as if someone —or something- was quietly witnessing our approach. Her eyes dart momentarily to mine before she steps across the fallen main gate and threads her way through the weeds and shattered glass lining the walk to the entrée principal.

If the exterior wasn't enough to scare off the squeamish, the interior certainly would. The house is massive and alarmingly chaotic. There's no electricity to light the place only the twilight that seeps through the broken windows and shattered doorframes. The villa is nearly empty, possessing no real furniture to speak of, mostly the remnants of construction, dusty tools, bags of cement and plaster, debris strewn about everywhere. It appears at some point in time an attempt at remodeling the entire villa had begun and then – for whatever reason- aborted. I reluctantly follow Audrey as she investigates the numerous hallways, rooms, baths and terraces, three levels of it! Everywhere is busted windows and locks; doors left ajar.

Without doubt, the most disturbing aspect of the sojourn about the ancient domicile are the rooms and hallways left half remodeled. Many of them throughout the entire three floors are half tiled, the workman's gloves and tools left at the terminus of the work, tiles neatly stacked ready for inclusion into the floor, the mud hardened in the bucket near at hand. It's strange and bizarre, as if the men had somehow inexplicably been *spirited away*. The entire place seems open to the elements and a gentle evening breeze wafts in, bringing with it the scent of the Mediterranean.

Eventually we settle on the large expansive mezzo terrace in the back commanding a stunning view of Nice and the Cote-Azur. She settles on a thick waist-high wall sporting a long row of classically designed urns, now harboring an assortment of weeds, and lights a cigarette. I drop my pack, avoiding the undergrowth and gaze about. Night is now upon us, the glorious orb of life having dipped below the horizon.

I study her a moment as she looks out toward the sea, the wind lifting the finer tendrils of her long honey-colored hair.

"You're not actually considering staying here tonight?" She turns and looks straight into my eyes.

"Oui. Of course," she says and I'm instantly ill at ease. I look back at the house. It looms above us quietly watching our every move, listening to our every word. All about us grows a wild plethora of brambles and overgrown fauna… and Audrey, under the starlight.

"This place is uninhabitable." She looks away and says nothing. I rub my forehead, pondering. It isn't just the building –so utterly vacant and in disarray- that distresses me, but more the place itself. It gives off an undeniably gloomy atmosphere. She addresses my reluctant manner, inquires as to what is troubling me. "This place," I say glancing back toward the house. "It's… strange."

"What do you mean *it's strange*?" she asks with a sudden irritation in her voice. "Life is strange… the house is stately and beautiful. It's an architectural masterpiece." I scratch my head. Indeed it's an impressive place yet I can't shake the weird and oppressive air the old villa seems to permeate. I confide my feelings to her. She laughs, a strange gleam within those dark pupils. I ponder the meaning behind that look and that laugh.

"Hey, come here… I'll show you something," she says gently taking my hand in hers.

She leads me down a wide flight of stone steps through a series of Romanesque arches to a long lower terrace extending some thirty feet out over the hillside that drops off into a vapid depression below.

"We can sleep here under the stars if the house scares you."

"The house doesn't *scare me* Audrey," I exhort in my defense. "My point is… what if someone is living in there?"

"No one lives in there," she replies. "Uncle Anton would never allow it."

"Anton? Mister Corbeau? What's he got to do with this?"

"This used to be his." This revelation shocks me.

"This house belonged to Mr. Corbeau?" I ask and she looks at me oddly.

"What about it?" she retorts and I really have no words with which to respond. I glance back at the bleak manor home towering over us.

"Are you sure there's no vagrants living inside? There are so many rooms, so many passages." She stares at me in the darkness saying nothing and the effect of her dark eyes is unsettling, or is it her sudden silence? "What about those blankets and junk?"

"Those were left behind by the workmen."

"The workmen?"

"Someone hired a work crew to remodel the villa," she says and her use of the word *someone* strikes me as odd. "Something must have happened, *they all left in a big hurry.* They didn't even bring their tools with them," she says in something of a mesmerized tone of voice. I can't help but to press the issue.

"Why do you want to stay here?" She hesitates and the moon above reflects a pinprick of white light from her pupils.

"Because… this is my house now." We stare at each other quietly. I've nothing to say.

I always travel with a Mag-lite, a small electric torch. With this as our guide we search the smaller house –still at least a half dozen sizable rooms- to the west of the lower terrace, built as a servant's quarters. We discover some wicker chairs designed like large giant bowls that hold futons. We then retrieve some blankets and pillows from the living space on the third floor of the villa and with these we produce beds for ourselves outside under the moonlight.

The night is warm and we choose to sleep on the enormous mezzo terrace –with its wall of urns- overlooking the city. Though the moon is bright, the coast is now invisible, swallowed in mist. The tiny lights of the city and the cars shuttling east and west along the Autoroute create a mild and enchanting feeling. We smoke and talk together about the people we have in common and my pensive mood slowly dissipates.

I'm amazed at how extensively traveled she is. I surmise she has friends and relatives in many places. It seems to me, by mentally taking notes, she has been on the road traveling quite frequently for at least the last five or six years. I question her about my observation. She admits it's impossible for her to stay in any one place for very long, that something in *her nature* drives her down the road and onto other destinations. This house, this villa, she reveals was purchased from the Corbeau estate and given to her by Emerald in an attempt to help alleviate this restlessness; but the place seemed to evade reconstitution somehow.

It is sometime later, deep into the night, when she begins to discuss *reality and dreaming*. I find myself intoxicated by her voice and words as if being read a story. She speaks about how living for her, is moment to moment; that this place we are in is like a dream that is continually reoccurring.

She talks about how necessary it is for her not to internalize the thoughts of others if their *energy* is contrary to her nature. Finding *one's nature* is of the utmost importance to her. I realize that her nature is extremely different than anyone else's I have ever met.

"*Reality*, as people describe it to me," she continues, "doesn't make sense because it's always based on past events or speculation about the future, both *which don't exist, they have no substance,* and rarely refer to what we are actually doing or feeling now, which is the only reality I know. Thinking is often in contradiction with what we're actually feeling. Feeling and thinking are often opposites... like you, I can tell, think a lot." I think about all this for a moment before asking her to elucidate. "There's nothing to elucidate about. Look around you, look where you are... like a dream you once had long ago as a younger man. You've left the home of your youth and are wandering in a dream, in a dream world with nothing to guide you but dreams... perhaps an odd sense that you've passed this way before, once long ago." She averts he eyes out over the thick terrace wall.

"When I was seventeen, my closest friend died in my arms," she continues. "And just to make hell out of it... in her pain, her mother, who had been my friend too, accused me of killing her. Everything changed then. When I realized that a person can leave you like that... or a close friend become a mortal enemy within an instant... everything about the future or the past started to change. It's not real... there's no real substance there at all." She looks at me, pressed against the eternal night sky.

"When you internalize the thoughts of others, it becomes reality in you. If you don't, then it's merely like *chatter in a dream*. Dreaming becomes reality *when you give it energy*. Just like when you recall memory, it again returns to reality, you can actually relive it." She lights another cigarette and blows a thin stream of gray smoke into the night. "Awareness is everything Willem. You should know that by now. The mind and its thoughts, are merely dreaming... chattering. Like this life we live, is nothing more than part of the collective grand dream, what they refer to as *the grand illusion.* How did the poet say it? *'Good little performers all.'* We're all walking through our parts... acting out our roles." She sees the expression in my face and exhales aloud. "Never mind..." She pulls her legs up and sits cross-legged upon the wall.

"You're saying that our lives don't mean anything?"

"Duh... the opposite. Our lives are everything... but not our thoughts, our thinking, our little private and collective dramas... only our awareness and its *direct connections*."

"What do you mean by awareness... exactly?" I ask and she stares at me placidly.

"Now."

"Now?"

"Yes."

"Now..." I say staring into the night. "That's awareness? Now?"

"Yesterday and tomorrow belong to the mind... *and it's a lie.*"

"A lie? How can yesterday and tomorrow be *a lie*?"

"Because it is... it doesn't exist... and in truth Willem... it never will. That's why it's a lie. A lie you've been taught since you were a child. All you'll ever have is right now... this moment... and the moment is endless."

"Audrey, that's a bit… out there."

"Right. Exactly. It is out there… and inside."

"What are you talking about?"

"Everything comes from and flows back into the invisible. All things, you and I, come from it and will return to it. Therefore the invisible is the essential thing, and the invisible only exists now, and now… now, is eternity." I stare at her in the moonlight.

"Uncle Lucien should have already taught you all this… that the solidity of material objects is an illusion. Solid matter is almost entirely empty space. You don't need uncle Lucien to tell you, just pick up a current issue of Scientific American." She points her cigarette toward the night sky above us. "So what is that vastness out there?" she asks then points toward her heart. "Or in here? That empty space that permeates all life, all matter?" She seems to wait for an answer but I only stare at her. "It's the same!" she expounds. "Everything comes from it, and everything returns to it. That immensity surrounds and permeates everything. You'll feel it someday, if you learn how to shut up…" she looks off into the distance.

"What? Loneliness? I know it," I say with remorse in my voice. She tosses her cigarette and turns toward me, extending her legs back onto the flagstones.

"No… not loneliness Willem… not loneliness. *I'm talking about Love,*" she says.

"Love?" I say incredulous.

"Yeah… and not the pretty pink concept of it either… *but the huge endless enormity of it.*"

That night I awaken from a dream, or did I? I'm gazing up into an immense starry canopy, darkness all around, the sounds of crickets and frogs. From the gentle embrace of night emerges the image of a woman, silhouetted against the canvass of the starry Mediterranean night. The vision is like a photograph, a still moment captured from a moving picture. She turns toward me and I wonder how those eyes can reflect the dim light that extends from the tiny stars so far away in the heavens. She returns to a quiet meditation, becoming frozen again in time and space like a still photograph pinned against the background of an eternal fathomless sky.

In the morning when I awaken, I'm alone; her makeshift bed left askew. I stand and stretch, breathe in the warm dry air of the cerulean French coast.

Assorted smells from the city and the sea below float on the gentle breeze. The bright Mediterranean sun has risen, the morning already becoming hot. I breathe deeply and the scent in my nose mixed with the brilliant azure sea reminds me I've been here before, once long ago… a thousand years, perhaps even more. My mind refuses the feeling to linger and diverts my eyes elsewhere.

I see the movement of cars and trucks below on the autoroute and workmen have commenced their labor on the chantile next door. I watch the Tunisian and Algerian laborers carrying bricks, mud and heavy objects upon their heads and backs while the booming voice of the foreman accompanies their every move. I wonder to myself what conditions are like in their native lands that push them so far from their homes and families.

Cigarette butts litter the terrace floor and the thought occurs to me that she must have stayed up nearly all night. It's then I notice the faint sound of a radio, playing rock and roll, emanating from the lower terrace.

I follow the massive stone steps under the arches leading to the servant's house and trace the music through several vacant plaster rooms eventually spilling into a secluded courtyard. Audrey, in only underwear, is washing her hair beneath an ancient faucet that feeds into a large stone basin big enough to contain a person. I stand in the doorway mesmerized by her slender form at the weathered stone, her hair flowing with the water gushing from the fountain. I find myself wishing I were a painter or photographer or even yet a poet.

I watch as she squeezes the moisture from her long caramel tresses, the water cascading across the stone beneath her bare feet, seeking out the crevices between the tiles that compose the floor of this amazingly timeless place. She spies me and smiles.

"Bonjour. Comme ca va?"

"Good morning," I reply, averting my eyes. She wraps a towel around her torso and begins brushing her hair. An old Cream tune begins playing on the tiny blue transistor radio that sits atop a stack of broken slabs of marble.

"I have to go to Monaco to meet with my mother, would you like to come?" she asks.

"Emerald is here? In Monaco?" I ask with excitement and surprise.

"No, my *other mother*," she says flatly. The idea sounds enchanting. "There's some soap and shampoo if you'd like to take a bath," she says pointing towards the basin. "Sorry but there's only cold water."

"Yes, I'd love to take a bath," I say.

"It's an Artesian well. Just release the wire that cinches this pipe and *the water just flows from the earth*." She demonstrates by releasing the fold in a long section of black plastic pipe that immediately releases a gush of clear cold water into the basin. "This actually dates back to Roman times," she says holding the pipe toward me and I study it. "Not the pipe dumbhead... the well. This is the oldest part of the property. *The villa is built on top of an old Roman enclave.*"

The entire courtyard is filled with slabs of marble and masonry. There are several broken statues of women and a small nude child with wings still intact. They appear to have once been pieces of a fountain.

"We have to get my car from Noelle. It might take some doing," she says tossing her hair over her shoulder and pulling a white t-shirt over her head; I notice she doesn't seem to wear a bra. She pulls herself into a beat pair of Levis and I smell her freshly washed hair on the dry breeze. She catches my eye and smiles wryly, "Enjoy your bath," then goes to leave. At the door she stops and looks at me silently for a moment.

"What is it?" I ask and she seems far away for just a fraction of an instant.

"Strange... just now..." she says softly, her eyes fathoming me.

"What?"

"You... here... this place..." She gives her head a slight shake. "Nothing. Dump all your stuff and come on up when you're finished."

We begin the trek back down toward Nice and within five minutes hitch a ride with a sporty young man who is obviously taken by Audrey and didn't care much to conceal it. Once in Nice we again visit the apartment where we had parted company with Noelle. No one answers the bell so Audrey leads the way to a nearby garage which houses, much to my surprise, an immaculate cherry-red Ferrari Testarossa. She hunts beneath the frame until she produces a set of keys, opens the driver's door and brings the car to life.

The ride into Monaco on 59 is sunny and relaxing, the blue Mediterranean dropping off to hundreds of feet below the winding roadway that cuts a ribbon across the bottom of the European continent. I have never been to the Principality and find it impressive and lively. We drive down the Boulevard Princess Charlotte through Monte Carlo and park down near the marina. We wait at a table for nearly an hour I drinking Carlsberg beer while Audrey sips Campari and water on ice.

At approximately one o'clock two very distinguished women join us. The Italian, I surmise, is in her late-forties and possesses an air of someone well experienced with the world of finer things. She is cordial yet I can tell is scrutinizing me from the periphery of her vision. She wears a light aqua-colored dress, elegant yet appropriate for the warm weather. The other, an American, is younger, perhaps mid-thirties, and seems somehow amused by my presence.

The women kiss one another in typical European fashion. Before any introductions can take place, mother and daughter converse extensively in Italian. I can only sit and look attentive. The younger woman, a brunette, produces a pack of Marlboro Lights and begins to smoke. When the waiter arrives, she orders for them, in French. The conversation between mother and daughter has obviously come around to me, judging by their quick fleeting glances. Audrey introduces me to Anna her *other mother* who graciously extends her bejeweled hand and speaks in exquisitely accented English.

"A pleasure to meet you… this is my colleague Margaret, she too is from the *Etats Unis,* from *the States.*" Margaret only nods, seemingly uninterested in shaking hands. She exchanges a rather strange gaze with Anna, raising and lowering one long thin eyebrow, saying nothing. Mostly out of nervousness induced by the following, and thunderous, silence I ask Margaret if she currently resides in the United States.

"Yes… occasionally," she says looking at Audrey and shrugging. She is having fun at my expense. The drinks arrive and Anna pays for them with a gold credit card requesting something additional from the waiter.

"Where do you live in the States?" I ask Margaret and have to wait until she puffs on her cigarette.

"New York," she replies, "and Los Angeles… sometimes Chicago."

"Oh," is all I can think to say. I look to Audrey to interject but her chestnut-brown eyes are dreamily taking in the blue expanse of ocean. Anna finally breaks the silence.

"Are you touring, or just visiting William?" she asks misstating my name. I hesitate briefly, quite enthralled by her manner.

"Just visiting," I say. She sips Kir from a crystal glass. I notice her ring is an ostentatiously large diamond in what I am sure is a platinum setting.

"Magnifique," she says smiling. That's it for me. With a slight bow of her head she returns her attention to Audrey quickly engaging in a spirited conversation in her native tongue. I watch and listen as they converse together, sitting beside one another at the table, Anna studying her daughter closely, Audrey talking with a detached air as she watches certain young men walk by. Occasionally Margaret is asked to respond on some topic and I can tell she is a novice of the language. Mostly she seems content to sit and chain-smoke, gazing out to sea, past the tiny towers crowning the breakwaters that surround the Marina Monte Carlo proper. Huge expensive yachts bob in the calm waters of the marina. It is an absolutely stunning day, a mild pleasant breeze blowing in off the sea. Suddenly Anna addresses me.

"Audrey tells me you spent the night with her at the villa in Fabron," she states directly. I pause and look to Audrey who gazes at me without concern in her eyes.

"Yes, I did. It seemed that her cousin Noelle-" Anna interrupts me.

"I'm sorry William, but I'm not concerned with Noelle," she says, a concise and deliberate tone in her voice. "I'm curious," she continues, biting at her crimson painted nails, "what are your immediate plans? Are you possibly in need of cash perhaps?"

"Pardon moi?" I ask surprised by this question.

"Do you have an itinerary? Have you appointments?" I'm a bit confused and she senses it, gently clasping my wrist. "Let me be more to the point," she says pausing and collecting her thoughts. "My daughter…" looking towards Audrey, "well… she can be very silly, do very strange things-" Audrey immediately interrupts, obviously at odds with Anna's choice of words. They argue in Italian for several minutes before Anna returns her attention to me. "What I'm saying is judging from what she has told me, you are a close friend of the relatives? Perhaps you may have time to stay on?" She waits for me to respond. I feel the blood rush to my face. "The thing is this William… I'm concerned about her staying alone at *Santana*. You've seen it yourself, it's not… secure." She pauses a moment to sip her glass of Kir. Audrey stares deeply into my eyes, searching for something there.

"What she's getting at is offering you a bribe," and Anna scowls at her.

"Why do you say such things?"

"Because that's what you're doing."

"Non, non... this is not it at all," she says focusing on me. "What I'm suggesting is offering you work if you like. Perhaps for a few weeks, whatever your calendar allows. You seem like a man of ability. Are you an experienced jardinier perhaps?"

"A what?"

"A gardener," Margaret interjects.

"The villa is completely overwhelmed... you saw... and the locks are in need of attention... perhaps you can do these sorts of things?" The waiter suddenly returns with a box of Dunhill cigarettes and hands them to Anna.

"Madame," he says with a polite bow. He then hands back the credit card and engages her in a rather animated discussion in French for several minutes culminating with him presenting her with a mauve colored envelope with some kind of embossed writing on it and bows once more.

"Oui, merci beaucoup," she says tipping him generously and he bows and leaves. She holds up the envelope and smiles to Margaret. "We've been invited to a soiree this evening, at the casino." Margaret smiles in mock surprise.

"Why imagine that," she replies in an animated tone and Anna laughs, amused by her response.

"Margaret dear, you are so cynical you know," she says laughing softly and placing the envelope in her purse and immediately returns to our conversation.

"My daughter has this crazy notion she would like to spend time at Santana. I haven't had the chance to have the work restarted." She tears at the plastic wrapping on the pack of Dunhills and extracts a cigarette lighting it. I realize she is waiting patiently for a response. What I think she's alluding to, is completely unexpected. "Of course I'm not asking the impossible of you. Things too difficult... electricity, the pipes, things of this sort are best left to professionals, oui? But just do what you can to help us assess the needs of the place." She pauses to smoke her cigarette and study me. "What do you think?" she finally asks.

"Well... although the place is in disrepair it's certainly not a complete shambles. The structure is sound enough. It seems to me just a few days cleaning is all that's necessary before bringing in a subcontractor." They all just stare at me. "Despite its current state, the villa is actually rather impressive. If it were re-organized it could become a potentially lucrative enterprise. How much are you willing to pay for repairs?" I ask and instantly feel self-conscious about my lack of tact, however Anna jumps at the question.

"Not much quite frankly," she says, a quick furtive glance toward Margaret. "Unfortunately, I'm forced to under rate your talents... but what I could arrange-" I interrupt her.

"No, I'm not talking about myself, I'm suggesting you hire a contractor." She drifts off a moment and whispers with Margaret who assesses me tenuously, shrugs a lot and pouts her lips frequently. Anna returns her rather mesmerizing gaze to mine.

"I could go a thousand Euros a week with you." My mind tries to fathom what is happening.

"I don't think you understand, I'm currently under the employ of Audrey's uncle," I reply and Audrey vaguely seems to smile.

"Oh please, that crazy old man? The one who sees ghosts?" Anna says. "You hardly belong with him, a handsome young man as yourself belongs here. Nice is exquisite. We'll arrange your own room and bath at the villa, and a private phone," she says her eyes fix on mine and a gentle smile curves the corners of her painted lips. "I'll send Margaret by tomorrow with a prepayment, chin-chin," she says toasting her glass and Audrey and I just stare while Margaret smokes.

Later that night, I have an unsettling dream. In this dream I'm lying on my back in the middle of the great mezzo terrace. When I sit up I'm surprised to see the entire grounds neatly manicured. The cracked and broken urns are all intact and immense exotic plants fill them to overflowing, the entire place rejuvenated and golden.

I'm shocked to see Morgan standing amidst a host of people surrounding her. They are robed in finely made fabrics and are jeweled in gold. These persons are a strange mix of Byzantine and Peloponnesian. Mycenaean and Greek warriors line the perimeter of the grounds, their bronze helmets and shields glittering in the sunlight, their bodies wet with perspiration.

I rise and from my vantage point on the terrace, I can see several marvelous ships anchored in the bay below, their prows, used for ramming, are gilded in gold and gleaming under a huge vibrant sun somehow larger, brighter than in life. What is unique about this dream is I seem to be, in total control of my faculties. I know without hesitation I am walking amidst a dream.

There is something distinctly unsettling about the people that surround Morgan. They seem to vie for her attention and there's an artificial quality about them, their spurious glances in my direction.

With a mighty effort, similar to walking in deep water, I manage to approach her. She turns slowly and smiles at me, it is distinctly her and a deep desire to embrace envelopes the entirety of my being. She wears a beautiful shimmering white gown with a golden belt. Laurel adorns her hair and it amuses me somehow, as if I were participating in an old Hollywood movie, slightly overdone. I try to speak but cannot. When the others engulf her, she turns away. I attempt with great effort, to take hold of her arm when I'm forcefully held by several of the warriors. Their eyes are as black as coal beneath their garish bronze helmets.

I call out to Morgan but am unable to utter a single sound. I attempt to convince myself this is a dream but there is nothing I can do to break their icy grip. They proceed to drag me to the terrace wall under which there emerges an enormous chasm below. The ground recedes and crags and mist are all I can see as they set themselves to throwing me over the edge. One huge warrior with a red crest trailing from his helmet raises me above his head, I can smell his sweat in the air and I'm sure I'm about to be thrown upon the rocks below. I call out and see Morgan, without the slightest air of concern, watch from the distance with the rest of the crowd. Then with all the strength my body can muster I smash my fist into the faceplate of the warrior holding me aloft and the entire dream shatters like a mirror.

I'm suddenly awake, lying upon the mezzo-terrace under a starry night sky, Audrey alongside, shaking me. I'm sweating profusely. I realize the smell of perspiration I detected in the dream is my own.

"Are you alright?" she asks as I slowly collect my senses.

"I don't know," I murmur breathing deeply. All about is darkness.

"You were having a bad nightmare," she says her eyes like black jet in the dim moonlight. I rub my eyes and breathe deeply still trying to catch my breath. My chest feels heavy as if a weight were pressed against it.

"I was dreaming," I whisper. She places a cool palm across my brow.

"You're dripping wet," she whispers and stands, returning with the white t-shirt she had been wearing that afternoon and wipes my forehead with it. I lay my head back into my jacket that I've rolled up and am using as a pillow and close my eyes. I then feel the soft touch of her head against my shoulder soon followed by the warmth of her body next to mine as she lies beside me.

"It's gotten cold tonight," she whispers. "Maybe we should go inside." My arms, seemingly without the aid of my mind, pull her closer so that half of her body lay on mine and this is how we sleep until morning when I again awaken to find her nowhere in sight. In fact, she is completely absent from the villa.

Early that afternoon Margaret arrives in a black Porsche wearing an expensive gray pants suit. We casually stroll about the house and grounds. Her attitude is very different than the previous day, more relaxed and friendly. I take the opportunity to ask her some questions concerning Anna's line of business.

"She does different things, real estate mostly. She's a bon vivant. She's currently involved with two film projects, one in LA, one here. Nice has a large film studio, Victorine Cote-Azur." This is interesting to me. I tell her that my work in cinema is what connected me with *Karras and Corbeau* initially and how I came to know Audrey. "Yeah, I heard something about that. Did you know that girl has modeled for some big publications?"

"I'm aware of it but she never talks about it. Which publications?" I ask.

"Fashion, her sister is a fashion photographer in New York, incredibly talented. I saw a private show of her work once in Soho, all black and white portraits, amazing photography. Anyway, I think it was her that set all that up, but Audrey doesn't think it appropriate to involve herself with 'an industry that caters to vanity' quote end quote."

"Oh, that's rather commendable," I say. Margaret looks at me strangely, laughs and shakes her head.

"Well, don't let her fool you," she says as we pace the grounds, stopping beneath one of the numerous cherry trees. She reaches up and picks a handful of cherries that have dried on the limb and puts a few in her mouth before offering some to me. "Try these, they're delicious, like raisins." I do, and they are. She gazes at the chaos around us. "It's a shame the way this place has gone to ruin."

"Do you know much about the history of the villa?" I ask.

"I believe it was built before the turn of the twentieth century, by an eccentric who died just before the building was completed; a labor of passion, he built it for his wife... or maybe she died... either way, it remained empty for quite a period of time. It eventually turned into a casino, in the thirties I think, that became infamous in its day with the death of some famous king or duke, up on the third floor... and under very bizarre circumstances apparently because the authorities closed the place down for awhile."

"Really? That's ominous."

"It reopened just in time for the second world war and the Vichy government allowed the Nazis to occupy it. Legend has it, they used the place to interrogate members of the

French underground, but I don't know if this is actually true or not." She lights a cigarette. I stand in silence thinking over these rather foreboding thoughts. "Whatever was going on here was serious enough that the Allied command had this place strafed, several times. Possession of the villa went back to the original family who subsequently sued the French government for damages."

"Sued the government? Why?" I ask.

"I guess a lot of people sued the government for damage to their property after that war... who else could they sue? Anyway, Audrey's real mother acquired it a little while back... along with the house in Cannes." She gestures across the landscape below with a wave of her arm. "Can you believe this view? Incredible."

"Margaret, why are the rooms all half tiled?" I ask.

"Anna hired a Polish work crew to remodel the place. One morning, *everyone was gone, just vanished*, literally overnight, and without collecting their personal affects... or even their pay. Weird huh?"

"Why? What happened?" I ask. She shrugs.

"I've no idea, but they've not been able to keep a work crew here ever since." I scratch my ear deep in thought while she inspects a series of glass doors that open out from the house into the mezzo terrace. "These had all been repaired with leaded glass, now they're all busted." She rejoins me brushing her hands together. "Crazy," she whispers.

"Margaret... Audrey mentioned to me that this was her house," I say and she smiles, laughing gently.

"She did, did she?" I wait for her to continue. "I don't know how much you know about her..." she says looking at me her eyes a deep hazel and quite lovely. She seems to be waiting for a response.

"Not much actually."

"She's a bit strange this one. Anna's concerned because she doesn't seem to exhibit any interest in doing anything. She can't seem to settle down." She drops her cigarette and twists it underneath her shoe. "Do you know anything about her father?" I confide that I know nothing about him other than he apparently lives in Los Angeles.

"That's right, he's an entertainment lawyer, big time. Do you know anything about her grandfather on that side?"

"Nothing. Does he live in LA too?"

"Oh no... San Marino, he's the quintessential Italian gentleman," she says. "He's involved with Ferrari at Imola."

"Formula One," I say.

"Yeah, all that," she says nonchalantly. "I don't really know anything about it, just that he's heavily involved with racing. Vittorio is an engineer, a chief mechanic, something like that." She chews on some more dried cherries deep in thought. "I've only met him a couple of times. He lives on a gigantic estate, a vineyard... very old... I think it's been in his family for centuries. Anyway, he spends every single waking moment tinkering with cars. How to make them go faster, more aerodynamic, more fuel efficient, all that sort of thing," she says. "I know absolutely nothing about cars but if you follow racing you'd love meeting him. Actually, on second thought maybe not. He's a bit absorbed... one of those people who live and breathe the artform, you know? Everything else, and I mean everything else, is unimportant. Well... except wine and grapes." She becomes silent a moment.

"I suppose there's something to be said about being focused on one's work," I say to fill the silence and she laughs softly.

"Yeah, I suppose," she tosses another cherry into her mouth. "He adores Audrey, he gave her that Testarossa she drives when she's here. Just gave it to her. A one hundred thousand dollar automobile." She looks at me for a reaction but I really don't feel inclined one way or the other about it. Again she laughs softly under her breath about my reaction and resumes her stroll. "Anyway, they send her money whenever she asks for it. Anna complains about it but she does the same thing. They foster this... this *laisse-en-faire* attitude because of what happened." She stops mid-sentence and flashes me a strange sideways glance. "Why am I telling you this? It's actually none of your business... is it?" I shrug. She shakes her head. "Odd, I'm not usually this chatty. I'm not paid to talk. It's probably better if I just refrain." After a momentary pause she says: "I'd appreciate it if you keep this to yourself... our conversation."

"I've no reason to speak about this with anyone else. I was just curious."

"Well, they're an interesting bunch."

She begins pacing the grounds again. I tag along silently for a moment before breaking the silence.

"Margaret, do you mind me asking... what is your relationship with Anna?" She stops walking and looks squarely at me.

"What do you mean?" she asks, apparently put off by my directness.

"Well, you don't seem like just a secretary," I say. She studies me closely for a moment before commencing her slow pace of the grounds again.

"Let's just say we're more friends than associates; she helps me, I help her." I understand her reserve. She suddenly stops and turns toward me. "Audrey says you're from San Francisco. I've spent a lot of time in San Francisco. Is it possible we may have met before?"

"That's somewhat odd, why do you ask that?"

"I rarely open up, to anyone… but you don't seem like a stranger to me, yet I don't recall if we've met through the families or some other-" her voice trails off as if in thought. "You don't believe we've ever met, before yesterday?"

"I'm certain I would have remembered." She nods, her eyes looking deep inside mine, just the hint of a smile at the corners of her mouth. She shrugs off the topic and resumes pacing the grounds, both of us in silence. Suddenly, and without looking at me, she breaks the quietude.

"Did she tell you she has a four year old daughter?" I'm uncertain to whom she refers.

"Who do you mean, Anna?" I ask and Margaret laughs.

"No… Audrey. Her daughter lives with her dad, in Los Angeles," she says and it's just like being blindsided. I stop and stare at her. She quits walking and turns, silhouetted against a dense growth of cypress along the western approach.

"No one's ever mentioned that, I had no idea," I say my voice conveying surprise. She emerges from under the branches, her eyes emphatic.

"Don't get me wrong. Audrey is… well… she's got a lot of insight for someone her age. I like her very much actually. It's just… I hate seeing her waste her talents. She's extremely intelligent. You know she speaks four different languages? Fluently. I can barely speak French. My Italian is pretty much a wash." She looks at me inquisitively. "She knows people all over the world and she's only twenty four."

We stand there in contemplation for a moment before the clatter of her cell phone punctuates the silence. She quickly retrieves it from her shoulder bag.

"Allo? Oui, comme ca va? D'accord." She smiles looking at me. "Yes, I'm with the *jardinier* now," she says for my benefit, a brief smile then a sudden seriousness. "Comme?

Pour quoi?" She turns aside and quiets her voice. "Pour quand? Partout ou… toutes les fois que…" a quick furtive glance in my direction, "non, n'importe… merveilleux, le ouvrier merveilleux… oui, tres bien… oui amoureux, a'bientot… bisous."

Margaret inspects the remainder of the house, opening doors and closing them, commenting about the deplorable condition of the locks and windows, which apparently had been secured at some point. Fixtures from the numerous baths and lavatories are missing or broken. Shattered glass is everywhere.

After all of this, she presents me with ten one hundred Euro notes for the first week, loosely outlining a general maintenance program for me to follow. As she leaves she adds:

"Whatever you can do around here is great, but more than anything else Anna wanted me to indicate her concern for Audrey's welfare. She's strange this one. She does things like… sleep in people's cars when she has *Carte Blanc* to take a room in the best hotel. Sometimes she wanders around all night without the slightest concern for her safety." She pauses thinking deeply. "Basically just keep an eye out for strangers and if squatters show up again send them out. I'll have a phone reinstalled sometime in the next few days and have the electricity turned back on." She glances about the impressive main hall where we are standing. It tells of a former glory. A large ornate fireplace that must have greeted hundreds of guests from all over the world with a bright cheery glow is now quiet, neglected.

"Unforgivable," she says staring at the vaulted ceiling. "They've taken the huge crystal chandelier that hung here. It's a shame." She shakes her head and turns to me. "In response to your question earlier about this house belonging to Audrey, it's true. Her mother, Emerald Montaigne, acquired this villa hoping that Audrey would settle down here and take care of it... and Rain."

"Rain?"

"Her daughter... Audrey's always been very fond of Nice and the whole Riviera. At first it seemed it might work but after a few months, one day she just walked out the door leaving it wide open... now look at it. Crazy." We turn and exit through the front door and she takes a moment to hand me a card with several international phone numbers printed on it in embossed lettering.

"Giovanna Manella, Los Angeles... Nice, France... San Marino..." I mutter aloud.

"You can phone any of those numbers night or day and get Anna or myself." She reaches her hand out to me. "Best of luck."

I walk her to the car, an immaculate black Porsche with French plates. She climbs in behind the wheel applying dark sunglasses over her eyes. She looks at me, a slight smile forming at the corners of her mouth and turns over the engine. It rumbles to life, a finely tuned machine.

"Well, ciao," she says and speeds off down the Rue de Fabron. I stare on, well after the car is out of sight before turning and walking back inside the old house with its dark history and secrets.

It isn't until twilight when Audrey returns parking the car inside the main gate I've been repairing. She looks tanned and refreshed and says she has spent the entire day at *the plage* and dinner with *a friend*. She wears the same pair of

Levis and leather sandals but a new white Armani shirt, recently purchased. She also seems to be wearing some new silver jewelry. Her eyes sparkle and wisps of her hair are strewn about her head and shoulders from driving the Ferrari with the top down. She looks lovely. I see many of her mother's attributes in her comely face but she lacks Emerald's intense blue eyes in lieu of her own deep perfect brown irises, most probably from her father I surmise. She holds out a bag to me. Inside are several croissants and a liter of ale.

"I thought you might be hungry," she says. "Actually I'm surprised you're still here." I don't say anything to this odd comment but reach in and begin munching one of the pastries.

I watch while she canvasses the pruning I have done around the entree principal. She kicks at a few piles of debris with her toes before turning and says with a rather serious tone in her voice, "What's all this? What are you doing?"

"*Jardeniering,*" I say popping the top off the beer with my pocketknife. She walks up and places herself squarely before me, the smile disappearing from her face.

"What's the meaning of this," she says, pointing to the newly trimmed hedges and trees surrounding the front entrance. I choke down the bread I'm eating and stare at her a moment, confused by the sudden change in her persona. "What do you think you're doing?" she asks and I'm not exactly sure her meaning.

"I'm clearing the garden," I say.

"What? Oh good Lord," she says diverting her face towards the rapidly fading sun now low on the western horizon. "I don't believe it." She raises both hands to her head and stares at her feet for a moment. "You can't possibly be that moronic?" Total confusion.

"What do you mean? What are you getting at?" I ask not masking my frustration.

"This!" I'm shocked to see tears welling up in her eyes that only moments ago were filled with serenity. "Who said you could do this?!" She is shouting now. "What right do you have to come here and screw with my house?" I reach out to touch her shoulder but she shuns me and points her finger very near my face demanding that I promptly return everything I have done back to its original state. I realize this is not merely some ridiculous request but an expectation on her part bordering on the insane.

"Listen, just this morning I was paid to work on the grounds. That's what I did... what I was hired to do."

"You idiot!" she says grabbing the bottle of beer from my hand and smashing it upon the flagstones. "Can't you see they're using you? Once the work is complete they'll take it from me!" I ponder this amazing notion a moment. She evidently feels quite certain about it.

"I hardly believe that's anyone's intentions," I say softly. "They're just concerned about-"

"I don't need their concern!" she interjects. "I don't need it or want it!" she shouts.

"Audrey, they just want to see the place cleaned up."

"What's wrong with it? The way it is?" she asks and I'm speechless for she is totally sincere. "It's beautiful the way it is... unique... *look at the wild flowers*," she says then breaks. I take her arm but she pulls it away sharply. "I knew it, I knew you were a fool. I knew it in San Francisco." She shades her eyes to hide her sorrow. My body instantly, without thought, embraces her. I cradle her head in my arm and feel tears roll over my forearm. We remain like this for several minutes as the last rays of the sun cloak us in a rich golden glow, the sound of Vespas racing back and forth on the Rue de Fabron.

In a timeless moment, there in this wild garden coated in gold and pink hues, I experience a deep and profound affinity for her and this *unique* place. I look upon her with wonder, brush a strand of her golden-brown hair from the corner of her mouth and I feel a smile form upon my face.

"I almost forgot. Your cousin Noelle came by with her boyfriend earlier, around four." Audrey says nothing but turns to stare up at the first stars just glimmering in the indigo sky to the east; wiping tears from her eyes with the sleeve of her cotton shirt. "It was difficult to understand them but I'm pretty sure she was asking for her car." I look at her, no response whatsoever. "Did you hear me?" I ask softly. She sighs aloud and flashes me a perturbed look.

"That car is mine. It was given to me," she says. "She believes it belongs to her family because my uncle Giovanni is… a conniving bastard." I don't really react and this explanation seems adequate as far as I'm concerned.

I decide to finish repairing the main gate and spend the next hour doing so, securing the Ferrari firmly behind the two large wooden gates. When I return to the mezzo terrace all our bedding has been cleared.

I can see a faint glow on the third floor and make my way through the old villa with its bleak rooms and darkened passages eventually making the large main room on the third level. There's a double couch in the centre of the room separated by a common back and a couple antique chairs that have somehow been spared destruction. A small kitchenette sits off to one side of the room. She has lit several of the candles we had purchased earlier cloaking the room in a comfortable glow. I see a makeshift dinner of fruit and tomatoes, bread and cheese. There is a bottle of wine, several, of older vintage that she must have procured from somewhere within the villa. I pour a glass and sip it. The wine is extremely rich and excellent.

She is engaged with an old leather bound book and not particularly talkative. I help myself to the tomatoes that have been dressed with red wine and olive oil.

"Sorry about your beer," she says after some minutes without looking at me.

"I prefer the wine, it's excellent." She glances from behind the book she is reading. The title *Egypte*, in embossed gold, is underscored with a subtitle written entirely in French.

"The wine is from a hidden cellar down below," she says. "That one is a forty seven." She returns to her book. I look at the label and it's so old and provincial that it's unreadable, but it is perhaps the best I have ever had up to that point in my life.

I decide to write in my journal and we both become preoccupied for the better part of an hour until she closes her book and sits near me on the sofa.

"What are you writing?" she asks munching on a piece of baguette and pouring some of the second bottle I have just opened into one of the crystals which seems to have survived the sacking of the place.

"My journal," I say rubbing my eyes. She looks over my hand toward the page.

"You keep a journal?" she inquires and I nod. "About what?" I shrug not exactly sure of the question.

"About everything." She looks at me intently.

"Everything? Everything that you do with the company, with uncle Lucien?" I stare into her eyes wondering if this is going to bring some kind of adverse reaction.

"Yes." She looks over the page.

"You write about me?" she asks drawing closer. I can feel her soft warm breath on my neck.

"Sometimes," I say. She returns her gaze upon the page.

"I can't read your handwriting, it's terrible."

"I know, sometimes I can't even read what I write," I say and this makes her smile. I realize when she smiles it's like looking upon something precious, when she's upset it's like storm clouds and lightening. Suddenly, I take her cheek in the palm of my hand and kiss her gently, serenely, and for a fraction of a moment all these troubling things weighing upon my mind disappear; my life back in the States, the film work and the music industries I've left on the wayside. Her lips are sweet, like strawberries. She slowly retracts and stares deeply into my eyes.

"Why did you do that?" she whispers, calmly awaiting my answer to this question.

"Because…" I stop and she studies me intently then slowly shakes her head infinitesimally side to side.

"No…" she says as softly as falling snow. I watch her in the dim light, her eyes dilating wildly. "*You're betrothed*," she says and I'm awestruck by these words.

"What did you say?" I whisper.

"You heard me… you belong to Morgan… you're just very far away… and alone." I turn away and stare into the room.

"Morgan's left my life, it's finished," I say returning my gaze, remorse in my words. Audrey picks up her glass and sips the dark crimson wine while her eyes burn into mine.

"You don't understand what's happening at all. One part of you does… the stupid part doesn't."

"The stupid part?" I ask and she nods.

"Right." Her gaze is unrelenting. "You actually have no idea what she gave up for you... do you?" I'm uncertain her meaning, saying nothing. This reaction causes her to rise and stroll the dark room and study me from afar. She slowly begins to extinguish some of the candles. "She's given up everything because of you." I'm shocked by this proclamation.

"What do you mean?"

"What do you think I mean?" she asks and waits. I shake my head. "You've no idea?" I'm at a complete loss as to what she's saying or if she's rambling. She extinguishes the last candle except the lone one between the double sofa upon which I sit. She takes the other couch opposite me, the candle's flame between us, reflecting within the pupils of her eyes.

"I'm afraid I don't understand you at all," I say eventually and this makes her smile, but it's a mocking smile and it makes me squirm.

"She left her lover because of you."

"What are you talking about?"

"Severin."

"Who is Severin?"

"I just told you... her lover... and, unfortunately, her employer," she says. I can't hold her gaze any longer. I stare at the candle flame as it burns without the slightest movement, like silk. "I would never believe it could have happened," she says quietly, "out of the blue..." I look at her as she stares into the light and the flame leaps softly. "I mean... she didn't understand it either. We talked about it all night long, over and over, until dawn. Several nights. I told her not to-" She catches herself and I see the reaction in her face.

"Not to what?" She looks at me squarely.

"Not to get involved with you," she says and the same intense look emerges within her eyes. "Now… now I'm not so sure," she says, a slight smile curves the edges of her mouth. "I'm beginning to get it."

"Get what?"

"What's happening… in New Orleans, it all comes together somehow… and it would never have happened if-" she stops again and shakes her head.

"What? If what?" She looks at me hard in the meager light, taking one last, long sip of wine, draining the glass.

"Never mind. Go to sleep," she says rising, picking up my blanket and pillow and tossing them atop where I sit. "You can go sleep by the door Casanova," she says but I'm already deep in thought about what she's been saying. Part of me is concerned by this discussion yet another part of me feels a deep longing. I watch as Audrey clears things to the kitchenette and begins brushing her teeth with a bottle of Evian water. When she's finished she returns to the couch and begins to undress. At an appropriate point, she blows out the candle flame and finishes undressing in the dark. I see her form silhouetted against the night sky that frames the terrace windows in a deep indigo blue.

"Go sleep in front of the door," she says from the darkness.

"What?" I say. "What's wrong with this side of the couch?"

"You heard me, over there," she says. "In case someone tries to come in, you'll know it."

"Someone? Like who?"

"Do it you chickenshit," she says and her sandal lands squarely across my forehead.

"Ouch! Dammit!" I shout and I can hear her muffled giggle from beneath her blanket.

Reluctantly I move to the door and stretch my body out across the cold stone floor. What a strange creature a woman is, I think to myself; men too I think, look at me, agreeing to be a human doorstop! Eventually I become lost in thoughts about Morgan. I ponder the things Audrey has said. Betrothed? What does she mean? I roll these thoughts over and over in my mind until I'm engulfed in a deep and soundless sleep.

Suddenly, I'm wide-awake and disoriented in the darkness. I've forgotten where I am. It takes a moment before I realize I'm in Nice and Audrey is kneeling beside where I sleep.

"What's going on?" I ask and she shushes me. I sit up and stare at her in the moonlight. "What are you doing?" I ask and she holds a finger to my lips.

"Please be quiet will you and listen," she whispers.

"To what?" I ask and she is very close to me.

"*Someone is in the house.*" These words immediately grip my heart like a vice. We both sit quietly listening, nothing, utter silence.

"I don't hear anything."

"I heard someone… voices," she says almost on top of me. I strain to listen and think she is imagining things when I do hear something that brings all my senses to bear. I begin to make out the sounds of someone, more than one person, *downstairs within the villa.*

"Get dressed, but be quiet about it," I whisper and she does this. I put on my socks and boots and find the length of steel pipe I had picked up the previous evening and had on hand, for just such an emergency. I carefully open the door and commence to exit the room when a hand grabs my shoulder causing me to start.

"Where are you going?" she whispers intensely. "Don't leave."

"I need to see what's going on. I'll be right back." I slip outside into the absolute blackness of the hallway and peer over the railing that separates the third floor landing from the stairwell. I carefully descend the darkened stairs to the second level and gaze around the disheveled chaos of the hall staring back at me in a vacant stillness. Just at the point I think I must have been hearing voices from the street, I see the beam of a flashlight cutting through the darkness below and the unmistakable sound of men's voices. As I watch from the shadows, I realize that a group of strangers are unmistakably making their way through the house room by room. I quietly return upstairs.

"Find something to wedge beneath this door."

"Who are they?"

"I don't know… men, they seem to be searching the house."

"Why? They're trespassing. Get rid of them. Tell them to leave."

"They're speaking in a foreign language," I say. She curses and immediately scours the room stumbling over something.

"I can't see!" she says, lighting a candle.

"They'll see the light," I say but she isn't listening as she looks for something to secure the door. I curse under my breath.

Suddenly there's a commotion from the stairwell and I can see a flashlight beam beneath the door. They've seen the candlelight. There's really no choice but to confront them. I yank open the door and shout.

"Who are you? Leave immediately!" I'm instantly cloaked in the light of a bright flashlight. There's shouting down the stairwell and the sound of footsteps upon the stairs. We're

instantly confronted by three dark strangers their flashlight
blinding our eyesight.

"What do you want? Leave before we call the police," I
shout and they mutter to each other. I hear the word
Americain repeated. When Audrey appears over my shoulder
and shouts at them in French their responses are not to my
liking at all. I hear –and sense- a distinct unsettling tone in
their words and meaning.

They *push* their way into the room and we've really no
choice but to recede back into the chamber and keep a
distance between us. Although they are in shadow, just
enough of the candlelight reveals three very unpleasant faces,
pitted and ugly, and a dread begins to creep inside my chest.

They look about the room with impunity as Audrey
exchanges a very animated dialogue with them until they
begin to shout, obscenities apparently, and she recoils behind
me growing quiet. When one of the men suddenly advances
upon us grabbing for her arm I swing the pipe, catching the
knuckles and he curses violently. I begin to realize they are
probably workmen from the chantile next door and have been
watching our coming and going, in particular Audrey. It
becomes quite evident when the leader of the group suddenly
speaks to me in very broken English. He asks if I'm
American but I won't answer him. When he approaches I try
to strike him with the pipe and he curses loudly.

"What do you want? Go away. Leave us alone!" I shout at
him and brandish the pipe menacingly. His response is to
withdraw a large switchblade and engage the blade. He then
tells me to leave the house, that they are only interested in *the
car and the girl*. I can feel Audrey's grip upon my arm
tighten. I tell him what he can do with his knife and his
friends laugh. He orders one of them downstairs and the man

begrudgingly heads below taking the flashlight with him, cursing all the while.

The leader and his accomplice begin to rummage through our belongings and curse at each other when they seem to find nothing much of value, arguing over my camera.

"Get out!" I shout and they turn their attention to us, the other man also extending a stiletto.

"Hey man, give me keys to the car. You go... leave the girl... okay? Cool?" he says and grows irritated when I say nothing. "You leave man, now, or I cut you!" Audrey shouts at them and they laugh at us. I keep Audrey behind me with one arm and attempt to lunge and take out the first's knife but he's too quick and immediately counter-thrusts grazing the top of my forearm. "Quit fuckin' round man, go!" he shouts thrusting the blade menacingly. The other tries to grab Audrey who screams and I nearly cave his head in but he ducks just in time, reeling backward swearing to beat the devil. The two speak together in French and Audrey whispers in my ear:

"They're going to attack us at the same time, from the sides," she says, desperation in her voice. I tell her to stay behind me.

Just as they set up for this attack, which I know will end badly for us *we hear the most horrible scream from downstairs within the villa*. It is a bloodcurdling scream of horror. The men freeze, staring at each other, then at the door and question each other. They listen intently and we hear again, more fainter this time, what sounds to me *like a man in the throes of death*. One of the assailants, the second, goes to the door and shouts a name down into the darkness and waits for an answer that never arrives. There's a flurry of words between the two men and I ask Audrey what's going on.

"The one man is ordering the other to go downstairs... to find out what's happening," she whispers in my ear nearly breathless.

"What *is* happening?" I ask.

"I don't know... something weird. Something-" She's cut short by a horrid scream that seems to end abruptly, and the entire room, the entire building, is frozen in an absolute silence. The first man shouts then grabs at the second, shouting and slapping at him to go below and the man, extremely reluctantly, goes out calling the third man's name. The leader immediately turns on us.

"What you doin' man?" he says in a sudden fear induced rage. "What shit is this?!" he spits, then shouts the question again. He then wipes his brow with his shirtsleeve. "Okay man," he says, "keep the bitch, just give me keys," he says then brandishes the knife. "C'mon, c'mon give me keys!" he orders. I whisper to Audrey just behind my left arm.

"Maybe we should do as he says."

"Up yours!" she shouts at the man, saying to me, "that car is a part of me. It has a consciousness. I'm not giving *her* to this... ape!" I feel a heavy weight grip my heart.

"Stupid bitch!" the man spits venomously. "C'mon man, give me keys and you go," he says and Audrey curses at him in French. "Stupid bitch!" he screams and lunges at me with the knife. I keep him off us with the end of the pipe. "Huh man?!" he spits. "You gonna get fucked up man!" We are forced to back up, circling the couch, his thrusting and my parrying. Audrey throws one of the bottles of wine across the room. He ducks it cursing at her, an onslaught of what I perceive as the most foul words and ill desires.

This horrid game goes on for what seems an eternity. I want to bash his skull in, but he's obviously skilled with a knife and fighting. I realize if this continues he will eventually breach my defense. He suddenly crosses over the island that the couch presents knocking over the candle and the room goes nearly black. I realize our situation is beyond perilous. I tell Audrey when he attacks me that she needs to run for her life and wake the neighbor next door.

Then the most unbelievable, most unnerving and incredible thing I have ever witnessed happens. Just before what I know will be a fatal attack upon my person there is a sudden commotion at the door and just as if watching some kind of grotesque horror film, an enormous gaping shadow enters the room and arrests all our attentions. I hear Audrey gasp from behind me, feel her nails cut into the flesh of my arm.

The shadow apparition is a frightening hunched form that *growls and spits fury incarnate*; it seethes with a primordial rage that shocks me to the core of my being. This thing, this man, whatever it is, emits a horrible heavy animal-like breathing, a thick viscous guttural intonation. The man with the knife screams out –not like a man would scream but like a cornered animal in a mortal dread. He brandishes the blade before him, dim in the meager moonlight.

The creature, takes up the furniture that separates them casting it aside as a man might discard a toy, then exhales the most vehement howl into the face of the assailant who simply crumbles, dropping the knife and whimpering like a sick cur, backing into the bank of terrace windows. The hunched form paces him, in a predatory fashion, shadowing his every step. Suddenly in an explosive lurch, the creature lunges into the assailant shattering the panes and we watch in horror as the man goes backward over the railing, falling three stories to the flagstones below.

This unworldly being pauses a moment upon the parapet. I see its form clearly under the moonlight. It rages, howling into the night, a chilling canine like wailing. Then, slowly *it turns toward us.*

I feel Audrey bury her face into my arm, her nails drawing blood from the flesh of my arm. The thing approaches us in the darkness in a long staggered lurch that bears no resemblance to the human gait. I'm completely frozen in the sheer horror of the moment, locked stock-still with fright. Its labored breathing is most frightening and foul and quite unearthly. I fear we will be torn asunder by this *demon in the dark.*

Then a most amazing thing transpires. The creature stops before us, breathing heavily, an absolute black silhouette against the shattered glass reflecting shards of moonlight. It stares at us unrelentingly for what seems forever; then ever so slowly it *retraces its steps and disappears over the railing.* I feel the vice-like grip of her fingernails release and I'm completely in awe as we stand silently in the darkness. Audrey again buries her face in my shoulder, apparently at pains to comprehend what is so utterly fantastic as to seem like a dream, or more appropriately a shared lucid nightmare.

The creature suddenly rages from below, a bone-chilling howl. It takes all my reserve, but I manage the fear that grips me and force myself to the terrace, carefully threading my way through the busted door frame and peer over the railing in time to see the man dragging his horribly disfigured leg, toward the direction of the boulevard beyond. I realize one of the cherry trees must have broken his fall, and his leg. I scan the area below and spy an enormous dark shape, slip over the east wall *like a shadow gliding under moonlight.* I watch as it winds its way silently down the vast hillside ravine, soon obscured by overhanging trees and is gone.

When I return to the room Audrey is standing alone amid the total wreckage of the apartment. She is shaking, her entire body physically convulsing. As I calm her I inadvertently gasp. I realize the shadow has returned within the frame of the door leading downstairs. We both watch as *an ebony form silently penetrates the room.*

I then remember I still possess the Mag-light upon my belt. I retrieve it and turn it on and we are both startled by the *outre visage of a dark, brown-skinned woman clothed entirely in black!* Her head is wrapped in an ebony scarf and her entire body is enveloped within a flowing black garment. I'm about to retrieve the pipe to defend us when Audrey firmly takes my arm.

"It's Madame Houri."

The dark woman holds up her hand shadowing her face from the glare of the light and I'm shocked to see strange inscriptions –*and a tattoo of an eye*- upon the face of the palm, eerily looking back at us. Audrey catches my wrist lowering the flashlight. She searches and quickly procures one of the candles, lighting it with the butane from her pocket. The candle sheds a soft luminous glow and I stare at this *shadow woman* and she stares at me before turning to Audrey.

"Audra, have you been injured?" she asks in the deep and accented voice of the Middle East.

"No," Audrey answers, "we're… we're alright." The dark woman's gaze returns to me and her eyes are deep ebony jewels reflecting the thin light from the candle creating a mysterious and unsettling feeling within my chest.

"Who is this man?" she asks and Audrey tells her. "*So! This is the acolyte. The one of which I've heard spoken,*" she says in a most queer manner and slowly approaches me and stares. She then extends a long garbed arm holding her hand out to me. "I am Houri," she says. After a momentary pause, I take her hand in mine and she clasps it for several long heartbeats as if unwilling to relinquish her grip. "*I have desired we meet,*" she says.

After an uncomfortably long and silent stare she turns toward Audrey again.

"Audra… why is it you are afraid? Do you not understand? This is now your home. Nothing ill shall befall you while you remain within these walls. This… horrible event tonight, these evil men… this was unfortunate. You've nothing to fear, *it has been resolved,*" and the way she says these last words make me involuntarily shudder.

She takes up Audrey's hand. I clearly see she's ill at-ease with the dark Oriental woman. "You're trembling… why?" she asks. Audrey looks at her and even in the darkness I can see the tears welling up in her eyes. "Surely you know Anton cherishes you above all. He would never allow… *anything,* to harm you. You are safe here. To do whatever you chose." She looks over at me. "To be with whomever you chose." Audrey nods, saying nothing. Houri seems to accept this reluctant acknowledgment. She then paces about the room, canvassing the surround, the sound of broken glass beneath her soles. "Shall I acquire assistance in clearing the damage?" she asks staring blankly at the ruined windows and torn and shredded furniture.

"No Madame Houri, that won't be necessary," Audrey says quietly. This seems to placate the woman's concern.

"Very well. Is there anything you require?" she asks and Audrey shakes her head.

"No." Houri bows her head gently and embracing Audrey, kisses her on both cheeks and looks upon her approvingly.

"You are so very lovely my dear... so very, very lovely. It is our desire that you are joyous here, upon these grounds. Santana is now *your* home... please, relax yourselves." Audrey looks at her and smiles but it is not her genuine smile, it's the one I see when she is at odds with the conversation, but it has the desired effect for the strange woman beams –if the word applies- and she commences to leave. "Au revoir, mon petite," she says. Audrey simply nods. As she begins to exit, Houri stops a moment to gaze intently at me. "Enchante, monsieur. To finally meet... as the English say it... *person to person.*" Again a sudden chill courses my body.

"My pleasure," I choke out. Her eyes seem to dilate in the darkness and after the briefest pause she flows silently out the door.

I carefully follow her and peer over the railing of the stairwell to witness how she can navigate in such utter darkness but it's as silent as a tomb and she's nowhere to be seen. I cannot even hear the tread of her feet. When I return to the room Audrey is frantically packing her belongings.

"What are you doing?" I ask.

"Getting the hell out of here." I watch as she moves quickly through the room collecting her meager things and packing them in her tiny bag.

"You're leaving me here?" I ask and she freezes at this comment staring at me, the most incredulous look upon her face.

"Are you serious Willem?" she says. "You stand up for me, then ask me a question like that? That's the kind of person you think I am?" she shouts and I watch helplessly as her eyes tear up again. "Why are you so goddamn obtuse?" she shouts. I stand there like I've been slapped. She places her face in her hands for a moment then looks at me. "Look, I'm sorry, but you're so… so…" She clenches her fists then lets go. "Of course you're coming… the car seats two. That's unless you *want* to stay here for some reason?" I assure her of the contrary. "Then get your shit together!" she shouts.

We load what little we have in the cramped space the Testarossa offers and she immediately speeds off into the night, not even taking the time to secure the gate behind us. When I ask her about returning the money I had been paid that morning she ignores me.

We get onto the westbound Autoroute A8 just outside of Nice quickly climbing to the speed of one hundred and seventy kilometres per hour and never slow down. We cut through the slower moving cars and lorries lumbering their way west like a predator bird soaring through the slow movement of clouds.

I attempt to converse with her, to come to grips with what has happened, but *something inextricable* locks her attention solely upon the road unwinding before us like a cascade of dark water. It's as if she's gone catatonic. The quality, the sereneness of her eyes and manner, has given way to a dark intensity, an intensity that is unnerving to some aspect of my mind. I stare into the night rushing in on us like a man caught within a torrent.

A8 soon turns into A7 north of Aix-en-Provence where I succumb to a kind of inner surrender. The hum of the machine and smooth rapid flow of the road –coupled with the night's taxing unreality- eventually lulls me into a deep dreamless sleep.

I awaken just before dawn, two hundred kilometres south of Paris, the world awash in an antediluvian gray twilight. Audrey stares ahead, transfixed by the road unwinding before us, fully engaged with the machine. I glance at the speedometer, just over one hundred and eighty kilometres per hour. I try to talk with her. She mutters some incoherent words without lifting her gaze from the on-rushing stream of concrete and asphalt. She seems inextricably mesmerized by the press of the road. All about us is a constant onrushing of time and space. I reach for my cigarette pack and find it empty.

Dawn breaks, pink over the rolling fields. Sporadic patches of dark forest, tinted in golden morning light, appear mystical, and are immediately gone. I look at my mysterious traveling companion and attempt again to open conversation but I quickly realize whatever has enveloped her attention is inexorable.

The speed of the Ferrari is no longer alarming but the antithesis. Despite the auto's speed, I watch the onrushing road with a strange, compelling attachment, *as if I wish the road never to end*. I know she is intrinsically locked with the vehicle, as if one with the machine, fluid, the woman and the car moving together, breaking when the slower vehicles get in the way and then rapidly accelerating to speed, the engine humming under the high velocity. I stretch and settle back into the seat, cracking the window and absorb the roar of the wind outside.

When we make Paris, it is well into the morning commute and already hot. The traffic is thick, the smell of the ancient city saturating the orange misty haze. We vie for position within the maw of cars, lorries and motorcycles until we arrive at the Gare de Austerlitz with its iron beam surrounds and contingent of people, baggage and trains.

After washing the blood from my arms in the men's lavatory, I wait at the car. Audrey disappears for the better part of an hour; when she finally returns her manner, albeit more grounded, is still detached. She confesses the need to return to the States, to New Orleans, and asks if I might meet her later at a certain cafe in Saint Michel. My mind appeals to it but something inside me knows it will be the last I will see of her on this trip.

Indeed, this turns out to be the case. Our rendezvous that afternoon in St. Michel is a traditional Parisian cafe. I wait, sipping black coffee and writing my recollection of this most extraordinary experience until the sun tires and grows faint. I pay for the table, tipping my gracious waiter one of the hundred euro notes Margaret had given me only twenty-four hours prior.

"Your friend, the girl, she, no show?" he asks in his broken English. I shake my head. He clicks his tongue in mock sorrow. "C'est un femme," he says shrugging both shoulders and taking up the note. "Merci mon ami… adieu."

Slinging my weathered bag across my back, I wander off into the electrified Parisian evening. All sorts of thoughts and feelings pass through my mind, a kind of melancholy caused by the loss of her companionship –coupled with the macabre nocturnal encounter of the previous night- burdens my progress through the dank cobblestone streets.

I make my way to the company's office in Saint Denis; really nothing more than an apartment, an old relic, that sits atop a bar, *The Richlieu,* just off the principal boulevard, the Rue de St. Denis. I stare at the building and laugh aloud to myself. She has delivered me from deep within the Sud du France almost to the company's doorstep.

I retrieve the key from Andrico, the proprietor of the Richlieu. He is shocked by my appearance apparently, for he fails at first to recognize me.

"Marde! What have you been doing?" he inquires passing me a bottle of the Beaujolais Noveau newly arrived from the south.

"Where do I begin?" I say. He refuses the bill I hold out.

"On the house effendi, you need it." He disappears down the length of the old mahogany bar, like a wooden barge laden with salty men adrift in a sea of tranquility.

Ascending the slow curving staircase, cut entirely of stone, I unlatch the door and enter. A musty familiar scent greets my nose and memories of earlier days, my first days here, flood me, nearly overwhelming me. I drop my things where they lay and despite my desire to bathe, I only accomplish opening the wine.

As I sit within the silence of the apartment, I'm enveloped with a deep longing for Morgan. I think deeply about her, wonder about her, what she's doing at this moment and fight the most earnest desire to phone her in New Orleans. All of our days and nights together pass through my mind *moment to moment from the very first time my eyes saw her.* The more I delve within these memories the more I'm overcome with sorrow. I long to understand the reasons behind why we are apart.

As the minutes slowly become hours, the loss I feel begins to give way to a sense of inner fascination. A fascination of the mysteries of life; the sad yet wonderful duality of the human experience, the human being, *alone yet one with the immense unfathomable universe,* and strangely, I become cognizant that this same energy, this same flowing, that brought us together is the same energy that pulls us distantly apart; like a sudden rogue wind blowing a ship off its predestined course onto a new and stranger destination unknown.

The Damned

I land in Heathrow from Roissey and take a cab to Soho, right to the front door of *The Riker Pub*, requesting the cabbie to wait at the curb. In truth I have not a pound left and have misplaced the company's credit card, which had come up missing during the rapid departure from Nice. I had phoned Beryl Collins, the company's implacable chief controller, from Paris and in her excruciatingly proper English manner told me: *'See Philippe upon arrival, he'll have the necessary recompense in hand, then report to me immediately.'*

"She's waiting for you," Philippe says in his particular accent –from France's Basque region.
"Who is?"
"The accountant," he says giving me a look. I slump onto one of the stools and order a stout. "Tsch-tsch…" he says shaking his head, "you don't look so good." He places a pint of ale before me. "Je travail?" I drink deeply and think about telling him my recent experiences when we simultaneously spy an all too familiar door open in the rear of the bar and the proper image of Ms. Collins emerges, cutting a direct path through the smoky environment in my direction. Philippe excuses himself under false pretenses and cowardly slips away leaving me to face her alone.

Beryl Collins is another enigma. A more pragmatic and practical woman I have never met in my life. She's the centerpiece of the company's varied arrangements and capital expenditures. Nothing escapes her keen intellect in the matters of travel or finance. How such a woman became involved in a company such as *Karras and Corbeau*, with its mystical and bizarre enterprises and its strange amorphous cast of characters coming and going is the principle part of the mystery.

She sides up to me at the bar, eyeing the drink in my hand, and without uttering a word slaps a manila envelope on the bar beside me.

"Beryl," I stammer, "I've no idea how I lost the company card. It may have been when-"

"The card has been cancelled, the new one is in the packet. You'll need it Stateside," she says in an uncharacteristically casual tone.

"Stateside?" She stares at me blankly through her horn-rimmed bifocals.

"Surely you've been in contact with Lucien, you've spoken?"

"No... I've been a little out of touch. What's it about?" Her response is patented.

"Why should I know the details dear boy? Here is your transit packet. You're flying in three hours for a meeting in New York... and you'd better get cleaned up. She's some kind of socialite. A magazine editor, or some such nonsense." She looks me over, head to toe, exhales loudly and retreats back to her private domain and I'm left to ponder what has just transpired. I examine the envelope as Philippe finds reason to amble back over.

"Incroyable," he mutters low. "The head," he says tapping my forehead hard with his index finger, "-is still on." I rub my forehead, and open the package; an airline ticket from

Heathrow to JFK departing in three hours, eight one hundred dollar bills in American currency, the new credit card and an address and time of meeting.

"Ms. Severin Marchaud, senior editor, Perle Magazine," I whisper aloud. The package also contains a telex from Lucien. *'Pls meet w/Ms. Marchaud re: Morgan's estate in NY. Ms. Marchaud is her editor and confidante. Lucien.'* I look at Philippe's wondering expression. He gazes at the note in my hand sensing my concern.

"Comme?"

"Morgan's employer in New York."

"Who is Morgan?" Philippe asks. I can only stare at him.

I arrive at the warehouse studio in New York well in advance of the meeting with Ms. Marchaud. I gaze up at the building, the now familiar gothic façade. This time it's as if reuniting with an old friend, the strange peculiar building looks down at me in a welcoming manner.

Inside, I switch on the lights and pull back the heavy black drapes that cover the wall of glass overlooking the street below. The camera and flash equipment are nowhere to be seen, nor the Macintosh computers and monitors, but the magazines and photographs remain.

As I again stroll the old warehouse I become engaged by the artwork. I study the large canvasses more closely and realize that the artist is none other than she. I'm shocked this detail had escaped me earlier. As I survey the tables and desktops I begin to take notice of what I perceive as inertia. There's a coat of dust forming upon the tables and their contents. Also the workspace has become littered with ashtrays full of cigarette butts, scores of empty beer bottles and a few empty bottles of Glenlivet scotch. The girls have been visiting.

I decide to make a cup of coffee and grind some Kona beans. I open the refrigerator door to double check if there might be cream. The coffee is delicious and soon the pensive feeling in my mind subsides, just in time to witness the door open of its own accord and an attractive blonde woman –who I believe to be in her early fifties- peers in.

I rise to my feet surprised I hadn't heard the bell when I realize she has let herself in with her own key. She starts a moment when I stand, then gently closes the door and addresses me.

"You're the man from Karras and Corbeau?" she canvasses the apartment as if expecting someone else.

"Yes," I say extending my hand, "Willem Furey."

"Has Morgan arrived with you?" she asks shaking my hand, a large sapphire ring and thin, jeweled wrist. I'm uncertain how to answer and wait for her eyes to meet mine, deep dreamy blue irises, active, aware. Her hair is very stylish and her dress shows her elegant figure. "She's here?"

"No, I'm afraid not." She withdraws her hand and looks at me.

"Can you tell me where she is and how I might reach her please?" her manner becoming intense, a person who expects answers to her immediate questions.

"Louisiana," I say not breaking her gaze and she silently stares into me for a moment.

"I thought she was in San Francisco, at her mother's home?"

"Yes she was, however, now she's in New Orleans at her family's estate." This information seems to affect her strangely, her eyes exhibiting a mixture of impatience and concern. She pinches her lip with her perfectly manicured fingers.

"Is there a reason she isn't returning my calls? Has something happened?"

"I don't know how to answer that," I say and she studies me intensely. "Please sit down, may I make you a cup of coffee?" She doesn't respond to this question, only taps her graceful fingers upon the table and gazes about the apartment, obviously considering something more important than a cup of coffee. I decide to make her one anyway. When I look back, she is closely studying the photography on the worktable.

"I'm sorry there's no cream," I say over my shoulder.

"Black is fine." She is looking over a series of photographs printed on glossy paper, proofs I assume, of a thin young woman in ripped blue jeans and a black suit coat walking a corgi, some markings upon them in light blue pencil. She takes the cup and nods at the photography. "This was the last campaign we were working on," the accent in her voice more noticeable, Swedish I believe, mixed with French, "our last project," she says softly, becoming aloof. I study her closely a moment before looking over the proofs.

"Very nice," I say and she snaps back from her reverie.

"Can you guess the product?" I look closer at the photography. The model looks to be approximately twenty so years of age with thin wispy brown hair. The cuffs of what looks to be a man's dress jacket are rolled up the arms. I study the model's face and consider the various elements within the frame; the earrings too insignificant and the hair lacks the polished sheen always prevalent in hair ads. Her make-up is nearly non-existent. There's nothing really special about the jeans or shoes. I point at the watch, a rather large affair that struck me as dramatic within the frame.

"It's either the watch, or the jacket."

"You're correct, but which?" I take a moment before answering.

"The jacket," I say and she smiles, a slight curving of her beautiful mouth.

"Why?"

"I believe it's a man's jacket she's wearing."

"Are you a photographer?"

"I used to work in cinema, currently I work for the firm."

"Karras and Corbeau."

"Yes."

"And what sort of work do they do?" I'm hesitant to jump into this question.

"What did they tell you when you called?" I ask and the dreamy quality in her gaze diminishes.

"I know Mr. Karras," she states flatly. "Very well. I have a high opinion of him. In fact, he helped me in the recent past. Something very personal... that I appreciate dearly." I recognize the reaction, the desire to speak about something profound but the inability –or reluctance- to put to words. "I phoned him regarding Morgan."

"What did he say?" I ask and she stares at me oddly.

"He said to expect your visit."

I tell her everything I know, or feel I can divulge to her. She thinks deeply about it all for several minutes, then states abruptly:

"I would very much appreciate your arranging a meeting between Morgan and myself in New Orleans... immediately, I'll cover all expenses, your fee as well."

"I appreciate your concern, however, I'm incapable of arranging it."

"Why is that? Is she in some kind of trouble?"

"Not in the least, she's safely with her family."

"Why then?" she presses and I confess to her that we are currently incommunicado. She compresses her temple with the ends of her fingers and I can see that something is suddenly troubling her.

"Am I to believe you've had no contact from Morgan about this, whatsoever?" There's a long intense look as she studies me before she extracts a hand written letter from her bag, post marked San Francisco, and hands it to me.

Dearest Severin,

Please excuse my last phone call, and what's happened, my disappearing again. I'm sure this feels all too familiar, however life takes me in sudden and unexpected parallels. I'll soon be traveling east, to New Orleans. I've made up my mind to do so. I realize we are at a critical stage with the campaign, you've made it all too clear, however there's really nothing I can do about it at this juncture. This involves my mother and my family.

Regarding your last message, I'm alright Severin, I don't want you to worry. This is a confusing time and I'm not purposefully avoiding you, however, something has been set into motion and I must see it through.

I miss you terribly. I need you to understand, that I do care about you, and think of you daily. It is this love I hold for you that compels me to tell you, something so very painful. Something else has happened, something unseen, unexpected. I have fallen in love Severin, amidst all this turmoil in my life. I didn't seek it, nor desire it, and for what it's worth, I'm estranged from him now as well, he who holds my heart. So,

I've hurt him deeply and now you. What shall I do? What can I say? Please forgive me.
Always, M

I feel myself go numb, like falling into ice water. Holding my head in my fingertips, I just stare at the letter. When I do raise my eyes, her gaze grows misty and the cerulean irises glisten.

"It's you, isn't it?" she says. "You are the *he* in the letter." I don't know what to say so I say nothing. She places her hand across her mouth momentarily, then slowly, mechanically takes a card from her purse and sets it upon the table and quietly moves to leave. At the door she pauses. "We obviously need to talk... but, I can't... not tonight... tomorrow," she says and leaves, gently closing the door.

That night I can't sleep. My mind continues to mull over the week's events. Lying upon Morgan's bed, I breathe in the scent of her hair from the pillow beneath my head and I become lost in memories of her. I recall an evening in San Francisco after watching a film. This is a week, perhaps, after my return from Bratislava.

We're having drinks at a small dessert bar and I bring up the subject of her employment again. She has consistently avoided speaking about the topic for days and I press the issue light-heartedly.

"Your boss is going to fire you," I joke and suddenly a most dramatic change comes over her. In awe, I watch as her tranquil green eyes cloud over and tears begin to fall into her wine. I cannot believe this rapid transformation, or why the subject of her profession would cause it. As I attempt to press her about the sudden change overcoming her, she takes up her purse and abruptly exits into the night. I'm at a complete loss.

I race after her, chasing her down the block to the next intersection. I take her shoulders and try to look into her eyes but she won't make eye contact with me. I ask her what's wrong, she won't tell me. When a cab approaches she waves it over, the cabbie pulling up to the curb and in total wonderment I watch as she gets in, closing the door and the cab speeds off. When I return to the house on Sutter Street it's in complete darkness. I ascend the stairs and carefully enter her room. She is asleep on her side facing the window. I gently lie down beside her and wrap my arm across her. She doesn't stir nor make a sound and this is the way we sleep until the morning.

I'm dreaming. I know I'm dreaming, aware of a sense of volition... to move and think. In the dream I'm back on the photo shoot with Morgan but it is no longer the pastoral Palace of Fine Arts but an enclosed and darkened environment, like a studio or soundstage. Everyone is milling about her. When she moves, I'm shocked by what I see. She is strikingly tall, perhaps seven feet in height and entirely clad in black, not cloth but a kind of black poly suit that is littered with tubes and wires. When she turns and shakes her head it's not the gentle dark tresses of her natural hair but a series of tubes and wires jutting out the back of her head that rattle with a thin metallic sound. Her face is there, somewhat, but the entirety of her head is like an electrical contraption and I realize, almost a horror, that she has *become a living machine.* Her right eye carries a large lens that pops and whirs and she snaps away at an *endless parade* of strange and weird persons that pass before her, some in garish costume, some naked or scantily clothed. She spies me and moves to where I stand watching. Her left eye looks into mine but the right, really just a lens, buzzes and whirs, even the tips of her fingers are small cameras and lights. Again they crowd about her obscuring my presence. She moves side to side snapping pictures through the cameras mounted in her skull and the cables and wires extending from the back of her head, trail down to the floor like long flowing hair. Once more, she strides over to where I stand and says in a weird ringing voice:

"Just a few more and we can leave." Again she's swallowed by the melee, the minions all gathering about her great ebony form. I'm so uncomfortable I know I need to wake myself from this strange and bizarre dream but I can't seem to muster the presence to do it. I suddenly overhear a dark group of people standing around me discussing someone. Try as I might, I cannot see who they are.

"She'll be back, and it will be like nothing ever happened," someone says.

"Who? Who are you talking about?" I suddenly hear myself asking aloud. There's some muttering and whispering.

"You're not wanted here, *she belongs to us*," they say demurely. I force myself away from this sullen place, away into blackness. When I awaken, I immediately look at the digital clock beside the bed that reads: 5:05 AM. For some unexplainable reason I clearly see, S:OS.

The following evening, Severin and I are seated together at Nobu restaurant. The environment is muted. I watch her from the recesses of my vision. She orders for us. I'm happy to have her do it as I feel my mind is not working at all. It's as if it quit working in Nice... perhaps it was earlier, the desert.

Her choice of fare is excellent and she orders a bottle of white wine.

"I had gone to a small gallery in The Village owned by a friend and saw the most incredible black and white photography... people mostly. The photographer showed exceptional ability, not only on a technical level, but also a psychological... or perhaps I would even say *a spiritual* level... the sensitivity of the eyes, the look of these people as if in their natural environments without a camera in their face. You know... that's a rare feeling in photography, the sensation that the camera doesn't exist at all. I bought the entire collection for the offices at Perle Magazine, after all what a wonderful contrast to the work Perle was shooting at the time, which was a bright, all color palette, primary colors with very little reference to the human context, the human experience... which is exactly where we went next."

"After Morgan joined your company?" I ask and she softly laughs.

"Not initially, not at first. I started her on really small, drab assignments but it wasn't long before clients were requesting her unique style of shooting. Eventually one particular client, a very prominent client, wanted her to shoot all their campaigns, that set it in motion."

"It?"

"When the magazine started making a name for itself." The waitress brings the appetizers and this keeps her preoccupied a moment.

"So she burst like a bright flame upon the scene?" I say more to break the ensuing silence; again, the gentle elegant laugh.

"Hardly I should think," she says softly. "She had sold nearly her entire studio. It took a bit of... husbanding, to bring that girl in, she was… just a little bit wild," she says oddly. "But it became almost like an obsession with me. After all, brilliance is undeniable. It took a year before she became one of our A-list shooters, a lot of work… a lot of… time…" She seems to falter and even in the meager light I can see her blue eyes cloud over with moisture, however, she's a person of self-control, used to running an agency and quickly covers her emotions. "We've been together many years," she says and our eyes lock.

"Professionally? Or… personally?" She looks into my eyes. I'm enthralled by the depth of her gaze; an inner knowledge. She closes them for several heartbeats and when she returns her attention, her eyes are moist, reflecting the soft light of the room.

"I've broken her heart," she says. "Oh yes, not just once… a number of times. How can I tell you… a complete stranger? I'm vain. I admit to it… but Morgan…" She stares into the room, past the walls and people, out into infinity. "Morgan should never have happened in my life. She's beautiful you know… how could you not fall in love? Such a unique, sensitive woman…"

The following silence is excruciating. As if to break it, she addresses the sapphire ring on her finger.

"This sapphire… she gave it to me. Do you know about the sapphire?" she inquires and I shake my head. "The Buddhists believe the sapphire can open the spirit to man… that it produces more peace than any other gem… but to wear it, one must lead a… unencumbered life. Perhaps I've no right to wear it… but I'll never take it off… not in this lifetime."

The entrees arrive. We quietly set about eating together, her table etiquette impeccable. She then asks me a series of questions about myself, eventually about how Morgan and I came to know each other.

"It's important, you know," she says, "this thing we call friendship. Why it is there. Where it comes from. It should never be taken for granted. I doubt there's a single close relationship I possess that doesn't owe itself to some kind of commonality, some kind of... *quiet connection*, with the other... the words that are spoken..." she shakes her head. "I don't understand it really. I just know it when I feel it," she says gazing deeply into my eyes, "when I see it." I wonder what she's thinking as she studies me unrelentingly. "I see it in you. Why you've come together. I believe it was Voltaire who wrote, *'Chance is a word void of sense.'*" She places her finger across her mouth and narrows her eyes. "It's impossible to explain it, put it to words, but I see it. I know it. Somehow I know... her life and mine... will never be the same, will never be as it was. Whatever that means, whatever form that feeling... that notion takes... I know it to be true." She then excuses herself. When she returns, her eyes are moist and red. The rest of the meal is spent in near silence. When the check arrives, she insists on paying it.

Outside it's starting to rain. We cross 57th street and dash to where she's parked her car, a black Bentley Azure. The doors close tightly, like a capsule sealing something for eternity. We sit there in silence, her staring into the street, water cascading down the windshield. She's deep in thought; I know she wants to tell me something. Finally I can no longer contain my curiosity, my trepidation.

"What is it?" I ask. Whatever it is remains unsaid, for several heartbeats later we are moving, absorbed within New York traffic.

When we arrive at the apartment, I'm shocked to see a girl, *a doppelganger*, who looks exactly like Audrey standing in the recess of the doorway. As the car pulls up and stops in the loading zone, I cannot take my eyes off her. Rain has darkened her golden-brown hair, soaked the shoulders slender, but the face is exactly hers, the eyes gazing up the street.

"What are you looking at?" a voice asks from the quietude.

I turn and gaze at the woman beside me; her wondering eyes the color of the ocean, her hair the color of sand.
"Severin... do you see a girl standing in the doorway?" She peers and I actually expect the opposite of what she says.
"Yes, I see her, a very pretty girl. Do you know her?" she asks but I'm already pulling on the handle of the car door.

I instantly feel the cold fingers of the falling rain take hold. There's a part of me that's certain this is a different person, her sudden inexplicable appearance here and in this way. As I slowly approach, her gaze locks on me and sends a dull chill through my body like the pulse of a pile driver. Her normally light hair looks nearly black. I'm uncertain it is she at all; something about her eyes... the eyes are darker, stormy.
"Audrey?" I call out as I near, rainfall dancing across the concrete. She simply stares, awaits my approach. I feel as if I am walking in a dream. It is only until we are face to face, that there's no doubt whatsoever, *it is her, standing in the doorway in the rain.* "Audrey?" I ask again. *"Is that you?"*
Without a word she reaches up and embraces me, her wet cheek against mine, frigid from the rain.

"Where have you been?" I hear her say, the voice thin and raspy. "I've been waiting for hours," she whispers. I look into her eyes; they are deep amorphous pools of wonderment.

"What are you doing here?" I ask holding her arms. She feels like a *stickman* beneath the saturated denim jacket.

I hear a voice from behind. Severin has followed me over. The falling rain dots her dress rapidly saturating her arms and shoulders. She shelters her face beneath her purse.

"What's happened?" I nearly cannot speak.

"It's Morgan's sister." Severin looks at the girl standing in the thundershower.

"The model?" she asks, Audrey strangely reticent. "Yes, I recognize you... you were on some of our covers." Audrey's reaction is odd, reluctant. "Is everything alright?" Severin asks her. No response. "Shall we go upstairs?" Nothing. "I'll go up and start some tea," she says to me then rushes to get out from under the downpour. I stand there getting saturated like a prop man in a derelict carnival.

"Let's go inside. When did you get in? Did you fly from New Orleans?" I ask, pulling her elbow. She resists, just stands in the deluge looking at me strangely.

"I need to show you something," she says, rain cascading down her face.

"Let's go inside and dry off first." She looks up into the falling rain that enshrouds us, the neon casting a deep scarlet glow like blood falling from heaven. She then reaches out, takes my hand, it feels like ice. *"Come..."* She begins to pull me toward the street. Something in me hesitates. In fact, something inside me is strangely ill at ease regarding her behavior. She looks at me. "What's the matter? Why are you suddenly afraid of me?"

"I'm not afraid of you Audrey, I just think you need to come upstairs and warm yourself, you're as cold as ice." She instantly embraces me, her arms wrapped around my shoulders and her head beneath my chin. We stand this way, in the rain for several moments, her unwilling to relinquish her embrace.

"Okay, what is it you want to show me?" I whisper and she slowly retracts gently taking my hand –like one takes the hand of a child- and leads me down the street to where a bone-white 1959 Cadillac Eldorado Biarritz sits patiently waiting at the curb. The car seems to shrug, indignant regarding its current situation, left sitting in the rain.

"*Come,*" she says unlocking the passenger's door and getting behind the wheel.

"Where did you get the car?" I ask looking it over. It's immaculate throughout, crimson leather upholstery and the chrome reflects the streetlight; the raindrops bead up and roll off the paint. She starts the engine. I'm surprised when she pulls out and we're moving along the dark Manhattan streets.

I shake the rain from my hair and arms but she just drives. I turn up the heater and the moisture condenses filling the windshield until I adjust the blower.

"Where did you get this car?" I ask again. Obviously this is what she wanted to show me so I'm surprised –and concerned- when she doesn't respond in the least to my question. I've witnessed this before, on the drive from Nice to Paris, when it was like she disappeared into another world. Perhaps she really is mentally off, I hear myself pondering.

Her quiet state is both alarming yet fascinating to two separate aspects of myself, two very extreme perspectives. The half that is alarmed is the part of me back at the apartment with Severin, warm clothes and hot coffee.

Another part of me is nearly the opposite. It has become fascinated by this odd series of circumstances. This part of me is in total wonderment as to why Audrey is here and what we are doing, where we are going. I look about Manhattan slowly passing and suddenly realize she is heading toward the Holland tunnel and the New Jersey state line.

"You can turn off here," I say pointing to the last exit, "or we'll end up in Secaucus." She drives past it uncaring. I look at her in the darkness of the vehicle and that part of me that wishes to be back at the warehouse boils up. "Now we'll have to loop back, it'll take another fifteen minutes." No response. "You realize Severin is waiting for us?" I say and she takes several moments to answer.

"*It doesn't matter.*" I'm uncertain how to read this sudden admission or the discordant way she's verbalized it.

"Perhaps it doesn't…" I mutter, "but she's waiting for us." Nothing. When we make the New Jersey side I point. "Take this exit, we can circle back here," but again, as before, she resolutely drives past, picking up speed. "Audrey, you've shown me the car, we've driven it," I say, and she looks at me darkly.

"Have you gotten stupid again?"

"What?" I ask, incredulous.

"I'm not interested in a car you idiot," she says and a part of me wants to grab the wheel and stomp on the brakes but I intentionally control my anger.

"What's this all about?" I ask and she flips on the car's old radio, AM-band static, several voices and odd noises intermixing in a weird amalgam of sound. "I'd appreciate it if you'd answer my question," I press on.

"*You'll know soon,*" she says cryptically and an odd feeling engulfs me.

I remain silent for several minutes. When the next exit presents itself I gently, but firmly, take hold of the wheel and begin to force the turn. She digs her nails into the back of my hand and it's like a thousand volts of electricity coursing through my knuckles. I release the wheel, shocked that her fingernails could cause such an intense electrical sensation. Blood is flowing from three small gashes.

"Are you losing your mind?" I shout. She doesn't even flinch. "You're acting crazy," I say sucking the blood flowing from my hand. She points a wicked finger at me.

"If you touch the wheel of this car again... I'll kill you."

I stare at her. I cannot believe what she's just said. One more dark ominous look in my direction and she reverts back to a quiet oneness with the onrushing road, her speed elevating.

I'm left to ponder over this new and disturbing situation. Kill me? What does she mean? Does she mean it literally? How could she? Is there a gun or possibly a knife hidden in the car? I wonder. As if reading my mind she suddenly says:

"I'll force the wheel and roll the car. I'll break your neck." I stare at her awestruck.

"You'll kill yourself," I say and she looks at me in the most unnerving manner.

"Don't be too sure of that," she says mysteriously and scrutinizes my reaction. "If you weren't such a dullard you'd know what I'm talking about." I've no idea what she's talking about and say as much. "You're an idiot!" she says.

"Perhaps I yank on the wheel and kill you?" I say and immediately regret it, thinking it will unleash another barrage of demeaning rhetoric but her reaction surprises me.

"It wouldn't matter." She realizes I'm dumbfounded. "Morgan has become everything to us. If we lose her, *half of*

me will disappear." She studies my reaction and a rage suddenly emerges in her. "What are you thinking?" she shouts.

"That's what this is all about, Morgan?" I ask and she stares at me silently. "You're afraid of me being with Severin, that's the reason you came."

"That's what you're thinking?" she asks, a most incredible expression on her face. She suddenly starts laughing, a very weird extraneous laugh.

"What are you laughing about?"

"You!" she says, looking at me like someone gazing at a monkey in a cage.

"You know what I think?"

"Stop thinking! I don't want to know what you're thinking, stop it." I think she is losing her faculties. "I hate your mind! How can you stand it? How can you live with it?" I'm now certain that she has gone insane.

"Audrey, I know someone here in New York who-"

"Get out of yourself!" she shouts. "When we get *there* and this... *you*... is all we have... then we're completely screwed!" I haven't the slightest clue about what she's railing on about except it's apparently the ravings of a schizophrenic mind. I stare into the night overtaking us and wonder what to do. After a moment she says quietly:

"Do you hear me Willem? Are you there now? *Have you returned*?" she asks as if addressing another person.

"Audrey, I think you need help," I say and it's like lighting a fuse. She slams her fist upon the dash.

"I hate your mind! Just shut up! Don't say or think another word." She then becomes rigid and silent, watching the darkness of the road unwinding ahead. I decide I've had enough and take the wheel firmly in hand at which point she reaches over touching the side of my head and I'm struck by what feels like electricity shooting through my brain, currents of energy and I feel myself go numb then black, a heavy opaque sleep enveloping my consciousness.

When I awaken, I'm peering through a rain-streaked window at a rapidly retreating countryside, mostly in mist. As I slowly –painfully- rise from where I sleep, in a foggy daze, I realize I'm still in the car.

I look over at my driver. Audrey clutches the wheel, her attention bent upon the road. She has removed the denim jacket and wears a black shirt. Her usually golden hair is dark and stringy from the previous night's rain. She glances over at me, looking fatigued, nearly exhausted. Her normally vibrant face and skin has an odd pallor, an almost gray hue.

"Where are we?" I croak, nothing, not a word. I look about, lush green countryside, what looks like higher ground in the distance but cloaked in mist. I spy a road sign rapidly pass by, highway 85. Amazingly, she takes the very next exit and I realize we're at a gas station outside of Alabama.

I immediately get out of the vehicle, stumbling, my body sluggish, unresponsive. I take a moment to orient myself. We're surrounded on all sides by fields of green glowing in the new morning sun. I stare up at the red horse with wings that advertises the station. It looks at me discerningly, seemingly at odds with my appearance… or perhaps my state of mind. I decide I'm going to use the ragged old payphone that sits beneath it. When I reach for my wallet, it's missing. I rejoin her at the pump.

"Where's my wallet?" I ask and she holds it up.

"We ran out of money, we needed the credit card for gas. The car uses a lot of it." I snatch the wallet back and proceed to check its contents. Everything is there except the company's new credit card. I ask about it and she pulls it from the back pocket of her jeans. I grab at it, vindictively, which shocks me actually, as if watching someone else and this action seems to pain her; in fact her whole demeanor has changed from the previous night's intensity. She now seems exhausted and vulnerable.

"Audrey this is insane. Do you even know where we are?"

"*It doesn't matter where this is*," she says oddly.

"What the hell are you doing?" I ask and a shocked look surfaces on her face.

"Are you serious?" she shouts and I'm beside myself.

"This isn't New York, that's for sure," I say and it's as if she nearly collapses.

"This is all a mistake," she says through the fingers across her face. "A waste of valuable time," she says beneath her breath. "We should have... have done something else," she mumbles. "What we should've done..." she begins to say then shakes her head, "no... that wouldn't have worked..." she says biting her fingernails. She becomes lost in some weird train of thought, talking to herself. I wonder silently how I'm going to find her psychiatric help.

"Listen, let's find you a doctor to talk to, someone who'll-"

"A doctor?" she rages. "A doctor? Really? A doctor is going to solve our problem?" she shouts aloud and the man filling an old stake-bed truck on the other side of the pump watches us intently.

"You just need rest," I say and she looks at me as if on the verge of collapse.

"Yes. We need to sleep. I can't go any further. You'll have to drive the rest of the way. I feel like... like I'm dissolving," she says staring at her hands then immediately crawls into the back seat of the Cadillac.

"Hey, wait a minute!" I call out but it's of no avail.

"Just follow the highway," she says, "the highway will take you."

"Where do we go now?" I say but she doesn't hear me, she's asleep. I curse under my breath and finish filling the tank, then get in to move the car off to the side to think over what to do. The car feels good and is smooth and responsive. I decide to quit the confines of the lonely gas station, with its winged horse, to find a cafe or a more active spot. Once I'm back on the highway the car picks up speed nearly of its own volition, as if it were in a hurry, and I suddenly realize I'm driving Colonel Emory Montaigne's Cadillac Biarritz and that I'm going to drive it to New Orleans, our current heading. I glance at the girl in the back seat as the wind buffets her hair wildly about her sleeping form. She looks dark, and as thin as a rail.

When I pull in through the iron gates and up the gravel drive of Maison Magenta, they are all there, waiting; Colonel Montaigne, the aunts, and –incredibly- Emerald. Also present are two lean white men and two older black men. It's just on the verge of twilight. The women solemnly embrace me, each one, Emerald, Monique, Magda, the blind Pearl and the silent Angeline. They gently roust Audrey from the back seat of the Cadillac where she's slept the rest of the trip. She looks weak and frail and they usher her inside the great house. The Colonel clasps my hand, speaks to me in French apparently because I cannot understand a word he says until I hear him say:

"The old girl got you here in good time." I'm certain he's referring to the car. He introduces me to his nephews, the two brothers, Jerome and Cristobal. They both have a lean wiry physique; Cristobal slightly shorter and heavier than Jerome, sports a mustache while Jerome's face has a salt and pepper five o'clock shadow. He then introduces me to the older black men. I recognize them from Morgan's paintings. It's Robert Anthony, the guitar player whose eyes gleam and his brother Carter whose gaze is dull and listless. They seem to only speak Cajun. Monique takes my arm.

"Come to the house Willem, you need to eat," she says in a rather serious tone.

Once in the house, I eat voraciously. It's a spicy seafood gumbo in a tomato base. When the aunts join me at the table, I'm overjoyed to see Emerald. She is thinner, much thinner than the last time I saw her and her eyes are not their usual radiant crispness, but weary. She clasps my hand in hers and I feel the warmth in her touch.

"I'm so glad you've come."

"How are you Emerald? Are you well?" I ask and a thin weak smile crosses her dark countenance.

"I am dear... *I've been freed of the entity which had taken hold of me...* we were successful," she says. I look into her eyes. I see —or feel- the pain she's gone through. I ask about Morgan. Emerald squeezes my hand tightly, her face etched in despair. All the women seem as if in mourning.

"Did Audrey not tell you what's happened?" she asks and I shake my head.

"She was oddly uncommunicative," I say and her brow furrows.

"Of course she was..." Monique interjects, "how could it be otherwise sister? She's not yet skilled in *the art of the Shade*," she says then turns toward me. "It was not she that went for you Willem." I stare at the two twins completely mystified. Emerald releases my hand.

"It wasn't exactly Audrey that went... *we sent her Shade*," she says. I stare at them in disbelief, their expressions unmoving.

"What do you mean?" I ask and the twins exchange a long knowing look. "It was certainly her, she just wasn't... she just *wasn't herself*," I say. They shake their heads.

"Surely Lucien has spoken to you about *the Shade*?" Emerald inquires and Monique stares at me, expectation on her svelte features.

"No... I don't recall it," I say. The twins seem nonplussed. "What's *the Shade*?" They both seem reluctant to answer.

"There's not time for this now, a tragedy is upon us," Monique says. I look hard at Emerald.

"It's Morgan," Emerald says on the verge of tears.

"What's happened?" She bows her head as if unable to speak.

"Mon Dieu," Monique interjects, *"Willem, she is with the dead!"* I stare at her as if she were speaking in some unintelligible tongue. A low moaning permeates the room.

"I'm sorry aunt Monique, I don't believe I heard you correctly." She places her hand atop my wrist.

"She has ventured into the *Isle du mort*." I stare, not sure I understand her.

"What on earth are you talking about? What is the... *Isle du mort*?" I ask and Monique goes rigid.

"*The Island of the Dead*," Emerald says through her fingers. "A place no living person should ever go."

"Yet she is there," Monique says with intent. "*She is enmeshed within the Damned*," Emerald's double whispers and a deep mourning encapsulates the family. Angeline is crying and Magda hides her face behind her apron and cannot control her emotions. Pearl sits like a woman who has lost a child. I take up Emerald's hand and gaze into her azure eyes moist with tears and worry.

"What's happening Emerald, what's going on?"

"We were remiss Willem... she's progressed so well, so very rapidly. She went out into the bayou... something went amiss... she lost her way." She looks to her twin whose eyes narrow.

"She was mislead sister, make no mistake," Monique says, the two women exchanging a deep silent stare, like someone looking into a mirror.

"Whatever the reason," Emerald continues, her voice fraught with despair, "she's become trapped within the Isle du mort. *The dead have possession of her.*" There is more wailing from the maid and everyone's heads bow in a deep remorse.

"Then I'll go there and take her out," I declare and it's as if banging on a bell, the entire room's attention on me. I look at Emerald who studies me with a profound expression. "I mean what I'm saying Emerald, tell me how to get there... I'll not return without her," I proclaim with the utmost conviction. There is an immense reaction from the women as they commence to gather around me.

"Merci bon Deux!" Monique says genuflecting, her eyes alive. "You would be her champion? You would go there, *among the non-living*?"

"I'll not return without her," I say and it's almost like *a laying on of hands* as I'm surrounded by the love of her family. The sounds of despair die out as all ears key upon our soft circle and in a hushed tone Monique speaks.

"The *soulless* surround her, obscure her... feeding on her light, reflecting illusion back upon her. *She knows not with whom she dwells*. They seduce her with phantasm. There is no reality... it is illusion only. *Willem, the horrors feed on her light.* As surely as dawn will come they will steal it from her... until the flame dies, and she will be left *a shell*, as one with them... *the Damned.*" There is another cry as Magda is unable to control her sorrow.

"The Damned?" I echo solemnly.

"Those that walk this earth without a soul," Emerald says, the black pupils burning into my vision. "They are the shadows of those who have lived and died on earth refusing all spiritual light, lost within the mire of matter... those whose souls are so wicked so filled with hate and loathing for their fellow man that the immortal spirit has fled them." They all cross themselves to a man.

"Where do I go Aunt Monique? How do I find her?"

"Out there, amidst *the Damned* young Willem," she says, her onyx ring pointing, "deep within the heart of the bayou... *the dark heart, the Isle du mort*, where naught birds nor animals nor even serpents dwell. Where but a century ago, men and women of color were murdered and hung from the mangroves. *This heinous act has forever left its mark in this place.* It is an *evil* abode without light, for anything living any sentient animal *that reflects* is reduced of its life through an insidious manipulation. Just as the mortal vampyre takes the physical blood from the living and sequesters it *within the corpse that resides within the grave, these creatures nourish themselves on the light of the living... hiding themselves from the eternal knowing flame of Life.*"

Everyone bows their heads in a kind of supplication, some crossing themselves. Monique gently touches my arm.

"Willem... to go there, amidst this place... one must be ignited."

"Ignited?"

"One must be immersed with *the flame*." I look to Emerald who takes my hand in hers.

"*The Fire of Love...* it is the only thing they fear," she says her eyes pouring forth a profundity of emotion. All eyes are upon me, even the blind.

"When can I go?" I ask and you could hear a pin drop as the women all look between each other. Eventually all eyes rest upon Emerald. She seems distressed by the question, as if unable to answer, when Monique places her hand directly across my heart.

"Every moment they surround her they take of her light," she whispers, "the light of her heart... *the sacre Coeur...* the light bequeathed her by the Holy Muse." The women cry again, a soft pitiful wailing. I immediately stand, feeling a fury mount within my chest.

"Let's waste no more time."

Outside, the men are stoking a large bonfire. As I fit myself into a pair of hearty boots a row erupts. The old Colonel is berating the men.

"What is it father?" Emerald inquires.

"These, weak men... won't even second him," he says looking at me abashedly.

"Second me?"

"You need a second... someone to second you... they won't do it! They're afraid!" He gestures at them and there's a general pall over the group of men. Jerome is silently shaking his head.

"C'est le Isle du mort Colonel, muy pelligrosso... c'est dangereaux!" Cristobal says in a thick Cajun accent and the men all nod in unison.

"You damn cowards!" the old man shouts then rails on in French. Emerald takes him in arm.

"Father, please don't chastise them so," she says, "can't you see they're afraid? You can't send them out into the darkness. You'll be sending them to their death. Look how *the fear* is upon them."

"Fear? Damn it to hell, I'll go! I'm not afraid to second this man, a man willing to sacrifice himself for my grand daughter, fetch me my stick!"

"Father dear... the journey is far too arduous for your old bones," Monique says and he knows what she says is true. He glares at the men.

"Hell boys, you'd just... send him in there alone?!" he shouts at the men who silently brood. I see it, in their eyes, the gravity of where I'm going. Robert Anthony, the old guitarist croons:

"Mon Colonel... c'est le *Cite du mort*." He looks at me and I see distinctly the awe in his eyes. "*The Duppy owns it...*" he says to me then looks at his brother Carter.

"*Le Diable*," Carter murmurs low and shakes his gray head, crossing his forehead with the tips of his fingers. The old man turns toward us.

"But they know the way! How can he expect to find the way? He don't know the bayou... and at night no less! It can't be done!" he shouts his cause to the men when Jerome suddenly erupts.

"Parlay, parlay Colonel. Un chien, un chien!" to Magda, "Magda, un chien, s'il vous plait, allez allez!" Magda turns to the Colonel.

"They want me to fetch Majo."

"I know what they want fool woman! Go do it!" he shouts and she is immediately off. "And Morgan's sash from the hook," he shouts as she races back to the house. The Colonel kicks at them. "Your very own cousin that you grew with... you'd just leave her out there with those devils!"

They speak in Cajun. I see they are growing weary of the old man's ranting, yet I see distinctly the fear about going and I wonder deep inside *what awaits me out in the bayou.*

"Father dear, you're distraught. Please don't anger them further," Monique says softly.

"But she's the first born, blood of your blood!" he says.

"But we have her champion." She looks at me glowingly. "Look! He's become ignited. The fire is in his heart. See how it burns within him," she says in a kind of reverent tone, her eyes wide with expectation, looking through me.

Suddenly the dog bounds around the large ornate porch. The Colonel claps his hands.

"C'mere boy… c'mon," dog and master converge. He rubs the rib bones that show through the animal's coat. "Good boy!" The old man looks at me. "This here old Ridgeback's eyes are dying but he still has a good nose. A damn good nose, don'tcha boy?" The dog whines and whips his wiry tail. Magda –hiking up her skirt- quickly joins us carrying a dark piece of cloth. I recognize it from San Francisco, Morgan's sash. The Colonel holds out his pistol, a US army issue Colt 45. I hesitate, uncertain what to do.

"Mon Dieu Papa! What use is that to him against *those already dead*?" Monique says. The old Colonel's arm goes limp under the weight of the pistol.

"It just don't seem right," he says, "to send a man into war without a weapon."

"But he has a weapon father." Emerald says. She steps up to me placing her hand upon my heart. "He has *the fire* within his heart that will find her and take her from the shadows." I take Emerald's hand.

"I'll find her. I won't come back without her," I say and Emerald's eyes are a'wonder.

"Merci bon Deux," Monique whispers quietly and genuflects. "Go now, while the flame burns."

"He has no second," someone says and a sudden pause eclipses the moment, when suddenly a voice sounds from the darkness behind us.

"I'll go." All eyes turn. Audrey has come down from the house. She looks different than the thin dark person who drove with me from New York. She's distinctly no longer the stormy person in the Cadillac. Her hair is tied back and she wears a clean blue denim jacket. Her golden-brown hair reflects the firelight and her eyes seem their familiar rich brown color once again.

There's a sudden commotion about this. Creole splinters the air. I hear the words *non,* and *petite blond* repeated several times. It's quite obvious the family is in disagreement about this idea when Audrey's voice sounds out loudly. She speaks to them all in French before turning toward the Colonel.

"I'm going. You can't forbid it."

"You gonna just stand there and allow this to go on?" the old man says to his daughter and Emerald takes up Audrey's hand.

"No Audrey... not you."

"Mom, don't say anything. I'm doing this. I owe it to her." Her eyes glisten and she takes her mother's face in both of her hands. "Don't you understand? She saved my life in LA. I wouldn't even be here." Tears course the entirety of her cheeks. "We've become deeply connected. *I love her, mom.* I'm going and getting her out of there. She'd do it for me." They exchange a long heartfelt moment. Audrey then turns addressing the group. "There has to be a second... you all know that, and why. I'm not afraid." She turns to her mother and whispers, "I'm not afraid." Emerald looks upon her daughter, tears streaming down her cheeks.

"I know… I know that you're not. You've never been afraid. Yes, go… go ahead. Stay very close to Willem and for the love of God, be careful." The Colonel steps up to Emerald.

"Emerald! This frail young fille? Surely…"

"Yes father… she'll be the second… it's decided." They exchange a profound look then the old man takes up the sash and puts it to the Ridgeback's nose.

"Majo," he shouts loudly, "go find Morgan. Go find 'er boy… go find Morgan!" The old canine breathes in the sash, sneezes, then immediately plies his sense to the ground. He slowly circles the garden, his head moving rhythmically side to side across the grass and flagstones. At a natural break near the edge of the wood he bolts in. The old white haired man, his eyes afire, points and shouts: "There he goes!" I don't need anyone to tell me what to do next. I'm off in the direction of the dog, breaking through the foliage with intent. I can hear Audrey at my heels.

We trace the old path through the ancient wood, being careful to dodge the bogs and skirting the waterways. The overhang is thick and dripping, the sounds of the creatures of the night filling the gloom. The dog, although old and withered, is steady and determined. He follows the scent he's been directed by his master. He gets lost once or twice and we wait as he circles until he picks up the trail, pushing on relentlessly into the blackness. This goes on for several long arduous miles under the heavy oppressive canopy. We are deep into the night, a darkness so utterly encompassing barely a sliver of moonlight breaks through the overhang above. All about us is a dark, dank morass.

When we again halt our sojourn, I become increasingly aware that I no longer hear the sounds of the swamp or its creatures. It has become unnaturally quiet. I feel Audrey's grasp upon my sleeve.

"Why has he stopped?"

"He's lost the trail again." I study the Ridgeback closely and realize he hasn't lost the trail. "No… he's afraid to go on," I whisper. The dog paces and whines, retracing his steps back to where we stand.

"What does this mean?" she whispers in the darkness.

"That we've lost our guide. He won't go any further."

"But why?" I kneel down to the canine and he winces and whines, pawing the moss at my feet. It's clear to me something inexorable has occurred when suddenly Audrey cries out. "Look!" She holds me pointing, and in the midst of the blackness I see what has caught her eye; almost invisible within the total blackness is a soft luminance off in the distance. "What is it?"

"I don't know." I strain to see through the gloom. It seems almost more a mist than a light. I reach down and take her hand. "C'mon." We slowly, carefully make our way into the wood, the dog refusing to go any further.

Several hundred feet later we come to the edge of a dank dark hollow. What our eyes behold out there in the midst of that great swamp sends a shaft of horror to the very center of my being. It is Morgan standing, as if transfixed, *within the middle of a hundred black shadows!* They are black, solid ebony forms, blacker than the night engulfing us. They swarm about *her being* that gives off a shallow feeble glow.

"My God," I hear Audrey whisper in my ear and her nails dig into my shoulder. "My God look at that! They're all around her... oh my God, Willem!" I realize it's just as Monique said. The black figures, in the shape of human forms, vie about her relentlessly and there seems to be the transference of a thin ephemeral light into the void of their collective black mass. "They're sucking her soul light!" Audrey whispers echoing my thoughts and she drops her face into my shoulder and weeps. "Oh God, we've got to get her out of there," she whispers becoming overwhelmed by the macabre sight unfolding before our eyes. I suddenly feel something burn in my chest. It courses my arms and legs. I take Audrey firmly in hand.

"Let's go," I say and start to lead her but she stops stock-still. "What's the matter?" I whisper and see the hollow eyes staring into the maw. She's terrified.

"I... I can't... I can't do it. I'm afraid," she says trembling. I hold both her shoulders, looking directly at her.

"Don't be afraid, close your eyes and hold onto my hand." She grips my hand like a vice and I turn and *lead her directly into the abyss*.

When I think back upon this moment, this singular moment in time, I'm shocked that we were not engulfed; *taken*, might be the right word. For we penetrate the black body without regard and the chill and terror of the experience was crystalline. But there was a strange familiarity about it all, at the time, that kept me detached from the horror and misery we were entering.

For ten years I had worked as a touring cameraman on large spectacle entertainment; large venues, even stadiums. I had left my home, my comforts, my thin raft of family and friends and journeyed out alone into a world of strangers. To me, what saved my mind –probably our lives- from the dread we were about to experience was a strange familiar feeling of *moving amongst the throng*; moving through a mass of bystanders idly loitering about, waiting their turn to *experience the Madonna*.

I distinctly recall the feeling, as we began to penetrate that execrable maw, of an indifference to it, a lack of concern about their horrid features, the ugliness that they projected outwardly toward us as we passed. It wasn't a lack of empathy for their wretched existences, just an all-encompassing lack of interest in engaging in it, obsessing with it.

At one point Audrey screams. One of the horde has wrapped an ebony tentacle about her. I dig my fingers into it and move it aside, yet she's unable to continue.

"I can't do it, I can't go on," she whispers from my jacket collar.

"Don't think about them," I tell her. "Remember what you said to me on Sutter Street? Under the sodium lights that night?"

"Yes…" she whispers. "The dead can't hurt us."

"C'mon…" I deliberately push our way through *the black mass*. Some part easily, some I have to push aside like trying to move a stubborn horse. When Audrey cries out again, I take her to my chest, bury her face in my jacket and keep pushing forward, always forward, relentlessly, toward the center, toward Morgan.

When we finally breach the darkness of the horde and come into her light, a vague sense of recognition slowly crosses her features. Although she is being mesmerized by the bleak phantoms that surround us –her eyes caught up in the illusion, the awe of their infernal machinations- a sense of longing, acknowledgement, grows between us until incredibly she looks into my eyes and speaks my name.

"Willem," she whispers, our eyes locking. Her eyes wander to her sister. "Audrey. You've both come. You're here… both of you. I'm so glad." I embrace her and she feels frigidly cold. She touches my face and I touch hers.

"Morgan we've come to take you home," Audrey says but she seems not to hear. Morgan gestures into the darkness.

"Everyone has arrived, our friends… the banquet is all set… are you hungry? There's goose, boar and hare… or stag if you prefer. See? Everyone is here… all our friends."

"Morgan, did you hear me? We've come to take you home," Audrey says and Morgan looks at her wonderingly.

"Home? *Home*…"

"Magenta. Villa Magenta. Everyone is waiting for you, Mother, Grandpa…" Morgan reacts strangely, as if trying to fathom an enigma.

"*Mother?* But she's here… somewhere…" She peers into the nothingness. "Our friends," she gestures absently, "…our arrangements."

"Morgan, you've no friends here. Look around you. Who do you recognize… truly?" She scans the gloom her eyes growing wide with the illusions cast before her.

"But there's… there's…" pointing at nothing.

"There's no one!" Audrey says taking her arm. "You're coming with us… right now… c'mon!" Audrey pulls at her but she resists.

"No," she says, confusion on her face. She seems unable to make up her mind. The dark mass is responding, becoming tumultuous.

"Morgan, these are phantoms. We need to leave, right now," I whisper our eyes locking. I sense that part of her that knows, coming through. "You're in danger. We have to get you back to Magenta. These things masquerading as your friends are going to kill you."

A sudden unmistakable change overtakes her. Slowly her eyes scan from side to side.

"They all smile, speak glowing lilted words... but behind every smile, a dagger," she whispers. I put my arm around her shoulders and pull her to my chest, warmth cascading between us. I can feel her melt into me, our eyes locking and we *see* each other.

"Willem..." she whispers, emotion arising in her voice. "It is *you*... you *are* here," she says lovingly. "You're here..."

"I'm here Morgan," I say my voice strangely resonate. She again brushes my face, an immense weariness in her eyes.

"Yes. Take me home. Please, take me home... I-I want to leave this place," and she collapses.

I take her up in my arms, her head against my shoulder, and begin to push our way back from whence we have come. Audrey clutches my sleeve, and I can feel her put her weight into our effort.

The dark horde stirs and soon a reverberating violence begins to permeate the mob. I can feel it vibrate through their number. Some begin to wrap black oozing coils —once arms- about my person attempting to impede our progress. I fear I'm failing in my struggle to extradite us from the morass. I then feel Audrey pulling my arm as she attempts to push through the dull viscous mass blocking our passage. I hear her cough and spit.

"C'mon, c'mon don't stop!" she says pulling with all her might and eventually we manage the outside perimeter of that dark and odious union.

Many paces further on we gain a slight reprieve at the base of an enormous mangrove whose roots envelope us for the moment, sheltering us from the feral hordes that now seem set loose. We watch in terror as they dart about in the darkness whipping each other into frenzy, moaning low.

Exhausted by the effort of freeing ourselves from the black mass, I fall to my knees, still holding Morgan. She seems fragile, child-like, in a kind of trance, her arms wrapped tightly about my neck as if her body –perhaps without the aid of her mind- is holding on for life.

"C'mon, c'mon!" Audrey beckons trying to pull me to my feet. "Don't stop now, not yet." With a great effort of will, I rise to my feet and we continue on into the terrible night, the phantoms now screeching like banshees and the moment is truly horrifying.

Eventually we find ourselves standing in the middle of that great void unable to continue, black water obstructing our advance.

"I've lost the way," Audrey says frantically. "Willem, I've lost the trail, I don't know where we are!" We peer about in the gloom. All around us, shadows are in motion, darting about, swirling within the miasma of swamp gas and dark bodies. I open my eyes wide and for the first time since entering the horde, I realize the gravity, the seriousness we are in, for the things have begun to saturate the woods. I see their Stygian forms moving through the boughs and tree trunks, inexorably closing in around us.

"Where do we go now?" I ask.

"I don't know! I'm all turned around," she whispers frantically in the darkness. It's then we hear a thin rasping voice.

"This way... come this way..." it says and it's as if Audrey is compelled to follow for she starts in the direction of the voice. I shout to her.

"Audrey, no, don't follow that voice," I say. She's startled by something immediately behind us. I hear her gasp and turn to witness a most unnerving sight. In the darkness is the face of a man, *a withered man* and his expression is one of abject misery.

"In life I murdered for worldly gain," it moans, *"now I'm forever lost in the requiem."* I step back but the thing presses closer, stuttering. "I know where a treasure lies buried, a fortune! Near at hand! More gold than your dreams can contain, let me show you... follow me... no longer can it serve me now... follow me." Suddenly another spectre is there, the spectre of a woman, the face alluring.

"Follow not *it* that takes you upon the road to ruin. I have more than substanceless gold trinkets. Take my hand and I'll bring you everlasting pleasure." Suddenly the face of the old man turns evil incarnate and shrieks.

"Vile harlot!" and the woman's alluring smile turns rancid and evil.

"Demon!" The two spectres turn on each other hissing and spitting like two cats feuding. Audrey seems overwhelmed and hopelessness begins to cloud my reason.

Suddenly we are shocked by the sound of a low animal growl that emanates from the shadows. Audrey clutches my arm terrified by this new unexpected presence issuing from the darkness. We brace ourselves for the worst when – incredibly- we realize it is Majo! He's found us. The dog snarls viciously at the two horrific forms that loiter before us, blocking our egress. The animal's actions seem to cast the horrid creatures into an agitated state, perhaps a momentary confusion.

"Let's go," I say. We push past the shadows despite their attempts to cling to us. When we break through, Majo turns heel and begins to lead us out of that damnable place.

Thrice more, we are assailed by *the horrors* but each instance the old Ridgeback growls and snarls viciously baring its teeth setting them back just enough for us to pass.

As we journey forth into the immensity of the great swamp, I begin to see them in the gloom; their grotesque countenances, some sinister and horrific, others less so. Several cast alluring guises and I know to look upon them would slow our pace. *My second is of the same mind* as she cleaves through them, unwilling to give sway to their loathsome pining. She's focused entirely upon the dog, following it instinctively, pulling hard upon my arm all the while; and this is how it is until we clear the *Island of the Dead*, the dog leading the woman and the woman leading the man.

Once we are back upon the path homeward, the dark shapes and their whisperings –their incessant nipping at our backs- diminishes. I no longer see or hear them, only the immensity of the swamp, its symphony of night creatures and their song. A feeling of exhilaration possesses me. I feel invigorated. We have gone into the r*ealm of the dead* and returned again whole, cradled within my arms the body and soul of my true love, the heart of the family.

Eventually we break clear of the deep bayou and the last of the journey back to Magenta is by the light of the sliver of moon that follows us from above. She shines a brilliance far in excess of her slim frame, as if she were lighting the path before us in a soft effervescent luminance.

When we finally enter the confines of Villa Magenta's immense garden surround, a roaring fire greets us. I'm surprised they are playing music and singing. Jerome strokes an old viola while Cristobal presses on a brilliant gold and white accordion. There are the two black men, Robert Anthony playing the guitar and Carter scratching on a washboard and drum. Their voices ring out; an old Cajun ditty. When Majo breaks the inner circle, the music instantly stops and the entire host turns and beckons us; we are absorbed into the bosom of the family. The women engulf us. Their arms and fingers –golden in the firelight- stroke the girl's manes and slowly, gingerly, they ply Morgan's grasp from around my neck and lay her down upon the soft green earth.

Emerald is the first to try to raise Morgan to consciousness but something is apparently not right.

"She's not here," she says oddly. "Monique, she's not here!" she says a frantic tone escalating in her voice. Her twin is instantly beside her.

"Morgan, wake up," the double commands sharply, brushing the hair from her niece's eyes. "You're here now m'love, wake up," yet she fails to stir in the least, in fact she looks unnervingly still. Monique suddenly goes rigid. "Mon Dieu, they have her in the Astral. The devils. Morgan wake up!" She slaps her heartily across the cheek yet so still she remains, as if dead. When she raises her hand to strike her again, Monique's wrist is gently arrested by Angeline. All watch in silence as Angeline calmly kneels and takes

Morgan's head in her lap. She gently brushes Morgan's hair back and in a rich clear voice whispers:

"Morgan... do you hear me? It is aunt Angeline... do you recognize my voice?" All watch transfixed as Morgan vaguely seems to stir. "Morgan, no other possesses this voice save myself... you understand that?" Morgan then mutters, nearly indiscernibly:

"Aunt Angeline..."

"Come to me Morgan... follow the sound of my voice. Follow not the Sadducees that beckon you into the darkness. Follow me back here... back to Magenta... back to your family. We're here waiting for you dear." Incredibly Morgan says:

"I... I can't... they're blocking my way... they won't let me through..." Angeline gently brushes her face with the palm of her hand, cupping her cheek in her long thin fingers.

"But you are through Morgan... you're here with us already. Open your eyes dear... open your eyes Morgan and look at me... look." Then, like a dreamer waking from sleep, Morgan's eyes flutter then open wide and she looks at us all, each and every one. When her eyes rest on Emerald beside her on the lawn she says in a weak voice:

"Mother..." They lock in a deep impenetrable embrace and weep. The women gather around her and she's gently raised and she –and the *petit blond*- are ushered off into the villa.

As I stand breathing hard in the firelight I realize Monique has remained behind, standing beside me.

"Merci bon Deux," she says and genuflects. Her eyes are afire, glowing in the night. Was the firelight being reflected? She gently touches my arm. "The wise old wizard..." she whispers and her eyes are piercing as she silently stares at me, a thin smile etched across her face.

"Where are they taking her Aunt Monique?" I ask, more to break the silence, the intense look in those eyes.

"La bain," she says. "The bath. They will wash them in lavender water, then to sleep."

"Is she alright now?" She stares at me fixedly in the most intense manner, placing her long slender hand against my heart.

"La Coc ce'nell," she whispers and leaves. Then, the brothers dump two buckets over my head, drenching me in cold water, which seems to wake me from a dullness inflicted by the strenuous enterprise. They yank my pants down to my boots and laugh and shout. It seems a great jest until I realize my legs are covered with leeches. They extract embers from the fire and burn the grotesque things from my body then douse the bites with bourbon. I'm wrapped in a warm blanket and set before the fire and given strong drink.

The brothers pick up their instruments, the music resuming anew. They call me, *Bonaparte* and sing several songs in Cajun about the great French general.

I look at the Ridgeback at the boot of the old Colonel. He pants profusely, exhausted from the night's long march. He looks at me, our eyes making contact and I gesture him over. He joins me at my place beside the fire and we share a moment together. I stroke his coat as he sits, his mouth held wide, the tongue panting, a smile turned up at the corners of his mouth. I rub his shoulders and neck and croon softly. He seems resplendent in the firelight, a rich golden glow within his fur. I realize how much I appreciate him. I know he knows my feelings, his eyes looking into mine, smiling. After a few minutes, he rejoins his master who taps his heel to the music and drinks dark wine from a large crystal glass. We carry on like this, the men, deep into the night.

I awaken the next morning just before noon. I'm in the same bedroom, the guest bedroom, adorned with antiques that have been in place for a century. I hear activity below and descend the winding back stairs to the kitchen.

The women are busy cooking. Upon closer inspection, I discover they are engaged in canning tomatoes. Large boiler pots full of red tomato pulp seethe upon the old cast iron stove fueled by burning firewood. They mix the crimson pulp with large wooden spoons and ladle the mixture into mason jars that are sterilizing lip down in cast iron skillets, with just enough water to lick the edges. Everyone is perspiring and working away. Monique smiles at me but says nothing, her sleeves pulled up and perspiration across her brow; Angeline, even Pearl, are hard at work cleaning and cutting bushel baskets full of tomatoes from the enormous back garden. Dozens and dozens of glass quart jars full of red tomato pulp are neatly set across one of the large expansive countertops. Magda, her hair wrapped in a towel, pushes past me using her hip, busy feeding firewood into the stove. They all look at me differently. I feel a strong affinity with them all. I'm uncertain what has changed, just that there is a change. Aunt Pearl puts down her knife, ambles over and takes me in hand giving me a long heartfelt embrace, her white eyes blankly staring back. She informs me that Emerald is in the garden *having coffee with father* and that I should join them. I thank her and leave the bustling old kitchen.

In the enormous back garden of the estate, Emerald is sitting with the Colonel drinking coffee from a French press. They offer me a cup. I notice it's the same chicory laced flavor as before. They are watching as Jerome splits firewood with a maul. He's bare-chested, lean and brown from the sun, his muscular arms thin and wiry. He is making short work of large cuts of hardwood, slicing away with single blows. Each swing cleaves away another split, the stumps disappearing into a growing pile of firewood. He sings a Cajun ditty, the melody recognizable from the night before.

I sit next to Emerald. She smiles but the glow I remember in her eyes, is now replaced with worry.

"How are you Emerald, are you alright now?" I ask, placing my hand atop hers resting upon the chair arm. She takes mine and squeezes it.

"I'm very tired... but well. Thank you for your help Willem... not only last night but on my behalf as well. I'm indebted to you," she says. We gaze into each other's eyes.

"You owe me nothing. I would do anything for you," I say and she contemplates me for a moment. "How is Morgan, is she alright?" Emerald looks directly into my eyes, the brilliant azure irises cutting into my psyche.

"She's exhausted. I doubt you realize, any of us, how close we came to-" she stops, placing her delicate fingers across her mouth. I can see she's fighting to contain her composure. Her eyes glisten. "She's alright... don't worry... you were in time." There's a momentary gleam in her weary expression and I realize she has been through a very traumatic period in her life.

"What about Audrey? Is she okay?" She returns her gaze into the distance. "She's fine also, you mustn't worry... she's just very tired."

"Did she tell you?" Our eyes lock.

"Tell me what?"

"About Severin." Her eyes are stoic, unmoving.

"We know all about her," she says. Father and daughter exchange a look and Colonel Montaigne extracts one of his thin black cheroots and clips the tip off with a cutter.

"What happened Emerald? How could Morgan end up in a place such as that?" There's an excruciating pause as Emerald stares into space. I realize the subject pains her.

"Tell him Em, he deserves an answer," he says and this seems to distress her.

"What?" I ask but she seems obstinately reticent. I look at the Colonel who seems impatient with his daughter.

"*It was those damn pixies,*" he says and I'm certain I've heard him wrong.

"I beg your pardon sir? What did you say?" He grows visibly impatient with me.

"You heard what I said dammit, it was those damn pixies!"

"Father…" Emerald says and he looks at her.

"Well?" he huffs then rises and strolls off toward the edge of the garden to stare at a large marble statue of the Venus overlooking one of the long narrow walkways.

"Please tell me what he means Emerald." Her eyes are deep and emphatic. She sighs.

"It's as he says… *we believe the pixies mislead her.*"

"What do you mean by *the pixies*?" I ask. She looks at me strangely.

"The pixies of course… the little people that live within this world, that share this world with mortal man." I'm completely confused. I think they are having fun at my expense.

"Are you joking with me?" I ask. Her countenance suddenly grows quite severe.

"Are you saying you've never seen the elementals, the nature spirits? Never in all your years?" she asks. I slowly shake my head. This seems to annoy her, her brow furrowing and she grows quiet.

"Tell me about them," I ask and her blue eyes grow dark like a soft blue ocean turning gray beneath storm clouds.

"Honestly Willem, I don't know what to make of you! One minute you walk through *the unliving,* the next you ask silly ridiculous questions. I... I don't know what to do with you. It's quite obvious I've hardly the patience Lucien has."

I'm stunned and it must show for suddenly she softens, reaching out with her fingers and clutching my wrist. "I'm sorry. Forgive me. After what everyone's been through." She places her hand across her throat as if she were about to go to tears but when she returns her gaze the tranquil blue eyes are there once more. She smiles genuinely, looking me over as if summing up something invisible about my person.

"You are a conundrum my dear," she says softly, then says: "The pixies are the little people, *the nature spirits* who have dwelt upon this earthen plane for eons. Perhaps you know them as gnomes or brownies? They're everywhere. You've seen them... oh, I'm certain of it. *Your mind refuses to allow you to remember.* These are the beings in fairy tale and myth, the entire world over, all cultures and peoples speak of them in their literature, their heritage."

"What are they?" I ask. She can't seem to comprehend my question. I quickly change my inquiry. "How did they mislead Morgan?" This brings about a dramatic change in Emerald's demeanor.

"I'll get to the bottom of *that*, rest assured!" she says loudly a sudden intensiveness in her normally eloquent voice. "Some of them are very much like people," she says eyeing the fauna at the edge of the garden, "prone to mischievous, devilish behavior... particularly when it's in their best interests not to be so!" I realize her response is not meant for my ears, but as if someone were in proximity of our conversation. I watch in awe as her eyes flash, seem to spit fire, as she surveys the edge of the garden walk. I catch sight of the ferns rustling although the day is still, without breeze.

She quiets and gazes into my eyes. "True… most of mankind will never see them due their avoidance of people. Man's course treatment of Nature and the animal kingdom is repugnant to them, however, a sensitive like yourself will easily catch glimpse of them from time to time when their constitutions meld with this plane of existence." I can only nod my head. "Yes… we will certainly get to the bottom of it!" she rails again and something rustles in the hedgerow, startled by her outburst. She collects herself, looks at me squarely. "Morgan has been going out into the swamp everyday to commune, sometimes with her camera."

"Commune?"

"With Nature… with the vibrancy that abounds us… that sustains us. Surely you understand?" she asks, her eyes narrowing.

"Yes," I say, not entirely convincingly.

"Well, it was only a matter of time before they began to show themselves to her… romp and frolic. It was the same when Morgan was a child. They would romp and play about… hide and seek… mystery games… *all such things that the Innocents do together.*" I can barely believe my ears. I watch my elegant hostess as she fathoms time, returning to these memories. "The faeries and undines in particular, oh so lovely Willem… to look upon them was a joy… particularly Judith and Valory… such lovely little things… so delicate… such pristine beauty." She suddenly grows very severe. "They would never do what was done!" She slams her palms upon the chair arms and again something startles within the hedge. I watch in awe as Emerald's eyes once more turn to flame. "You little devils!" she shouts. "You imps! You'll get a taste of your own wicked poison soon enough! Mark it!" she rages and her eyes, in fact her whole manner becomes like a sudden tempestuous wind.

I'm shocked to my core, never having seen this aspect of her character before. Jerome ceases his singing and chopping and stares at us. The Colonel too, off in the distance, seems to take notice. Incredibly Monique is instantly behind us, I had not noticed her approach. She places her hands upon Emerald's shoulders.

"Quiet thyself sister... you're distraught. Don't create conflict where none belongs. A more diabolical source loiters in the shadows. The pixies were used m'love, mere tools. They are incapable of imagining such a heinous crime. A far more sinister... thing... dwells at the terminus of this evil act." She gently strokes her sister's shoulders. "Come Emerald, come inside the house... you need rest yourself." Emerald quickly quiets her emotions. She catches my eye noticing the shock on my face.

"Excuse me my dear, I'm needed in the kitchen... we're putting up the tomatoes for the season," she says rising and abruptly leaves.

The Colonel continues to meander the garden and Jerome whistles, catching my attention. He gestures for me to join him. I reluctantly do so. He holds out the maul towards me. I take it, surprised by its weight.

"Allez Bonaparte," he says pointing at the log that rests upon the cutting stump. "S'il vous plait," he says stepping back, wiping the perspiration from his brow with his t-shirt. I hoist the ax and with a mighty heave bury the head solid in the center of the stump. Jerome clicks his tongue. "Non-non Bonaparte," he says taking the handle from my hands, forcing the maul from of the wood. He then gestures along the outside edge of the log taking care to point at the wood's grain with his finger. "Je compre?" he asks. I nod getting the gist of his meaning. He wants me to cut along the grain on the edge of the stump. He emphasizes his meaning by cleanly cleaving off that part of the wood with one solid stroke. "Oui Bonaparte, compre?" he says handing me the maul. "Salut."

He spies Magda coming to collect more firewood for the stove. "Eh Magda, ma chere amie… biere, s'il vous plait," he shouts and they smile at each other.

"Oui Jerome, un moment," she says bending to pick up a piece of wood. He intercedes and does it for her, placing a few thin sticks of it upon her forearms before taking up several larger pieces himself. I see the glint in her eyes, the glow between them and it is instantly clear to me that they are lovers, a quiet unassuming love. I watch them walk to the house together side-by-side, she carrying her tiny stack of wood, he the larger.

I take up the maul, spot the grain pattern and swing down hard. The wood splits cleanly and the feeling is a strangely euphoric one. I spin the log for another stroke and repeat this process a half dozen times before the log is no longer a log but several clean jagged pieces of firewood. I commence this process upon the pile and within the hour I have cleaved nearly a rick of firewood. When Jerome re-emerges from the house, he seems quite impressed with my progress.

"Whoa, Bonaparte, ce bonne! Tres bien," he says punching my shoulder rather heartily. We laugh together and I return to splitting wood. I continue, unrelenting, until twilight.

That night, well after supper I'm writing in my room when I sense a strange feeling over my left shoulder. When I gaze up from my journal I'm astounded to see, placidly looking over my shoulder, a pretty, dark-haired girl perhaps ten or eleven years of age.

"Why, hello," I say and her large dark eyes gleam, looking into mine. She doesn't say a word but seems interested in what I'm doing, diverting her attention between the journal and myself. "What's your name?" I ask closing my notebook. She studies me for a moment before saying in the most odd way:

"Me."

"Me?" I repeat smiling by this response. "Me who?"

"Me... Montara... me," she says and in the pause while I ponder this response she says: "Montara... X-ray van," pointing at her chest. I cock my head to one side thinking.

"Montara... X-ray van?" I question her somewhat at odds with this strange response and she points at her chest again.

"Me," she says in the most resolute manner. I puzzle over this response a moment when she touches the side of my cheek with just the very tip of her index finger then points, "Willem... Willem Furey," she says loudly.

"Yes, yes... that's my name," I say and hold out my hand towards her. She points again and says quite loudly:

"Willem Furey," I'm uncertain exactly how to respond. I smile and nod.

"Yes..." I say and study her. Her eyes shine brightly and her long black hair, done in two long braids flows like obsidian. She looks me over a moment then sighs aloud.

"Morgan," she says and I turn my body in the chair addressing her fully.

"Morgan?" I echo and she nods her head.

"Morgan..." she says again and pouts. "Morgan... bayou... no..." she states emphatically and I'm quite taken by this.

"What did you say?" She studies me again.

"Morgan... bayou... no..." she says shaking her head before swinging her beaten old teddy bear. "Morgan... dreamtime..." she says scanning the room, looking about at the contents of the apartment when a voice from behind catches both our attentions.

"Montara, what are you doing in here?" It's Magda at the door looking in. Montara immediately points at me.

"Willem... Willem Furey," she proclaims loudly and Magda enters and takes her by the shoulders.

"Yes baby, that's Willem... now get on back to your bedroom or Aunt Magda won't read you a bedtime story tonight."

"Morgan... dreamtime?"

"No sweetheart, no *Morgan dreamtime* tonight... Morgan sick, remember?"

"Morgan... bayou... no!"

"Yes little miss... Morgan shouldn't have gone. You told her didn't you," she says kissing her cheek.

"Morgan... no... go."

"Right baby girl, Morgan *no go* but Montara do go... you go to bed."

"Magda... storytime?"

"*Magda storytime* if you git in bed right now sugar," she says.

"Montara... fly," she says and suddenly seems to jump nearly to the ceiling! Magda quickly grabs her by the waist and seems to settle the child back onto the floor instantly extending a boney index finger in her face.

"Montara no fly! Montara walk!" she says a severe look on her face. She flashes a quick furtive glance in my direction before readdressing the child. "You know what your maw said about that," and pats her sharply on the behind and sends her on her way. At the door the girl turns and studies us, a dejected look on her pretty face.

"Magda... storytime..." she says, tears welling in her beautiful eyes.

"Yes, if you get in bed right now," she says sternly. The mysterious young girl looks at me.

"Willem Furey..." she says softly, "Montara... *love*..." she says and Magda shoos her.

"Go, go... right now." I watch as she turns and slowly meanders down the hallway taking a brief moment to peer over the railing at the front hall before she skips down the hallway swinging her teddy bear in big concentric circles.

"Who is that?" I ask.

"That..." she says smiling, "is Montara."

"Montara... X-ray... what was it?" I inquire and the smile instantly disappears from her face.

"Montara Montaigne... that's Monique's child." I'm more than surprised by this news.

"Monique has a daughter? I didn't know," I say and Magda leans against the desk, crossing her arms and eyes me curiously.

"There's a lot you don't know about this family," she says. I mull this over as her dark eyes fathom me.

"What did she mean by... *X-ray van*... I think is what she said?" and the question puts an odd expression on her face.

"She says a lot of strange things... she's a very... special child."

"She seems rather old to be talking in monosyllables. Is she... well... disadvantaged?" I ask and Magda looks hard at me then laughs under her breath heading for the door.

"Disadvantaged? That girl is gifted... you've no idea," she says closing the door.

That night as I lay sleeping, I'm suddenly awakened by a violent peal of thunder. It is raining hard outside, I can hear it clearly through the windows left ajar due to the heat. The roll of thunder subsides to be replaced by sporadic flashes of lightening that give off no sound. It's a constant and sustained pattern of electrical discharge broken by the low rumble of far distant thunder. I find the moment intoxicating, the sound and smell of the falling rain and the quiet pulsation of lightening outside the windows. I rise up on one elbow to better see the storm *when I see it,* for just a split second, an instantaneous glimpse, a shadow there one moment then instantly swallowed by night.

I don't move, peering into the darkness of the room, straining to see, but there is nothing except the absolute black of the room's interior. It's only when the next flash of lightening enters that I again catch what appears to be *a shadow in the middle of the room near the foot of the bed.* Am I seeing things? I stare wide-eyed in wonder until the next pulsation of light brings home a stark and unnerving realization; *someone is standing at the foot of my bed, staring at my sleeping form.*

I feel my entire body congeal as if I had been thrown into a vat of ice water. I cannot move, staring into the darkness, waiting. When another flash of lightening erupts, I see the outline of a human form clearly.

"Who is it?" I call out. All goes dark and still. I repeat my question feeling my nerves crawl by the sudden oppressive darkness when a rapid series of discharges put to rest any doubts that I might be seeing things. *Someone is at the foot of my bed watching me from the darkness!* Whoever it is they say nothing.

The room has a glass kerosene lamp near the bed. I decide to ignite it and reach out for the box of wooden matches. With a great deal of nervous tension I strike a match and hold it out towards my nocturnal stranger. What I see in the match's soft illumination shocks me. It's Morgan, staring at me in the darkness. Her eyes are pools of ebony, the black clothes wrapped to her neck, the hair wild and flowing.

"Morgan?" I whisper in the meager light and repeat her name again. *Very slowly she comes to me.* As she reaches my side the match's flame bites into my finger and I drop it with a start. I reach for another when I feel the soft coolness of her hand upon mine. She gently sits down upon the bedside. I watch in awe as she, in total silhouette, takes both my hands and folds them together upon my chest. I cannot see her eyes in the darkness as she sits, holding my hands atop my heart.

"*My love... you've come,*" she whispers and I pull her to me, kiss her. Her lips feel cold but sweet like the smell of orchids. We share a long loving embrace. I cannot let her go. I feel her slender shoulders and she seems frail, thinner, than I remember. Her weight upon me is like a soft snowfall or the weight of a dove within one's grasp. I whisper her name and we kiss once more. It feels like breathing in the night, a rich living embodiment of night, of splendor and wonderment. I'm lost within her arms. I cannot let go until she gently pushes herself away, her hands resting on my chest. She stares down at me in the darkness.

"*You came for me,*" she whispers like a soft wind, her eyes piercing the blackness, the silence igniting the space between us. When I can't stand it any longer, I pull her to me and we hold each other for many heartbeats until she again pushes herself from me, her form etched across the solitude of the room. "*I'm with you Willem... always...*"

I kiss her hands but she pulls them away, not harshly but softly, like a gentle wind and soon I am lying in bed without her touch. I stare into the blackness and in a sudden series of flashes, I no longer see her within the space of the room. I call out. I throw aside the sheets that separated us and move through the dark, cursing the lightening that has chosen this moment to hide itself. I manage the door and pull it wide.

Outside, the hallway is entirely in shadow, just vague silhouettes of the numerous bedroom doors and the stairway surround. Another long electrical discharge offers me ample opportunity to see the length of the great upper hall. There is no one to be seen. I feel my way down the hallway calling out her name, eventually making the head of the stairs.

I hunger for her visage and as if in answer to that desire, the entire upper and lower hallways are suddenly lit up by a monstrous clap of thunder and lightening, brilliant and sustained. The entire house is etched in black and white bas-relief as the lightening makes the shadows dance and cavort. She is nowhere to be seen, only the bleak emptiness of the great house.

The commotion arouses the aunts. Soon I'm set upon by the sisters who emerge from their rooms like lightening beetles in the night. Their small kerosene lamps puff thin wisps of black smoke casting a magical glow about their dark and wondering eyes. I see Monique and Emerald like two halves of the same person and the thin pale Angeline looking ghostlike in her long white robe. They inquire about what has happened.

"It was Morgan, she was in my room," I expound and the women exchange eye contact as if speaking together without the use of words.

"I'm sure you were dreaming, such a night," Emerald says in her impeccable English, without the French inflection I hear in the voices of her sisters.

"No, no, she was here with me. I held her. It was not a dream," I say and Emerald pulls her gown tighter around her shoulders. There is an odd tapping, behind us and everyone turns shedding light into the darkness of the great upper hall.

"Comme?" Pearl says emerging from her room, tapping at the floor with her cane.

"It's nothing Pearl," Emerald answers, "go back to sleep." She ignores the request and taps her way to the circle where Monique's outstretched hand is there to greet her.

"What has happened?" she asks, her ghostly white eyes casting a most eerie reflection in the lamplight.

"It is nothing sister, young Willem had a dream which awoke him… go back to your bed."

"What sort of dream?"

"It was not a dream aunt Pearl… it was Morgan." This produces the most profound reaction, a silent exchange between the women. They look to Emerald who pinches the nightgown tightly about her slender neck.

"That's impossible… she's bedridden, recuperating. I'm certain it was only a… very poignant dream," Emerald says.

"Emerald, take me to her. Don't do this. Don't keep us apart," I say and Angeline holds her hand to her mouth to stifle a small cry. The women all defer to Emerald, her eyes, glimmering in the lamplight, a profound sadness there when she looks into mine. Then she closes them, turns away and disappears into her room, closing the door. I go to follow but am stopped when Aunt Pearl speaks.

"Wait!" She slowly taps her way to me, the lamplight flickering wildly behind her silhouette. She places her hand upon my arm, touches my shoulder and then my cheek. The dead eyes, void of color, stare at me from their shadowy recesses. It is as if she is looking straight into me and I'm awed by the moment.

The thunder and rain hammers relentlessly upon the panes of the old mansion groaning under the intensity of the increasing storm. Her eyes flash when the lightening strikes, reflecting a weird brilliance and it's as if her eyes were becoming aglow, as one blows on an ember to bring forth flame. She turns to her family.

"Tell him sister... *tell him the Story of Woman*." Angeline looks to Monique who cocks her head strangely and inquires in a thin voice.

"You would have me tell him sister?" she asks queerly. Pearl looks back at me, the white colorless eyes like tiny crescent moons.

"Yes. Tell him... *the Story of Woman*." They converge about me, and in a soft muted tone, like an elder child reciting stories around the firelight, she tells me this simple story:

"This is the Story of Woman, passed down our line fifteen generations... Darkness was across the face of the world, and upon the wind and waves, and upon the Man, he whom the great Creator Being and the Muse, brought into Life. The great Being begot the fire, the eyther, and when the eyther and darkness were mixed the light of consciousness was born unto this world and put inside the Man that he rose up from amongst the animals around him, fire and the darkness both, light and the void. As years turned to eon, the Man became fascinated with the fire, fashioning all array of things and spells from its breath and the fire fed the flame within the man's heart that he became not unlike the consuming flame itself.

So it came to pass that the divine Muse was left as lonely as an ocean is broad. So forlorn became She that one night, when the moon was in wane, She disguised herself in the trappings of a raven and stole into his chamber and took a rib from the Man whilst he lay sleeping and with this She fashioned Woman and endowed within the Woman the vastness of Her eternal cloak, all the stars and their creatures contained therewithin, the soft winds and the tempest both. And when the great Creator saw this, he breathed the eyther into her, but the great Muse swaddled her so, within the fabrics of the starry night that she might not fall all total into the fire and her heart become consumed by it. And so this is how it was and is to this day... the Man and the Woman."

The following morning I'm awakened early by a knocking on my door. I'm surprised to find the old Colonel fully dressed in his white muslin suit and tie, standing resolutely at the portal.

"Get your duds on son, we're taking the Cadillac into the city."

"The city?" I question him yawning.

"N'orleans... what other city is there?" he responds and heads downstairs.

I back the '59 Biarritz out of the barn where he keeps it. He has me put the top down and soon we're on the old asphalt road heading toward New Orleans, his white hair rattling in the breeze.

"Where exactly are we headed Colonel?"

"Meeting a friend," is all he says and leaves it at that.

We pass through a series of neighborhoods on an eclectic path of the Colonel's divining. We must look quite the sight for we seem to draw a lot of attention.

Eventually we make it into downtown, skirting the modern buildings of the bustling business district. He directs me into the heart of the French Quarter and the change from the modern downtown is a dramatic one, the buildings composed of that old world French faux and stucco, the blue enamel street signs set into the sides of the buildings; vine works clamoring about the second and third floor terraces with their black iron railings. French –the written word- is everywhere and the shops and residences possess a distinct air, a quality that sets the community apart from other American cities.

The Colonel is going on about William Frees-Greene as he meticulously directs me into an alleyway and into a large courtyard open to the sky but surrounded on all sides by two and three story structures. The court itself seems old, composed of cobblestones, well laid. An old stone fountain sits in the middle and trickles water through a plethora of plant life. I see two bronze frogs, long turned a beautiful shade of blue-green.

"Park there," he says directing me toward a corner of the courtyard. When I turn off the engine, we sit for a moment taking in the quietude. I breathe in the rich clean air for the place is inundated with growth, trees and vines, potted plants and flowers. "Let's go, he'll be waiting," he says prying open the door and picking his knees up out of the leg well.

"Is the person we're meeting an old friend?" I ask casually to fill the ensuing silence.

"A very old friend, very old friend indeed." We meander out of the courtyard without a word to anyone. He also tells me not to bother putting the top up.

There are several small innocuous shops along the way and the Colonel takes pause to stick his head into one of them, the Creole proprietor addressing him with an almost reverent composure.

"Hello Azalea. Is August in?" he inquires.

"He is not Governor, he's down in the ninth ward, at the community center. Shall I ring him?" she asks but he waves it away.

"No, no don't bother him, he's doing better things than wasting his time on me. Just let him know I poked my nose in."

"Of course Colonel. Oh, but he'd love to see you! He'll be upset if I don't call. Come on in here a minute and I'll phone," she says pulling him through the door. Inside I'm astounded by the contents of the tiny store. It's filled to capacity with dried plants and mushrooms, small tied bundles hanging nearly everywhere and dozens of glass containers lining the walls and shelves. There are books, incense and bells. She takes up the phone but he gestures her to stop.

"Zizi, we'd like to stay, but we can't. We've a luncheon at the cafe." She lowers the phone, her brown eyes and mouth frowns.

"Oh, but that's a shame. How about afterward?"

"If there's time," he says kissing her on both cheeks. She looks at me and her eyes sparkle. She accompanies the old man back outside.

"How is Emerald getting on? Has she improved?"

"Markedly," he says.

"Glory, that's wonderful, just wonderful. We were all so worried."

"I know, but don't fret. She's nearly healed."

"Thank the Goddess," she says, "she's in the best of hands."

"Take care darlin'... my regards to the family," the Colonel says extending another kiss on her cheek and we set off down the alleyway. I look back over my shoulder and she is still standing outside the shop watching us.

"Who was that?" I ask the Colonel. Without even a glance in my direction he says:

"Another witch," and plods on, his cane leading the way. I laugh under my breath and he looks at me sharply, the full white brows bristle. "What's funny?"

"Your choice of words," I say and he stops dead in his tracks.

"What about my choice of words?"

"Well, you obviously mean she's a healer," I say.

"What's the difference?" he asks. His eyes stare hard into mine and I regret breaching the subject.

"Well... a healer heals, and a witch... well..." I'm at a sudden loss for words and squirm under his aged stare. He huffs and exits the alley, making his way into the crowd on the street.

"There's no difference son, your definition of the word seeks reevaluation. I'm not talking about those narcissistic shrews who fiddle around with other people's lives. I'm referring to the true line of the art form. Some women naturally bond together son, it's in their best interests to do so. The reasons are plain," he says looking at me hard. "Women create life son, not men. Men take it, we're good at that part of the bargain... but women, generally, abhor the taking of life because they bring life into the world. Men don't bring life into the world... share the pain and wonder of it, so we don't fear the taking of it." He pauses and addresses me fully. "Men love killin' son, we love it so much we don't stop with the animal kingdom... hell, we'll set to our own kind, our own species, women and children even! Imagine it, men killing women and children on this planet, blasphemy!" he shouts, drawing attention, and resumes his gait. "Man loves to wage war. We can't get enough of it. There seems no end to it. Look at the world today, on and on since antiquity... despite our higher selves... our better natures." He looks at me. "You don't consider what I'm saying truth?"

"Well I think you have a way of overstating the situation." He cocks his head at me.

"Take yourself for instance... the person you are inside. You don't think yourself capable of it."

"Capable of what?"

"Killing another person son, open your ears!" he says and I'm rather shocked by the question. It must show for he continues. "Even the question alarms you, your mind evades it, can't deal with it outright. That's the dichotomy of it, our dual natures as men... *the human sacredness of life yet the animal desire to take it.*"

I'm somewhat at odds with the conversation when he gestures with the length of his cane. "There's our quarry now, he whom we track," he says pointing at a well-dressed man, clean-shaven, having coffee at one of the tables outside the Cafe Mystique.

As we approach the cafe I'm shocked to the core when I realize that the man in the powder-blue suit *is none other than Lucien!* He sits under one of the café's large green umbrellas reading a paper. As we approach, he spies us, folds the paper and stands smiling. When we greet, he extends a long hearty handshake with the Colonel.

"Lucien, you old opossum... how're you keeping yourself?"

"Fit Emory, you yourself look well," he says amicably.

"Looks can be deceiving you old carpet bagger. You don't look a speck different from the last time I saw you. Sit back down there... what're you drinking?"

"I'm having coffee and cream," he says and gives me a sharp inquisitive look but says nothing.

We sit together at the table and it's a fine sunny morning, a slight coolness on the light breeze. I stare at Lucien awestruck as he idly chats with Colonel Montaigne. Why is he here and why this sudden drastic change in his appearance? His hair is cut trim and he wears an immaculate suit and –amazingly- a silk tie. He glances at me, a strange gleam in his eyes, but focuses his attention upon the Colonel who seems completely unfazed by this sudden transformation and it occurs to me that, perhaps, this radical change in his outward appearance has something to do with this unexpected meeting with the old soldier.

With the shorter hair, and beard removed, Lucien looks much younger. The addition of the suit and tie lends the appearance of a sophisticated older gentleman, perhaps a corporate manager or company president. I can't come to grips with his sudden change of appearance and continue to stare at him. Lucien avoids any reference to it. We sit this way as the Colonel talks on about Maison Magenta, New Orleans, the weather, and his health. When the waiter arrives he immediately recognizes our octogenarian host.

"Colonel Montaigne! Comme ca va? How are you sir?"

"Fine Emil, is the old man up?"

"I'm afraid not Colonel, but he'll want to know you're here for sure."

"That's alright Emil, don't pull him from his bed, we'll manage aright. What's on the bill of fare today?"

"Oui Colonel, today is the California prixe fixe."

"California?" the old man mutters under his breath. "What's the skinny?"

"The prixe fixe is a three course menu, the first course is the salad Nicoise with Roquefort cheese, the second course our creme du garlic soup with wild chives and the main course an authentic San Francisco cioppino. It's delicious. The beverage pairing is a brown nut ale and the wine the house red. For dessert we have our chef's favorite, crème brullee." Colonel Montaigne doesn't even consult us he immediately orders this fare for us all.

"But nix that house red Emil, I want a bottle of the fifty eight Rothschild from the cellar," he says pulling one of his crooked black cigars from his leather humidor and biting off the end.

"Tres bien Colonel," the waiter says and is immediately off toward the kitchen.

"You'll appreciate the fifty eight Rothschild Lucien," he says lighting the cigar. "That was Magenta's favorite year, ya'll remember… and fifty nine. Those were two very good years."

"I remember," Lucien says smiling. "How are your daughters Emory?" The old man rolls his eyes.

"That bevy of witches?" he says huffing. "The same. They won't let me eat red meat, they hide my liquor and pinch their noses every time I light up. They'd be happy to have me just sit there and rot!" Lucien laughs softly.

"They worry about your health," Lucien says winking in my direction.

"Health? I'd be healthier if they let me have my cut of Filet Mignon on Sundays. And I've had a shot of straight Kentucky bourbon everyday of my life since I was seventeen. What do they think has been keeping me tickin' this long?"

"They've all suffered under the affects of alcohol in their lives," Lucien says quietly.

"Yes... they've all had a belly full of it, no mistake there. None worse than Monique, poor thing," he says and they both grow introspective.

"What happened to Monique?" I find myself asking and the men look long and hard at me.

"Why, son, haven't you noticed the right eye, the one with no iris?" the Colonel asks.

"Well, I've noticed her eyes are different. One is green and the other is..."

"Black!" he says loudly. "Go ahead and say it, black as coal. It is what it is," he says and spits off to one side of the table.

"What happened?" I ask reluctantly. The old man wrings his gnarled old hands a moment.

"That damn heathen she got married to after Shelton killed hisself..." he says gazing back and forth like a caged animal. "He got all liquored up one night and struck that precious thing so hard it knocked the color right from her. In a coma for three and a half days," he mutters, "three and a half of the longest days of my life..." He returns his gaze to mine and he is seething inside. "The eye went all black, black as night. That's when the visions started," he says waving a long boney finger at Lucien. "All that about seeing the Virgin Saint... and starting out on this path working for the poor. She's squandered her entire inheritance Lucien, her entire inheritance!" I look at Lucien and he sees the confusion in my face.

"While in the coma, Monique claims she was visited by Saint Angela Merici and asked to dedicate her life to the protection of young women... and the poor." The old man suddenly pounds the table with his fist.

"Damn lucky he run, that jackal!" he says to Lucien then looks at me. "Oh I went hunting for him, rest assured! I was fixed about putting a bullet into him, the mangy coward."

"It's a good thing you didn't Emory," Lucien says.

"I loathe any person that strikes a woman or a child. There's none lower in society, no one," he says loudly and Lucien agrees with him. "And that Baron, that German Baron, Em got tangled with after Seamus died... Eisenhammer... whatever the hell his name! I knew he was a drunken Nazi from the first day I laid eyes on him. Arrogant, abusive son of a-" he stops and curses beneath his breath. "You really let me down there boy," he says to Lucien with sudden intensity. "It was you who was supposed to marry my girl after Seamus died, not that damn kraut aristocrat. Why didn't you step into the middle of that, save us all the trouble?"

There's a long pause as the two men share a deep seated silence and I regret asking the simple question that brought up such a tirade from the old man.

"How is Emerald, Emory? How is she fairing?" Lucien asks seemingly no change in his demeanor and the old man sulks.

"You don't need to ask me that... you know... you always know," he says and Lucien's eyes are keen, intent upon him.

The waiter appears with an old bottle of wine and three crystals. We watch silently as he uncorks the bottle and pours a minute amount into one of the glasses and places it neatly before the Colonel.

"You may dispense with the formalities Emil, go ahead and pour the wine," he mutters and I sense his sadness, his regrets. We toast silently, each man with his own thoughts. The waiter abruptly returns with three plates of salad with a large wedge of cheese and freshly baked bread. Lucien and I start into our salads but the old man has fallen into remorse apparently either lost in his thoughts or perhaps embarrassed by his sudden outburst. Lucien reaches across the table and takes the back of the old man's weathered hand.

"Don't become lost in the past Emory, let's enjoy our brief time together, here and now. It's good to see you again old friend." The Colonel slowly raises his eyes and gives a soft curt laugh.

"Of course. It's just... hell, I'm only a few years from rackin' up a century of living. There's *a sadness* to it," he says looking at me, "living and dying."

"You've been dying for twenty years Emory," Lucien interjects and smiles. The old man huffs under his breath.

"I think Morgan's right," I say to lighten the mood and the men look at me. "That you're too ornery to die," I say and the mention of her name has brought about a sudden change around the table, my companions exchanging curious looks. I am aware that they are silently considering something. Eventually the Colonel breaks the silence.

"You, you know why we've come down here son, and why Lucien's here don't you?" I stop eating and look at them, the Colonel diverting his attention to his salad.

"No sir, I guess I don't."

"There's a plane leaving for the Continent in a few hours. Lucien came down to travel back with you." I set my utensils down.

"I beg your pardon... what do you mean?" I ask and Lucien coughs softly.

"The family asked me to accompany you back to Europe. We've some work building in France with Anton. We'll need all the help we can muster," he says and I'm perfectly aware that this tack is a smoke screen.

"Colonel Montaigne, I'm in love with your granddaughter sir. I've no intentions to leave here without her. I don't care if

I work on the estate or somewhere else. I've no intention of leaving her again. I don't care if you or your daughters want me to go, I'll not leave her… not again." He looks up at me and his eyes are full of a sudden sadness. He seems to want to speak but apparently cannot form words. He looks to Lucien, who says the words that freeze my heart, in fact, the entire world around me.

"Willem, it was Morgan who asked me to come."

Time ceases for me in that moment, it no longer possesses any meaning. I've no real recollection of any further details. I can no longer eat, talk nor think. I believe I just sit, listening in on the idle conversation until it's time to leave. Suddenly, we're at the airport, then the plane, flying high above the earth, moving about the cabin in slow motion. People talk to me –as if in a foreign language- but in truth I don't really understand or care what they say.

En route to Britain, while in the middle of the flight, a strange thing occurs. The cabin had quieted noticeably, most passengers in their seats reading, watching television or sleeping. I look over at Lucien asleep in his seat and *the image of a most beautiful, most radiant woman sits with him.* Her features are soft, angelic, and her hair is golden, perhaps white. Her elegant hands rest peacefully upon his shoulders and she seems to be sleeping also. As I stare at this incredible sight, she slowly, ever so gently awakens and looks at me *and the smile in her eyes* is knowing and euphoric. Then she softly fades as if dimming a light.

We set down at Heathrow. I recognize the airport and its customs but I cannot really engage with it. Beryl Collins has apparently impeccably arranged the flight.

There is an endless crowd of people, like a river, gently flowing straight into the English twilight. The cab ride through London is like moving through a dream. I see the city's magnificence and its sorrow. I realize sitting silently in the darkened cab that I appreciate Lucien; appreciate that during the entire trip, he has said barely a word. That was perhaps the most sublime part of it. That he required nothing from me but the dignity to be left alone, without the burden of words or thoughts.

When the cab arrives outside my lonely flat, I stare at it through the rain-streaked window. As I slowly extract myself from the vehicle, I recall an utter loss of meaning as I stand there upon the stone. Lucien gets out for a moment, the cab idling, and takes the spot next to me staring up at the dark building under the falling rain. After a moment of quiet, he places his hand upon my shoulder.

"To care enough for another human being to walk away from their destiny, from interposing one's own desires and fears in lieu of their experiencing life's critical moments, is the highest form of that beguiling and oft-times misunderstood thing we call *Love*. For what is love really but the giving and surrender of that which is most treasured, most precious… that thing we call *the heart*."

I could not prevent the welling of water within my eyes as he patted my shoulder and slowly returned to the cab.

"Lucien… what is *the Shade*?" I suddenly ask from under the rainfall. He stands at the door of the cab a moment before he speaks to the driver then closes the door and rejoins me at the curb, the cab limping off into the night. We stand a moment in silence, his face to the omnipresent sky raining down from above. After several moments he asks:

"Do you know why I sent away the cab?"

"No."

"Leaving in it would have been solely for your benefit. I don't need a cab to return to where my physical form moves and breathes," he says and studies me. I'm not clear about his meaning. "Every physical object has an *astral counterpart, an ethereal double*; I, you... this street... the entire city in fact. This is the nature of manifest reality. We've echoes not only in these denser lower planes but also in the lighter, higher realms... all things great or small. This is the nature of *the Shade* of which you inquire."

"What do you mean?" I ask and he contemplates my question a moment.

"Matter, the physical state, can assume the ethereal condition and back. The one melds with the other. *You yourself do it every night when you sleep.* This thing which stands before you now... formed somewhat out of the expectations of the beholder... is my ethereal double... what the mystics of old referred to as *the Shade*."

"I don't understand."

"There wasn't time to make the necessary arrangements, aeroplanes and tickets and such... or even the time to transit my actual physical body to New Orleans from the reservation on so short a notice. Inasmuch, it was expedient to send my ethereal body, *my Shade*, this that stands before you, myself in every way, possessing my memories and thoughts... my mannerisms. That part of me... the *echo*, that through the *force of my will*, can bridge the material and ethereal planes."

"I'm sorry but... what you're saying seems like... well... fantasy," I say and stare at him solemnly in the rain.

"Willem... your biggest obstacle in life is that side of your personality that refuses to *see the invisible*."

"*See the invisible?*"

"The visible effects of matter are merely the effects of force."

"What do you mean by *force*?"

"What you see or think of as matter is in reality nothing more than the aggregation of atomic forces."

"Yes, I accept that, but... you're in actuality here... physical... I can reach out and touch you," I say, and do so.

"I've already told you, *the Spirit –so subsequently its Shade–* bridges this material plane and the next, where matter becomes ethereal. Time and space are aspects of *this* plane of existence, *not the next or the others above and beyond*."

He grows quiet, staring up into the oppressive gray. I mull over what he's said, half of me amazed, the other skeptical.

"I'm sorry Lucien but I can't accept what you're talking about, or at least what you're alluding to. I accept that matter is composed of forces, energy, but... a person can't just... travel through the air... or be in two places at once," I say. He rubs his chin taking this in.

"Let me ask you a question. *Is a thought a form of power*? Power in the sense of *current*... energy flow?"

"The thought processes of the brain –as an electro-magnetic process– has been proven by science."

"Splendid... therefore the opposing power of *unbelief* and skepticism, if projected in a current of equal or greater force can *neutralize the other*, just as any wave cycle nullifies an opposite cycle?"

"*Neutralize the other?*"

"There's a line in the Christian bible... *'And he did not many mighty works there, because of their unbelief.'*" He studies me intently a moment. "Thus the power of Faith my friend... the power of believing." I can only stare at him the rain saturating my head and shoulders. "Perhaps... it would be more meaningful to just show you?" he asks staring hard at me. I shrug my shoulders at which point he turns and begins to walk down the street his outline rapidly becoming thin and diaphanous under the London rain and vanishes into thin air.

I stare on for many minutes, not quite able to grasp what has just happened, until I'm clothed head to foot in rain. When I eventually realize he has in fact disappeared, I turn and solemnly enter the building.

As I make my way up the lift to the third level and through the dim empty hallway to the door of my flat, I think over all these dream-like moments of the past weeks and months. I come to the conclusion that becoming *a human being,* as Lucien used the phrase, is perhaps the hardest thing I have ever tried to accomplish, more difficult than my career as a filmmaker or cameraman... all of it... *the rattling of the chains of existence.*

I unlock the door and enter the flat. It smells foul, unfamiliar to me. Have I been gone that long? When I engage the switch for the light nothing happens. I try the switch several times and decide the bulb must have burnt out. When I make the desk, feeling my way in the dark, the desk lamp won't ignite either. *Strange*, I think to myself, *the breaker must have sprung.* When I see the glow of the electric clock and other devices, I'm instantly ill at-ease. Suddenly a voice sounds from the shadows cast by the streetlight near the window overlooking the street.

"The lights are out Mr. Furey. I've willed it so." I nearly jump out of my skin, staring into the dark.

"Who is it? Who's there?" A small butane flame sparks and in the dim glow I spy a most repulsive face. It is the face of a man, possibly sixty years of age, a narrow aquiline nose and rather pointed chin. His eye sockets are sunken and hollow, the eyes hidden in the feeble glow of the small flame.

"Closer Mr. Furey," the voice beckons, "don't be afraid." I very reluctantly do so. As I approach the man –hidden in the shadows- his emaciated hand extends into the light and gestures. "Please… sit down."

"How did you get in here?"

"I walked in."

"The door was locked, you broke in. Leave now before I call the constable."

"Do you know who I am Mr. Furey? Any inkling whatsoever?"

"No."

"That's good… very good. It pleases me you don't. Rumor has it Karras is wasting his time on you. I'm inclined to believe it."

"Who are you?"

"All in good time Mr. Furey… all in good time."

"Get out of here before I call the police." He then extracts a hand pistol from the darkness and points it at my heart.

"Sit down. I want a word with you." I stare at the weapon etched in the streetlight that pours through the window. He gestures toward the chair opposite the one in which he sits. I carefully take the seat and watch as he places the pistol down upon the table beneath the window that separates us. He then lights a cigarette. All I can see of him from the darkness is this small glowing ember in the shadows and the silence is unnerving.

"I can't imagine you comprehend why I'm sitting in this exact spot at this exact window on this exact night?" I'm uncertain if he's asking a question. I remain silent, watching as he picks up the pistol and aims it at the street below. I realize the elongated barrel is in fact a silencer. "I knew Lucien Karras would be standing exactly... there... in that exact spot at this hour. However..." he says replacing the gun back atop the table, "he didn't exactly *show up*, did he... Mr. Furey?"

"I don't know what you mean?"

"Shooting his double would be... well... the waste of a good bullet. Wouldn't you agree?" I watch as the cigarette burns anew and eye the pistol. "Would you like to shoot me Mr. Furey... given the opportunity?" he asks from the dark. I watch the slow mechanical rise and fall of the ember in the dark.

"What do you want?"

"I want you to shoot me." Silence. "Not sporting... this evening... Mr. Furey?"

"Get out."

"All in good time sir... all in good time," another excruciatingly long pause. "I'd like you to do something for me... something simple." Silence. "I'd like you to deliver a message for me. I'd like you to tell Lucien Karras that I'm quite ill disposed to what they've done. Oh, I can hardly object to the small setbacks... one must expect it I suppose... but this business regarding *my exalted one...* is quite unacceptable Mr. Furey, quite unacceptable!"

"Your *exalted one*?"

"Yes... my exalted one."

"Would you care to elaborate on that?"

"Oh indeed I'll elaborate on it… and much more. *An eye for an eye*… Mr. Furey… a very old concept. They murdered one of my kind… this cannot go uncontested."

"Murder? Impossible. Lucien Karras wouldn't hurt a soul."

"*A soul*… a soul!" he hisses vehemently. "You tell Karras and that Creole witch they've complicated my plans for the last time. *Two eyes for the one eye* Mr. Furey… is the new bargain."

"What are talking about?"

"The Lover of souls! My exalted."

"The Burning Man…"

"Oh come now… such a dour misnomer, a rather discredited nom d'plume sir."

"You're talking about killing the medicine woman, Aphelia, for killing that grotesque thing."

"I'm talking about Monique Montaigne!" *he* shouts in a sudden unbounded rage. "You think that ignorant backwater savage could be the death of something so powerful?! It was that damnable Creole witch Monique Montaigne that was the instrument and by hell I'll have her on a skewer!" he screams and the moment is unnerving. "That… conjurer, will be dealt with accordingly," he spits, seething. He gathers his emotions somewhat. "All in good time sir," he whispers and exhales, a foul smell permeates the room. The following silence is horrifying. "You will tell her, Mr. Furey?" Silence. "Her life is forfeit… *an eye for an eye*. Oh… and her little helper… the neophyte." I'm aghast for I know he's referring to Morgan. "She's dangerous to me, and will be more so. Like a cancer growth that must be cut out before it's allowed to… metastasize. I'd prefer it that way. That she not be allowed to… mature." He stares at me from the darkness. "I orchestrated that quite nicely I thought." He suddenly leans forward from the shadows, half of his face cloaked in the dim light of the window; the eyes are hollow and empty *like those of a corpse.* "You proved quite resourceful in that little affair Mr. Furey... do you know that? In fact, I dare say you quite rather upset my carefully laid plans. Perhaps I've misjudged you. Perhaps, you too are more dangerous to me than I've reckoned."

I suddenly grab for the pistol but the moment I pick it up it sears my flesh like taking up a red-hot brand and I instantly drop it. The *Hollowman* laughs and the laugh goes through me like ice. I'm swallowed in a mortal fear.

"Impressed?" he asks. "A simple parlor trick, Mr. Furey... nothing more." He then stands, reaching down and retrieves the pistol. As he towers above me, it's as if he were entirely black, like a shadow lost of its distinctive features and the sensation is terrifying. I watch as he slowly retracts into the darkness of the room and it's as if he's disappeared. It's not until the apartment door opens that I see him. He stands in total silhouette against the meager light of the hall and stares. "It's been fun," he says and begins to leave, suddenly turning he says: "Oh, you will tell them Mr. Furey... won't you? If it's not an imposition..."

I awaken later that night drenched in a profuse sweat. It's as if I cannot breath. I force myself to the window and gasp in the cool night's air. I'm filled with an overwhelming fear. Was it real, or imagined, the dark stranger within my room? I feel a profound longing for Morgan and I silently call out for her... a deep calling from the centre of my being.

In my dream that night I see her, high above on the wing. She comes down from the skies and *steps within the twilight of my room.* She is beautiful, resplendent, the same willowy woman, but the eyes are wiser, not the soft tranquil gaze but deep and agleam. The caress of her fingers upon my brow and the touch of her lips make me feel anew. She looks into me, her eyes filled with wonderment and in words that pierce any unreality I hear in the voice that is hers:

"Dearest Willem... fear not my love, you are not alone. I do love, and tis thee. How my heart yearns for you. Surely you know my love, surely see, we are one, forever and enon. Come home Willem, on wings, come to me."

When I awaken with a start, I am alone in the darkness; the window opened wide, the curtains dancing in the wind under the moonlight like waves foaming along a midnight beach. I rise and go there. I look out into the night. The rain has stopped and a quiet stillness has enveloped the ancient city as if it sits silently on the edge of something, waiting. In that moment, a large ebony fowl alights and takes to the wing, heading south, inexorably into the distance and is gone.

Epilogue.

Garden of Night

Where art thou o' divine one?
Where hast thou gone?
Are thee lost, adrift and a' wandering?
Within Nocturne's garden alone

The seas are a' rollin'
O' slender one, thou beautiful thing
The night winds blow on and on
High upon the wing

Come back, come back to me
O' long lost love
Are you adrift below the sea?
Are thou with the moon above?

Where hast thou gone o' treasured one?
O' wanderer of the midnight breeze
Is it thou a' wandering alone?
Amidst the midnight trees

Hast thou forgotten me?
This heart so pure
A fire deep within the night
Cast away Tisiphone's allure

Where art thou o' divine one?
Spread thy wings and alight
Are thee lost, adrift and a' wandering?
Amid the garden of night

Fini

The author would like to thank the following
for their valued contributions during the
production of this book:

Don Mangione for his wonderful book design,
(this title & The Profound Art of Omens)
Mariposa Davis for proofreading the manuscript
Rie Koko & Joy French for the early reads
Bryan Uecker (Book Nook) and Erik Anderson

My family (immediate and extended) friends
students & mentors, precious persons all,
for their continued encouragement & light

Lastly, the great E.A.Poe who died penniless yet
left us such wealth, A.C.Doyle & Thomas Mann.